'What p[ossibly]
possibly [have with me?]'

'The most private business of all,' she replied, 'for I have come to ask you to marry me. This will be a purely business arrangement. In return for your agreement to all these conditions I shall pay off your debts.'

'What makes you think that you can trust me? Why should I not fall on you, once we are married, and take my rights? I am a rogue, am I not?'

'You may be a rogue, but I also believe that you are an honest rogue, and that, if we marry, you will be *my* rogue.'

Paula Marshall, married with three children, has had a varied life. She began her career in a large library and ended it as a senior academic in charge of history in a polytechnic. She has travelled widely, has been a swimming coach, and has appeared on *University Challenge* and *Mastermind*. She has always wanted to write, and likes her novels to be full of adventure and humour.

Recent titles by the same author:

THE DESERTED BRIDE
THE BECKONING DREAM
THE YOUNGEST MISS ASHE

REBECCA'S ROGUE

Paula Marshall

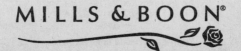

MILLS & BOON®

First published in Great Britain 1998
Harlequin Mills & Boon Limited,
Eton House, 18-24 Paradise Road, Richmond, Surrey TW9 1SR

© Paula Marshall 1998

ISBN 0 263 81035 6

Set in Times Roman 10½ on 12 pt.
04-9807-79690 C1

Printed and bound in Great Britain
by Caledonian International Book Manufacturing Ltd, Glasgow

Chapter One

1813

Will Shafto, his hat on the side of his handsome head, strode down Piccadilly, whistling merrily. The troubles which had haunted him since his early youth were over. Life lay fair before him. He had recently proposed marriage to Sarah Allenby, the woman of his dreams, and she—and her family—had accepted him.

That she was the woman of his dreams only because she was a great heiress, a golden dolly as rich as Croesus, and not because she was the youthfully charming beauty of the season who thought that it was her looks which had attracted him, troubled him not at all. The looks and the charm were a bonus for him, not a necessity.

For was she not—albeit unknowingly—about to rescue him from the Marshalsea, the debtor's prison which awaited him if he had failed to win her? The last decade spent struggling to appear rich and handsome on nothing a year, keeping himself afloat only by his wits, was behind him. He could truly be Shafto of Shafto Hall again, with all that that implied.

Oh, yes, the Hall could be repaired, the lands around it sold by his wastrel father might be bought back again and the Shafto family returned to its former glory. If the price were to be the sale of himself and his integrity to a woman whom he liked, but did not love, then so be it. He had his reasons, and so far as he was concerned they were good ones.

Moreover, many marriages between those of equal fortune were based on no more and no less than he was offering his heiress. He would be faithful to her, would be as good a husband as it was possible to be, particularly since she would be the means by which the Shaftos would be solvent again. Gratitude alone would keep him faithful.

He turned into the curtilage of the great palace in Piccadilly which a former Allenby had caused to be built in the Italian style of the early eighteenth century; a palace which would soon be his. He was visiting it in order to sign the marriage settlement which his lawyer, and those of the Allenbys, had been drawing up that morning.

Will stifled a grin at the thought of Josiah Wilmot, that clever shark of sharks, about the business of deceiving the Allenbys as to Will's true circumstances. The papers which he had been presenting to them appeared to show that Will was not only solvent, but magnificently so.

He was so lost in his dream that he did not notice the cold stare which the butler gave him, nor did the fact that he was shown into an ante-room, rather than the big drawing-room where he had always been welcomed on his earlier visits disturb him. He was still lost in his euphoric dream.

It gave him time to check his appearance in a Venetian glass mirror, to register that he was as well turned out as ever. His dark curls were brushed *á la* Brutus; his cravat was a spotless dream; his blue-black jacket was a perfect fit, as were his cream breeches and shiny black boots. He was not a vain man, but he was well aware that his looks and carriage were better than those of the common run.

Everything seemed to be in order. The butler returned to say, still cold, 'The family are ready to receive you now, sir.'

He was led down a black-and-white flagged corridor to a room which he had never entered before. On the way he passed a well-dressed young woman, with an obvious duenna in tow. The young woman responded to his obligatory bow with a stare as cold as the butler's. She was, he noted briefly—Will always made it his business to notice everything, one never knew when it might come in handy—of average height with a cold clever face in the ancient Greek mode. She was a beauty, but a severe one, with a straight nose, grey eyes and a high forehead below fashionably dressed chestnut hair.

The butler impatiently ushered him into a room where, instead of his beloved awaiting him, a group of men, all of them members of Sarah's family, were standing. Among them, Simpson, the Allenbys' lawyer, was an oddity in his decent black clothing, a crow among peacocks. The room was some sort of study where busts of antique philosophers were arranged along a high cornice.

At the far end of the room, behind the Allenbys, were two bruisers, instantly and unhappily recognisable to

Will as Bow Street Runners. Something was very wrong. He was soon to find out what it was.

John Allenby, Sarah's uncle and guardian, was the first to address him.

'You must, sir, being what and who you are, understand why we are receiving you after this fashion.'

Will decided to be brazen. It was the only thing left to him.

'No, indeed, sir. I am all at sea.' It was, perhaps, an unlucky phrase to use. John Allenby seized on it immediately.

'Would that you were, sir. Would that you were. Suffice it to say, as briefly as possible, that there can be no question of a marriage between you and my niece. Despite your own, and your lawyer's, lying assertions we have become aware, through the investigation undertaken by these men here—' and he waved at the two Runners '—that you are a penniless, landless fellow, heavily in debt.

'You are a rogue, sir, a miserable fortune-hunter, an adventurer of the worst kind. The ring you have bestowed upon my niece, and which lies on the desk before you, has not even been paid for. Your only income is less than two hundred pounds a year. Had we known of your true character and circumstances we should not have allowed you to speak to our niece, let alone propose marriage to her and be accepted.'

The world had fallen in on him. Will was like the man in the Eastern tale who, seated before a basket full of pottery, dreams of the fortune he will make by selling it, until, kicking his foot out in ecstasy, he knocks it over and breaks it all—and destroys his future.

The barefaced and insolent courage, which had sus-

tained him in the nine years since he had been left a
pauper at eighteen, did not desert him now.

'And your niece, sir? What does she have to say to
this dismissal of my suit? May I not speak to her?'

'What my niece may, or may not, desire is nothing to
you. She will obey her elders and betters and will not
be allowed to associate with you again. As we wish no
scandal to attach to her name through her unfortunate
connection with you we shall not bruit this business
about the world. You will leave at once, taking the ring
with you—and if you are so foolish as to argue this
matter, the Runners whom you see before you have their
orders to escort you to the door.'

Will made no move either to leave or to pick up the
ring from where it lay on the desk. Of all the dreadful
moments in his hard life this was perhaps the worst: a
public humiliation before men whom he had previously
thought of as his friends. He looked at Harry Fitzalan,
Sarah's cousin, who had introduced Will to her.

'And you, Harry?' he asked. 'You agree to this?'

John Allenby did not allow him to answer.

'Of course, seeing that it was his folly which brought
about ours in first allowing you into Allenby House and
then countenancing your courtship of our niece.'

There was nothing for it but to try to leave clutching
some shreds of dignity around him. Will bowed, and
turned to go before the bruisers removed him.

John Allenby called to his back in a jeering voice,
'Come, you are leaving behind your half-owned property,' and he threw the ring at Will's feet.

Will made no move to pick it up, but walked steadily
on his way to the door. He would neither defy the men
before him nor try to justify himself. Both courses of
action would be useless. He had been caught out in a

massive deception and he could only wonder what had caused Sarah's uncle to set the Runners on him. He was not a criminal, and had not associated with criminals, but if poverty were to be counted a crime in the eyes of the men who were judging him, then he was one.

Once at the door, and before he opened it, he turned again to hold his head high and say, in a distant, unmoved voice, 'I would have made her a better husband than any you are like to choose for her.'

It was, although he had no means of knowing it then, a prophetic statement which more than one present in the room had cause to remember. At the time John Allenby stared inimically at him. 'If you do not leave on the instant I shall order the Runners to throw you down the steps and into the street.'

Will inclined his head gravely. 'No need for that. You will present my compliments and my regrets to Sarah, Fitzalan. I know you to be a man of honour.'

Harry gazed miserably at him before biting his lip and shaking his head.

'So be it,' said Will, as his erstwhile friend denied him, and left. *He* had denied nothing, because everything that John Allenby had said about him was the truth.

And yet, not quite the truth.

Outside, in Piccadilly, the full horror of his circumstances struck Will hard. In the knowledge of his coming marriage he had borrowed money on it to outfit himself as a husband fit for such as Sarah Allenby. He had also laid out other monies, but not for himself, which would also now have to be repaid. He would not need to trouble about what the rest of society thought about him when the news of Sarah's jilting of him became public because he would be rotting in a debtor's prison.

His jaunty stride had declined to a tired amble, his head, for the first time in his life, hung low. He thus did not notice that a fashionable chaise with scarlet and gold armorials on its panelling was following him down Piccadilly. It stopped just outside Burlington House where a sturdy young footman sprang down from the box to accost him.

Will was so lost to everything that at first he did not respond to the footman's greeting and carried on walking in the direction of Hyde Park.

'Sir,' said the footman, 'my mistress would have a word with you. She is in the carriage there.'

'With me?' asked Will, bewildered at being spoken to by this stranger. 'With me?'

'If you are Mr Will Shafto, sir, then my mistress would talk with you for a moment.'

Will's gaze took in the man, the chaise, and the woman sitting in it. She was the severe young beauty whom he had seen at Allenby House. He walked over to the chaise. The woman lowered the glass panel in the door to put her head out and speak to him.

Seen close to, her looks were more classically severe than ever. She could well serve as a model for the goddess of wisdom, Athene herself, since she appeared to be on the point of handing out some unpalatable edict from on high. Will could only wonder why in the world she wished to speak to someone whom she must be aware was a disgraced adventurer—other than to reproach him, of course.

'Mr Will Shafto,' she said, and her voice was as cold as her face.

'Yes, I am he.'

'They have thrown you out of the house, I believe, and broken off your engagement to my cousin Sarah?'

'Is that a question?' said Will, a trifle nastily. 'Or a statement designed simply to put me down further?'

'Neither,' she replied, her lovely calm unruffled. 'I was merely making sure of my man.'

My man, indeed! What the devil did she mean by that? In no way was he her man—or anyone else's man for that matter.

'And I must introduce myself to you, seeing that we have not met before.' She continued, not a whit put out by his calculating stare, 'I am Rebecca Rowallan, and I am twice as rich as my cousin Sarah.'

'Congratulations and good day to you then, Miss Rowallan. And now, forgive me. I must be on my way. Not being an hundredth as rich as either of you, I have much to think about.'

'So you must, Mr Shafto, considering your changed circumstances. But, pray, do not rush away. I would wish to know two things. Where do you live? And may I visit you tomorrow morning at ten of the clock? I dislike doing business in the public streets.'

Of all strange things for her to say to him on this damnable day! Will finally lost his hard-won composure and gaped at her open-mouthed. The words were wrenched from him. 'What in the world for?'

'Not here, sir,' she answered him. She was as smooth and slippery as Lawyer Wilmot himself. 'I have just told you why, and I try never to repeat myself, but since your wits are a-wandering, for once, I will do so. I wish to do business with you. So, pray, tell me your address. Perhaps I had better reassure you that it will be to your advantage to receive me.'

Receive her? For what? And for what conceivable advantage to him? Surely it was her wits had gone awandering, not his.

'Ten, Duke Street,' he ground out. 'I have rooms there. On the first floor.'

Her beautiful eyebrows rose. 'Duke Street? Can you afford to live there?'

'Of course not. But needs must...'

'...when the devil drives. Yes, I know. I shall call at ten of the clock, remember. My companion, Mrs Grey, will be with me. We shall require no refreshments.'

Without waiting for an answer she called to the coachman, 'Drive on, James.'

Leaving Will staring after her as though she were an apparition ready to summon him to heaven or to hell.

Chapter Two

'No news from Josiah Wilmot, Gib?'

Gib Barry, Will's valet and man of all work, shook his head. 'None. I've not seen hair nor hide of him. But you know old Josh, he's so many irons in the fire he's probably on with the next one, now that yours is out of it and cooling.'

Will had been pacing around his drawing-room ever since he had reached home. Now he stood stockstill to stare out of the window.

'It's the end, Gib, you know that. Right up the River Tick, we are, and no mistake. If you wish to leave me to find employment elsewhere, I shall quite understand.'

'I know that. Faith, I've been your man since you were a lad—long enough to know what's what where you're concerned. But I like my billet here, and my little pension from the Army for my poorly leg means that all I need is a roof over my head. No, I'll not leave you, yet. No one else would be so considerate of a poor cripple.'

'But you will have to go soon, of course.' Will had begun his restless pacing again. 'For it cannot be long

before the duns haul me off to the Marshalsea and you'll
need to find another roof, this one having gone.'

'Wait and see, sir; wait and see is my motto. The
darkest hour is always before the dawn. Who knows
what tomorrow might bring?'

Such carefree optimism was beyond Will. Ruin had
been steadily creeping up on him for years until, meeting
Sarah Allenby, he thought that he had found salvation.
This very evening he had arranged to accompany her to
the Opera, but some other bright young spark would be
sitting beside her; knowing her, he doubted whether she
was giving Will Shafto another thought.

Her very shallowness had attracted him because it
meant that he would easily be able to satisfy her, make
her happy, but it also meant that she would not have
fought very hard to keep him. In the end, one man was
very like another to her, and she had chosen Will for his
bright good looks and his entertaining conversation as
much as for anything else.

If he had not truly loved her, then she certainly had
not, in any real sense, loved him.

His pride said, Go out and show yourself at one of
your clubs to prove that you are not set down by this
afternoon's work. His common sense said, What, and be
pointed and stared at as the man who was turned away
from Allenby House as an adventurer? He was sure that
more than one of the men present that afternoon would
talk of what had passed, regardless of John Allenby's
wishes that the matter be kept secret for Sarah's sake.

It was too good a piece of gossip to be kept quiet.
No, he would wait a few days before the brouhaha died
down. Not because he lacked courage, but if he were
once turned away from the fashionable haunts of young

men about town, he would be permanently ruined, never be received anywhere again, and he dared not risk that.

So, it was an early night for him.

Then it was an early rising the next morning and a manful attempt to eat Gib's good breakfast which, for once, tasted of the dust and ashes his life had become.

He could not even loll about comfortably in his dressing-gown for there was Miss Rebecca Rowallan to see, when he might find out what the deuce she wanted with him. He was glad that he had resisted the temptation to drink the night away for he was glumly sure that he needed a clear head to deal with her.

Gib dressed him as carefully as ever. He was not quite as glorious as he had been the previous afternoon, but glorious enough. For once Will did not examine himself in the mirror, taking Gib's word for it that he was entirely *comme il faut*. His face had become hateful to him. It was bad enough to play the fortune-hunter, but even worse to be exposed for doing so.

Miss Rowallan, he was not surprised to discover, was punctual to the very second. The small French clock on his mantelpiece was striking ten even as Gib announced her, and her attendant lady.

'Miss Rowallan has asked that her footman be allowed to wait in my kitchen, and so I have agreed,' Gib informed Will as he pointed the two ladies to a large French sofa.

Miss Rowallan, who was dressed in a demure morning gown of Quakerish grey with a white linen collar and cuffs, promptly seated herself, but her lady remained standing. Something which was explained almost immediately when Miss Rowallan, whilst drawing off her gloves, said sweetly, 'I must ask that Mrs Grey be allowed to join my footman. I prefer to speak to you alone, Mr Shafto.'

Will's eyebrows climbed—as did his servant's. He looked curiously at Mrs Grey, standing before him, her hands clasped, her expression mutinous, the perfect picture of a middle-aged duenna not being allowed to do her duty. It did not need saying, but everyone present thought it: no single young woman should ever be allowed to remain alone with a man. Particularly not with a young man.

'Is that what Mrs Grey wishes?' Will asked, more than ever intrigued by what Miss Rowallan had to say to him which her woman might not hear.

'No, it is not,' said Miss Rowallan calmly before Mrs Grey could answer him. 'But since I pay her wages she does my bidding, not I hers.'

The bitch! What a harsh thing to say before the woman herself—even if it were true.

'You are not afraid for your reputation then, madam? To be alone with me, I mean.' Will's tone was a trifle cutting, but that affected Miss Rowallan not at all. Her own reply was equally so.

'Who is to talk, Mr Shafto? Certainly not Mrs Grey nor, I believe, your man, whom I have reason to know is discretion itself where you are concerned. And if you were to make any such claim about my being here alone with you, who in the world would believe you—and not me?'

Who, indeed? The hard bitch had the right of it. He was discredited, was he not? Will shook his head to clear it. 'Very well, then, if that is what you wish.'

'That is what I wish. I will send for you, Amelia,' she told her companion, 'as soon as my private business with Mr Shafto is over. It should not take long.'

'There's a good fire in the kitchen, Mrs Grey, and some excellent tea,' Gib said encouragingly. 'Mr Shafto will only drink the best.'

This revelation of his reckless extravagance in view of his financial situation set Will internally wincing, but his guest appeared to take no notice of it at all. Her face changed not a whit.

Nor did Will's. He did not sit down, but moved to stand with his back to the window so that his face was in shadow. 'I am agog,' he said, 'to learn what private business you can possibly have with me.'

For the first time she smiled at him and her whole face was transformed and softened. For a brief moment he could see that she was related to the sweetly pretty Sarah—and then the resemblance was gone.

'The most private business of all,' she replied, without any form of preamble, 'for I have come to ask you to marry me.'

It was as well that Will's face was in shadow, for light would have shown that for a brief space he was thunder-struck.

He gave a short, harsh laugh.

'Marry you! Am I to understand that you are proposing to me? You must have known what passed at Allenby House yesterday afternoon and that I was rejected for being a penniless fortune-hunter.'

'Yes, I do know that, Mr Shafto. That was why I left. I did not wish to be present when you were interviewed, nor did I wish to undertake the unnecessary task of comforting my cousin for she needed no comforting. I have seen her more distressed when she lost her favourite doll.

'True, she wept a few obligatory tears when she learned that she was to lose you, but my Uncle Allenby comforted her by saying that with you well rid of she was sure to marry a Marquess, at least. That brightened her up wonderfully. I left her practising to be m'lady.'

'Well, *you* will never be m'lady, if you marry me,' returned Will shortly.

'True again, Mr Shafto. But you do appear to have a deal of common sense which most of the men around me lack.'

'Now, how can you know that?' wondered Will. 'Seeing that we have never met before.'

'Oh, I have seen a lot of you,' she said, almost carelessly, 'and heard much from Cousin Sarah and from Cousin Harry. From them both I have learned that beneath your charming manner you possess all the hard common sense which is missing in both of them.'

'And is it *your* common sense which has resulted in you proposing to me, a man you hardly know, and this not even Leap Year? You do know, Miss Rowallan, that it is not Leap Year?'

'Oh, I am well versed in the calendar, Mr Shafto, as I am in most matters not normally considered the province of the female sex. The law, for example. You must understand that my proposition is not a simple one. It comes attached to certain conditions which would be plainly set out in the marriage settlement.'

'It does, does it?' growled Will, who was beginning to think that there was something demeaning about being proposed to by a female.

Who and what did she think he was? A silly question, for she knew exactly what he was: a fortune-hunter. And had not almost her first remark to him been a declaration of her extreme wealth? Which should have told him something. He thought for a moment. For more than a moment.

'You are silent, Mr Shafto. You have not asked me what the conditions are.'

Her coolness, in view of the enormity of what she was saying and doing, was provoking. Will, normally a man whom little provoked, found it difficult to control himself.

'Because I am asking myself certain questions. For example, why, with all that money—twice Sarah's, you were careful to tell me yesterday afternoon—you are not buying yourself a Duke at the very least—if Sarah is considered to be worth a Marquess, that is?'

'I do not want a Duke, Mr Shafto. I am also well informed as to the marital eligibility of all the senior noblemen in England and a most unattractive lot they are. Particularly the Royal Dukes, who are both ugly and promiscuous. You, on the other hand, are most personable—if you will forgive me for saying so.

'But if I am to be allowed to usurp the man's prerogative by proposing to you, then I may also comment on your appearance, I hope, since it is commonplace for men to do that to the women whom they are trying to charm into marriage!'

Will closed his eyes. This was beyond anything. 'I am at sea,' he muttered for the second time in two days.

Miss Rowallan put her head on one side and, for once, looked at him almost coyly. 'A very apt thing for one called Shafto to say. You know the old song, "Bobby Shafto"?'

'Too well,' said Will bitterly, wondering where this mad conversation was straying. 'But my hair is black, not yellow, and I have no silver buckles on my knee.'

'They are unfortunately out of fashion and not likely to return,' she agreed. 'But let us leave that, Mr Shafto. It is not to the point.'

Will bowed at her, 'Oh, by all means, let us get to the point. If there *is* one beyond your original proposal.'

Was she straying about in her conversation to wrong-foot him? Will had met some criminals and confidence tricksters who did exactly that to their victims. Was he her victim?

'If you marry me, Mr Shafto, it will be for my benefit rather than yours. A husband will give me protection, not only from adventurers, whom, unlike you, I cannot trust, but from relatives whom I cannot trust, either, and who seek to dominate me because I am a woman. You must understand that a single woman on her own, beyond a certain age, and under another, is an anomaly, and an anomaly to be preyed on.

'That being so, I am prepared to marry you if you will consent to have drawn up papers and settlements which will keep you from ever touching my fortune. Privately we shall draw up other agreements—to wit, that you will be my husband in name only, that this shall not be disclosed, and that, if at any time after a period of five years either of us wishes to end this purely business arrangement, we are free to do so.

'In return for your agreement to all these conditions I shall pay off your debts and allow you an income sufficient to appear in society as a gentleman worthy to be the husband of one as wealthy as myself.'

Will turned away from her, and offered her something which no gentleman should ever offer a lady: his back.

He stared unseeingly out of the window at Duke Street. He scarcely knew whether he had been complimented or insulted by such an offer. On the whole he felt...

He didn't know what he felt.

'Well, sir? Have you no answer for me?'

Will did not immediately show her his face. He said, speaking away from her, his voice harsh, 'You are trying to buy me.'

Nothing disturbed her lovely calm. It was intolerable that she should look like a perfect lady and say such unladylike things.

'But why should that trouble you? Were you not willing to sell yourself to my cousin, for, in effect, less?'

He swung round to drop on one knee before her, and say, his face savage, 'But that was *my* choice. This is yours.'

If Miss Rowallan was frightened at this sudden change of manner from someone so usually mild and self-controlled, she showed no sign of it.

'No,' she told him. 'It is still your choice. Think, you can say Yea, or Nay. No compulsion. And think also, if you say me Yea, then all your troubles will be over. Furthermore, if we do marry and then agree to part, I shall ensure that you will not go unrewarded.'

Oh, the temptation was great—greater, indeed, than she knew. But what sort of man would it make him if he agreed to do as she wished?

Will rose and said in a stifled voice, 'What makes you think that you can trust me? Why should I not fall on you, once we are married, and take my rights? For that matter, why should I not do so now—and then refuse to marry you? We are alone. Are you not very trusting—too trusting? After all, I am a rogue, am I not? That was decided yesterday afternoon.'

If he had thought to shake her, to frighten her, he had been mistaken. She remained as cool as ever.

'Yes, I believe that I can trust you. Last night I was told that you said that they could have done worse than allow you to marry Sarah. I believe that to be true. You may be a rogue, but I also believe that you are an honest rogue, and that, if we marry, you will be *my* rogue.'

Her rogue, indeed! The thought choked Will. It stiffened his resolve to refuse her.

'No, I won't. I reject your offer. I must have some honour left. To marry you in such a fashion would destroy my remaining self-respect.'

'I cannot see that in marrying me, you would be doing anything different from marrying Sarah. What's more I do not ask you to be celibate—I only ask you to be discreet.'

'How can you speak so?' Will was gazing at her almost in horror. 'And you a single woman!'

Miss Rowallan shook her head at him. 'I do not think that you know women very well, Mr Shafto. In that you are like most men.'

She rose. 'In a moment I shall ask you to ring for Mrs Grey. You may have refused me now, but I shall give you three days to think over my offer.'

He glared at her. 'I shall not change my mind. You must find another dupe.'

All that she replied to that was, 'We shall see. And now, Mr. Shafto, I think that it is time that you asked me to partake of the tea of which your man spoke. We must part as friends who might yet be more than friends.'

She was ice, she was steel and, marvelling at her, Will did as she bid and rang for Gib and Mrs Grey.

He could quite understand why she had not wanted her attendant lady to be present at their tête-à-tête!

Three days! Three days to decide whether or not to marry a woman whom he had disliked at first sight, and now disliked even more after he had the misfortune to know more of her. Beautiful she might be, but it was the beauty of the Gorgon who struck men stone dead. She was cunning and devious, no doubt about it, for how otherwise had she known that Gib would always be faithful to him?

Had there been two set of Runners shadowing him? No, he had not the slightest desire to lay a finger on her, could not imagine ever being roused by her... She must find another half-man to make a half-husband of.

Will was still fuming to himself later that day when Josiah Wilmot at last showed his worried face at 10, Duke Street.

'I had thought to see you before this, Josh. Much before this.'

Josh Wilmot heaved a mighty sigh. 'What point in that, Will? The matter was over and done with before you reached Allenby House. They were waiting for me when I was shown in. A whole cabal of them, sanctimonious faces and all. I was not even allowed to open my despatch box. They told me that they knew all about you—and me, too. They had put Runners on to us, they said, and the only things which prevented them from handing us both over to the law was that they could not discover that we had actually done anything criminal, and that they did not want the business to become an open scandal.'

'You might have warned me,' Will reproached him.

'Warned you! They kept me prisoner there until after you had come and gone. Confess it, Will, we were engaged in a nice little piece of flim-flam, pretending that you are richer than you are. After all, you are master of Shafto Hall, your family is an old and good one, and it is not criminal for you to be poor, nor to wish to marry a golden dolly. Many have done it before you. Bad luck for us that they found out before the wedding and not afterwards.'

'Bad luck for me, certainly,' agreed Will.

'True, and I've even worse news for you, which was why, as your good friend, I have come to see you to-night. Your paper, your bills, have been bought up by Jem Straw and before the week's end he will have you in the Marshalsea. Your little gallop is over. Get you away from London, if you can.'

'Back to the ruin which is Shafto Hall,' said Will wearily. 'At least in London I have managed to live, but what shall I do there?'

Josh Wilmot's honesty might be dubious, but his friendship for Will was not. He put an arm around his shoulders. 'Look you, Will, I would offer you a clerk's post in my office, pen-pushing, only I know that it would not answer because it would keep you—and *only* you.'

Will paced agitatedly about the room as a wild animal does when caged. He stopped to say, 'Were it not for that, for my other commitments, I would accept your offer. I am sick of the life I have been living and which circumstances have forced upon me. I have barely been keeping my head above water, waiting only for the flood which will overwhelm me—and which has now arrived.'

Josh shook his head. 'Have you no friend, no relatives who might help you?'

'None. For God's sake, Josh, what does a man do who has only been trained to be a gentleman and is fit for nothing else? I thought that marriage to Sarah would…'

He stopped abruptly and walked to the window, then turned to face Josh. He was in the same place, the same position which he had occupied when Rebecca Rowallan had made her monstrous proposition.

'Yes,' prompted Josh as Will stood there, as thunder-struck as he had been earlier. 'You were about to say?'

'Nothing…something.' Only, he thought, that Rebecca Rowallan was offering him salvation. Earlier in the day he had not been so completely on the ropes as he was now, with the prospect of the Marshalsea before him.

'Yes,' he exclaimed, striking one hand on the other. 'Yes, come hell, come the Devil, I'll do it. I was pre-pared to sell myself one way, so why not sell myself the other? She was right, damn her! Where's the difference? She gave me three days. God help me, I haven't needed one.'

Josh stared at him as though he had run mad.

'Eh, what's this, Will? Make sense, lad.'

Lad! Josh hadn't called him lad since they were boys together, not yet knowing how cruel the world might be to the poor and lowly.

'Don't ask me,' he said. 'But I have a way out. I'll not rot in the Marshalsea, Josh, and for old time's sake, I'll try to ensure that you have a decent life, too. Our hard times are over.'

'But how, Will, how?'

Will began to laugh, helplessly. 'I'm going to be mar-ried, Josh, to someone even richer than Sarah Allenby and this time there'll be no last-minute hitch. I hereby invite you to the wedding.'

He laughed all the harder at the sight of Josh's dropped jaw.

'Come, lose that Friday face, man. You shall be my lawyer again and my best man to stand at my side whilst the Allenbys watch me marry cousin Rebecca Rowallan.'

Josh took him by the shoulders. 'Look at me, Will, and speak the truth. Has worry driven you mad?'

'No, I'm not mad, Josh, far from it. You might even say that I'm suddenly driven sane. Tomorrow afternoon, as ever is, I shall be at your office to explain all.'

Josh could get nothing further from him by way of explanation, and went his way, shaking his head and muttering to himself about men driven witless by lack of money.

Left alone, Will sat down and began to plan what he might say to Miss Rebecca Rowallan on the morrow. Please God that she had not changed her mind!

Miss Rebecca Rowallan had not changed her mind. Not about her proposal nor about what Mr Will Shafto might choose to do. He was, she was sure, certain to agree to do what she wished when he had taken the time to consider her offer more carefully.

As he had suspected, she had put men on his trail to far more effect than the Allenbys had. She knew something of Will Shafto's life in London, of his lack of money, but little about the means by which he had managed to live on nothing a year. About his life in Northumberland she had learned nothing. The villagers had refused to talk to the man she had sent there. Some old and fierce loyalty made them silent when accosted by a chance-come stranger.

All that he could discover was that Mr Shafto senior had gambled everything away, shot himself, and that the family had left the Hall after his death.

'And that's all?' the man had asked. 'Is the old man's wife still alive? Has the present Mr Will Shafto no brothers or sisters?'

But he had gained nothing in reply beyond a terse, 'Nowt to do wi' you.'

No matter. Miss Rowallan had found out all that she needed to know. Mr Will Shafto was apparently alone in the world, and desperate. She was sure that he would visit her, if not this morning, then the next.

It was while she was seated in her drawing-room, waiting for him, that she had other visitors, two of them, arriving together. Mr Beaucourt and Mr Hedley Beaucourt, his son. She wished to see neither of them, but politeness demanded that she could not turn them away. They were family, after all, if only distant family, and Mr Beaucourt senior had been her guardian.

She rose to meet them, her manner as cool as ever.

'Mr Beaucourt,' she said in greeting, giving his son merely a distant nod.

'Oh, uncle, surely,' the father said, smiling, while the son tried to take her hand to kiss it. He failed. Somehow it eluded his grasp.

'Not quite,' Miss Rowallan told him gravely. 'You were merely brought up in the same household as my late mother, and are consequently no blood relation of mine.'

'Come, come, my dear. You refine too much on a relationship which allowed me to be your guardian.'

'Which you well know was none of my wish. Pray inform me why you have honoured me with this visit?'

Regretfully she sat down. It would be mannerless to keep them standing, but they must do so whilst she remained on her feet. She motioned them to sit, which they did with great flourishing of their tailcoats. Father and son both aspired to be part of the dandy set. Miss Rowallan was in another of her Quakerish gowns, a dull blue this time.

'You are in looks, cousin,' said Hedley, raising his quizzing glass to inspect her, 'but then, you always are.'

Miss Rowallan made him no answer, merely repeated her question as to their visit.

'Now, my dear, you know perfectly well why we are here.' Mr Beaucourt sounded reproachful. 'I have spoken to you of the matter often enough. You are twenty-five years old, a great heiress who has refused to take part in the Season until this year. You should be married. Nay, you must marry. You need a husband to manage your vast estates and affairs for you, and it was long the wish of your mother and I that you should marry my son Hedley.'

At the mention of his name Hedley rose and bowed. 'It is my wish also,' he said unnecessarily, having said the same thing many times before.

Miss Rowallan doubted whether her mother had ever wished any such thing. She had disliked Mr Beaucourt, who had only become her daughter's guardian because of the sudden death of her father's brother, after her parents' death in a coach accident. This had left no one of substance to be appointed in his place by the courts, except the man sitting before her, who, only moderately wealthy himself, had long plotted to marry his son to her.

She did not know which of them she disliked the more. The father, or the son. She smiled coldly at them. 'As I have informed you many times before, I have no mind to marry at all. Unless, of course, I find someone who attracts me so much that he makes marriage attractive, too.'

The elder Mr Beaucourt leaned forward and put a familiar hand on her knee. She removed it. No whit disturbed he continued. 'Now, now, my dear. We are well aware that you do not wish to entrust yourself and your fortune to anyone who might wish to exploit both it and you. But no such problem attaches itself to the proposal which I am about to make to you…'

He paused diplomatically. Undiplomatically, Miss Rowallan jumped into the silence.

'I believe, sir, that you have made it many times before. And, no, I must repeat again that I have no wish to marry your son—if that is what you are about to suggest.'

The elder Mr Beaucourt gave a melancholy sigh; the younger merely looked aggrieved and began to suck the silver knob on his cane agitatedly.

'My dear, you do not consider sufficiently what you are saying. You can trust us, for we have your best interests at heart, but as an unmarried young woman you are always at the risk of being taken in by a pretty face.'

He got no further. Miss Rowallan rose to her full height. 'This is the outside of enough, sir. You insult me. What can have given you such an absurd notion? May I say, in order to end your importunings once and for all, that if pretty faces are the problem, then I am in no danger from your son.'

Young Mr Beaucourt nearly swallowed his cane before choking out, 'Oh, I say, cousin. Steady on.'

'I am steady,' she announced, 'quite steady,' and her grim expression bore out her statement. 'Before we all say what we might live to regret, I think it better that you both leave, and do not come back until you have decided to cease pestering me to marry a man whom I do not like and cannot respect,' and she swept out of the room.

Both men were so taken aback that neither of them recovered sufficiently quickly to answer her in kind.

'I suppose,' whined the son, 'that in the circumstances we had better leave.'

'No such thing,' roared the father. 'I shall at once demand to see her again. Were it not for her money I would not wish to see you married to such a virago,' and he made for the door, followed by his complaining son.

They were met by the butler, who was followed by the largest footman either of them had ever seen. 'Madam has asked me to be certain that you leave at once,' he told them, his face quite straight. He continued suavely when Mr Beaucourt senior began to fume at him, as though forcibly removing gentlemen from the premises was an everyday thing, 'Or I cannot answer for the consequences.'

Nothing for it but to leave, thought Mr Beaucourt senior, while muttering morosely, 'I thought it a good sign that she saw us without her damned duenna, but I doubt if she would have been so downright had she been present. But this is not the last of it. No one speaks to me like that. No one.'

By now they were on the pavement, to see a hackney coach draw up from which stepped Mr Will Shafto, dressed with great elegance and carrying himself with his usual consummate ease. Passing them without acknowledgment other than a tip of his hat, he walked up the steps to Miss Rowallan's front door, to be welcomed by the butler who had just threatened to throw them out.

Father and son looked wildly at one another.

'Now what the devil is *he* doing here, paying calls in the morning?' said the father.

The son, who had taken up his cane again, decided not to suck it but to say instead, gloom written all over him, 'Perhaps he's the pretty face you said that she was sure to marry!'

Will Shafto was only half-aware of the two men who had preceded him. He had seen both of them about town and liked the look of neither of them. He had no notion that they were in any sense close to the woman he was about to meet, and who rose to greet him without so much as her duenna with her.

It was, then, to be another confidential meeting which boded well for him. Will made a mental note that if he were to marry the lady he would see that she employed a better dressmaker. The clothes she usually favoured did nothing either for her face or her figure. All that would have to change if she were to become Mrs Will Shafto.

He had had so many disappointments in life that he always used the conditional tenses when thinking about the future: something which he had failed to do when he had thought that he was on the point of marrying Sarah Allenby. He had made a mental resolve never to tempt Fate by doing such a thing again.

Nevertheless his spirits were buoyant and remained even more so when she graciously motioned him to a seat directly opposite to her.

'No need for you to stand, Mr Shafto, since by your appearance and the early hour at which you have arrived, I believe that you have come to give me an answer which I wish to hear.'

There! She was going straight to the point just like a man. No shilly-shallying, no missish drooping of the head, or touching of the handkerchief to the lips. No, everything was downright with her. Will stared at her in wonder and decided to answer her in kind—if blunt was what she wanted rather than tact, then he would oblige her.

'Indeed, Miss Rowallan, since you wish to buy me, then I am here to sell myself.'

She offered him the smile which briefly transformed her face. 'Oh, bravo, Mr Shafto. I see that we are both going to know exactly where we stand, and what we are about. It will save so much time, will it not, as well as a great deal of hurt feelings.'

'True,' returned Will. 'And since the marriage mart is what we are engaged in, then honesty ought to demand that we abide by market practices so that buyer and seller cannot later claim deceit.'

'I see that I have chosen my man well. And, Mr Shafto, you do understand that this is a purely business transaction? We shall be partners only in that sense, not in any other. The marriage will never be consummated.'

Oh, her frankness with him was strangely liberating! Will had spent a large part of his life in dealing in polite evasions—particularly where women were concerned— so that to meet with a woman with whom he could consistently talk brisk sense in plain language was like finding himself in an invigorating cold bath, not a steamy warm one.

'Yes, I understand that fully.' He decided to be as demeaning towards her as she was being towards him. 'Not to have to consummate the marriage will be a great relief to me, I assure you.'

'Excellent! That you do not find me at all attractive, I mean. That relieves my mind, too. We shall live happily together like a pair of old maids.'

'Or a pair of old bachelors,' added Will, joining in the game.

'Quite. We shall have no would-be amorous *rencontres* in corridors or bedrooms to worry about.'

'Perhaps the occasional meeting of minds in the library, instead?' was Will's counter to that.

'Oh, you read, Mr Shafto? That is a blessing I had not counted on. I had thought you quite given over to pleasure and the difficulties of being a fine gentlemen with no money to back you. Yes, I shall be happy to meet you in the library and discuss The Rights of Man—and Woman, too, perhaps. Have you read Miss Wollstonecraft's noble work?'

'No, but I am acquainted with Tom Paine, and Burke's answer to him.'

'Better and better. I anticipate a happy five years in which we shall both enrich our minds. All that remains to us is to set the lawyers to work. Do I take it that you will be employing your dubious friend Mr. Wilmot?'

'Of course, seeing that I am dubious, too… I have promised him that he may assist me at the wedding. If you agree to that, I shall be prepared to agree to all those whom you wish to invite.'

'Fair enough. It is going to be a pleasure to do business with you. Indeed, as a result of this meeting I am prepared to give you considerably more of a yearly allowance than I had originally planned. A result, I assure you, of your total lack of gentlemanly piff-paff when talking to a woman.'

'Oh, you can certainly rely on me to avoid gentlemanly piff-paff,' returned Will gravely. 'I only practise it when I talk to featherheaded women—and you are certainly not one of them!'

'Excellent, Mr Shafto, you reassure me. I do not think that I could long endure very much light-minded conversation. You will not, therefore, be surprised if the rest of our tête-à-tête is conducted along purely practical lines.'

'On the contrary,' said Will. 'I shall be most relieved.'

'Then you will not, I think, object if I suggest that we do not immediately inform society of our intention to marry. Bearing in mind what has just passed between you and my Allenby connection, I think it would be wise if we went through a reasonably lengthy pantomime in which you courted me assiduously, and I responded enthusiastically. Not straightway, perhaps, but on a rising note.

'Furthermore, to save precious time I think that we may begin this very evening. I understand that you were to have escorted my cousin Sarah to the Opera last night. Instead, with the three tickets I have purchased you may accompany myself and Mrs Grey to one of the best boxes tonight.'

Now this was pushing things on with a vengeance. Will did not suck his ivory-headed cane as young Mr. Beaucourt was in the habit of doing when wrong-footed.

Instead he countered rapidly with, 'Forgive me for quibbling a little, but will not attending such a public occasion together be an overhasty declaration of intent? When, after all, were we supposed to have met and become so fascinated with each other that you are willing to be seen out with me so soon after the…débâcle…of my engagement with Sarah?'

She had an answer for that as she appeared to have an answer for everything.

'Not over-hasty at all, Mr Shafto. We met, you must remember, at Lady Cowper's ball at the opening of the season, and since you were already involved with my cousin Sarah, you could not, as a man of honour, give way to the burning attraction which you immediately felt

for me. Fortunately the Allenbys' untoward conduct towards you has given you an honourable release and you
are now free to pursue me—gently and discreetly.'

Will rose and bowed extravagantly to her as a mark
of respect for her lively mind as well as her lively
tongue. 'Charmed to be described as a man of honour,
I'm sure.'

He sat down again and resumed. 'But if I am to be a
man of honour I must assure you that I have no memory
of either having met you at Lady Cowper's ball, or con-
tracting there such a burning passion for you as would
excuse my over-hasty pursuit of you now that I am free
again.'

'Then your memory, Mr Shafto—I do not think that
I should yet call you Will—is at fault. Pray recall that
after being introduced we danced together, and then,
later, you joined me at supper and we discussed Tom
Paine, rather than the ballgowns of my fellow heiresses.
Come, come, my dear sir, you do not really suppose that
anyone will remember exactly what took place at a ball
some weeks ago. I find that most people are incapable
of remembering what occurred at one the night before!'

For the first time she had dropped her solemn and icy
manner and there was a touch of mischief in her face,
which together with what she had just said set Will
laughing.

Which caused her face to assume its basilisk set again
so that he muttered, 'Forgive me. As a man of honour I
must be solemnity itself when we discuss such important
matters. Of course, I remember, but I believe that we
discussed Lord Byron's latest work rather than Tom
Paine. But I will defer to you if you remember otherwise.'

'You are an apt pupil, Mr Shafto. Tom Paine it was,

although I believe that you mentioned m'lord Byron in passing. Do I understand that you will therefore call for us this evening and escort us to the Opera?'

'You may, Miss Rowallan. It will be my pleasure. You would prefer me to be not too splendidly turned out. Something discreet, perhaps?'

'No, not at all. Be as splendid as you wish. I intend to be quietly elegant so that before we astonish the world with the news that we are to marry I may gradually become more and more the picture of a young woman whose appearance blossoms in response to the devoted attentions of a lover.'

Miss Rowallan ought to be writing for the Opera, not simply attending it, her imagination was so fertile, Will thought, but he did not yet know her sufficiently well to tell her so.

She rose. 'I take your silence to mean assent. I think that we have done enough plotting for today. On another occasion we shall decide in more detail how our future campaign is to be conducted.'

'One moment,' said Will, rising also. 'Are you prepared for the criticism which you will receive from all quarters when you are seen to be encouraging me?'

'Oh, indeed, Mr Shafto. Not only am I prepared for it, but it will give me the greatest pleasure to ignore it, knowing that no one will have the slightest notion of what we are about. That, in effect, I am exploiting you, not you me. It will add spice to all our meetings, will it not?'

Of all the brass-faced bitches he had ever met, Miss Rowallan was undoubtedly the acme, the very top of the tree. Will's regard for her was of genuine admiration for such raw courage from a woman alone in a world of men.

So moved was he that without thinking what he was doing he took her hand in his and kissed the palm of it reverently. The result of his hasty action astonished him. Miss Rowallan blushed a brilliant scarlet and snatched her hand back as though she had burned it.

'I had not meant to surprise you,' he came out with, for something needed to be said.

'Never fear, Mr Shafto,' she replied, her face a normal colour again. 'Any surprise will come from me, not you. After all, you were merely displaying the correct conduct of the lovelorn man—which in the context of our recent conversation is no surprise at all. *Au revoir*, then. We shall meet again later.'

It was his *congé*, and all the way back to Duke Street Will wondered what had provoked the blush and such a fierce reaction from the cold piece Miss Rowallan undoubtedly was.

Miss Rowallan knew. She had been fully in command of herself and him during all their meeting. But so far she and Will had not touched one another. All intercourse between them had been carried out at a distance.

And Will had surprised her by what he had done. She had not been ready for it, and she certainly had not been ready for the sensation which had shot through her when his warm lips had touched her cold palm. It had caused a *frisson* of pleasure to shoot through her such as she had never experienced before—and caused by such a slight thing, too.

She excused herself by saying that, whatever else, Will Shafto was an extremely handsome man, and perhaps that knowledge had caused the strong effect which had followed when he had touched her.

But other handsome men had kissed her hand without

her feeling anything at all so she could not but wonder at herself—and try to dismiss the memory from her mind.

With little success.

She was still wondering when Mrs Grey came in, her face an emblem of disapproval.

'He has gone?'

'Yes,' replied Miss Rowallan shortly, turning away.

'May I ask why he came? After all, we know him to be a rogue. I am surprised that you even received him.'

Miss Rowallan did not reveal that Will had come at her invitation. Instead she said after her usual icy fashion, 'He came to ask us to go to the Opera with him tonight.'

'And, of course, you refused.'

'On the contrary, I accepted for us both.'

'You cannot be serious—knowing of him what you do. Forgive me, but what will your cousin Sarah think of you taking him up?'

'My cousin Sarah is incapable of thinking, and even if she were, what she thinks is of no matter to me. She is not my keeper. I find Mr Will Shafto interesting and charming, and I trust that you will be civil to him whenever we meet. Is that understood?'

Mrs Grey's face was a picture. The heavens were falling in. She said feebly, 'You cannot be encouraging him?'

Miss Rowallan gave her attendant her best basilisk stare. 'And if I were, what then?' and she swept out of the room to signify that the conversation was at an end.

Chapter Three

For once, the attention of the audience at the Opera House was not on the stage, but on one of the boxes. For there, dressed as demurely as usual in unadorned white, sat England's greatest unmarried heiress, Miss Rebecca Rowallan, beside the dubious Mr Will Shafto, whose engagement to her cousin, Sarah Allenby, had been so sharply and so mysteriously called off.

If Miss Rowallan was aware of the furore she was creating, she gave no sign of it. Instead, she appeared to have no other interest than the music, paying little attention to Will Shafto who sat between her and an inwardly agitated Mrs Grey.

If Mr Shafto was agitated there was no sign of that either: quite the contrary. He was dressed *à point* all in black after the fashion established by Mr George Beau Brummell. His cravat was his and Gib's invention, being so elaborate that they had named it The Floral Dance. His black clothing possessed the advantage of distinguishing him from the rest of the *ton* who were dressed more gaudily, as well as enhancing the fineness of his physique and his features.

At the first interval Miss Rowallan suggested that he

might like to take a walk with her. Before he could so much as rise to offer her his arm, the box door opened and a number of her friends and relations entered, their faces arranged in various expressions of surprise and distaste.

They all converged on Miss Rowallan and ignored Will. He rose and stood by the door, ready to defend her if she became overset by their fiercely muttered disapproval of his presence.

John Allenby began first, hissing at her, 'Cousin Rebecca, I cannot believe that you are allowing that... scoundrel...to be your escort in a place as public as an Opera box.'

Miss Rowallan, as demure as her dress, opened her eyes wide, and murmured from behind the white lace fan which she had just raised, 'You would prefer him to escort me in private, perhaps? I scarcely think so. And, by the by, I would rather that you did not address me as cousin. You are no cousin of mine.'

'Miss Rowallan, then, and pray do not talk nonsense to me. I would prefer you to have nothing at all to do with him.'

Miss Rowallan yawned openly at him. 'Your preferences cut no ice with me, sir. You may be Miss Sarah Allenby's guardian: you are not mine.'

What John Allenby was saying was not originally meant to be overheard, but his voice had risen and Miss Rowallan was not troubling to lower hers so that Will—and the others present—could hear her every cutting word.

It was plain that Mr Allenby's supporters were as scandalised as he was both by Will's presence, and by her support of it. Will, however, was trying to suppress

laughter at the spectacle of others beside himself being
subject to Miss Rowallan's scarifying wit.

As John Allenby began to splutter at her, she lowered
her fan and indicated to Will by a movement of her head
that she wished him to leave them in order to promenade
on his own.

He bowed in her direction and began to open the door.
Whereat John Allenby acknowledged his presence for
the first time and turned to thunder at him, 'You cowardly scoundrel, to leave the poor girl you are compromising to defend herself on her own!'

Before he could answer Miss Rowallan said sweetly,
'He leaves at my command, sir. And I am sure that he
understands that I am perfectly capable of defending myself without his help.'

Will felt that he would indeed be the cowardly scoundrel he had been labelled if he said nothing, even though
Miss Rowallan had defended him in her usual no-
nonsense style.

He said in his best society drawl, 'Miss Rowallan is
well aware that if at any time she needs my strong right
arm, or my tongue, to defend her, they are both at her
disposal. As it is, my lady's word is my command.'

He thought that John Allenby was about to drop dead
of an apoplexy. Miss Rowallan, on the other hand, inclined her head prettily, saying in a voice as soft as silk,
'My thanks to you, Mr Shafto. You are as chivalrous as
I had expected you to be. May I apologise to you for
the rudeness of these people who call themselves my
relatives. Wishing to save you pain I suggest that you
leave me to deal with them and take the exercise which
I am sure you require.'

Will opened his mouth to argue with her, but she

shook her head at him playfully, but meaningfully. She intended him to do as he was told.

And so he must: for he was there but to do as she commanded. He bowed again and made his way into the corridor where he found another group waiting to enter the box to speak to Miss Rowallan once the Allenby party left.

Among them was Harry Fitzalan who, on seeing Will, caught him by the arm, exclaiming, 'Will, old fellow, do not take it amiss that I did not defend you when the Allenbys turned you away. It was a cur's trick, I know, but my allowance depends on them, and a poor devil I should be without it. You do understand, I'm sure.'

Oh, yes, Will Shafto understood only too well. He also understood that Harry Fitzalan's idea of poverty was very different from his own. But he said nothing, merely clapped Harry on the back in return, and nodded his agreement that Harry was not to be condemned for letting a friend down.

'But what the devil are you up to now? What I don't understand,' Harry rushed on, 'is what you think that you are doing by escorting Beck Rowallan to such a public place as the Opera. And so soon after Sarah's jilting you.

'As for Beck, that cock won't fight, old fellow, we've all had a go there with no luck at all. The woman's an icicle, determined to be an old maid. You'll be wasting your time and money if you start chasing her, and you know you can't afford to waste either. Why not try to find some Cit's daughter who'd be only too pleased to marry a gentleman?'

This kind advice fell on Will like a ton of bricks, as the saying had it. First of all, he was furious to hear Miss Rowallan referred to so slightingly—something which surprised him. Secondly, he was not Harry Fitzalan's old fellow, and thirdly he had tried chasing Cits' daughters, only to discover their fathers were a deal harder to pin down than Harry supposed, demanding both station *and* money in exchange for their offspring.

Restraining himself with difficulty, and at the same time beginning fully to understand what he was letting both Miss Rowallan and himself in for once he had agreed to her strange proposition, Will said, 'I'm grateful for your kind thoughts, Harry, but pray allow me to be the best judge of my own interests.'

Harry clapped him hard on the back again, saying tactlessly, 'Only trying to help you, old fellow. Know how you feel—well, not exactly, I've never been jilted and thrown out of the house into the bargain, but who knows? Need to marry money myself.'

Only because, although you have an allowance large enough to solve my difficulties, you insist on gambling it away, was Will's unkind thought on hearing that.

On stage the curtain had risen, the music had begun and people were finding their way back to their seats. Will became aware that the Allenbys were leaving Miss Rowallan's box and that he was directly in their way. By allowing Harry to corner him, he had nullified her kind attempt to save him from insult by sending him away from her box.

John Allenby marched up to him, frustration written on his face. Will could only imagine what his supposed beloved had been saying to him and his cohorts.

He stared fiercely at Will, exclaiming, 'I have told that foolish young woman what a dishonest fortune-hunter you are, but she refuses to listen to me. I would have thought that what happened to you after you had been cunning enough to entrap my niece, and been found out, would have deterred you from engaging in such adventures in the future, but no! You immediately find another silly young woman to exploit. It all goes to show that women are unfit to be left in charge of their money without supervision... The empty-headed creature in there thinks that you are in love with her! Pah!'

He paused for breath. Behind him a chorus of 'Hear Hears', and 'Yes, indeeds', was supporting each unkind word he uttered.

'Have you quite finished, sir?' Will enquired politely. 'I must point out to you that it is only your age which prevents me from knocking you down immediately for insulting a defenceless young woman to the man who has so recently become aware of what a pearl she is. Pray allow me to pass before I forget myself. I have no wish to miss more of the entertainment than I need.'

He thought to himself that Miss Rowallan's brass-faced impudence must be catching, since he was busy practising it now. It was plain that John Allenby thought so, too.

'You are a fine pair,' he almost shouted. 'And were it not that the young woman needs my protection, I would consider that the best thing to teach her a lesson would be for her to be so unwise as to marry you...'

The man standing immediately behind him caught his shoulder. 'Come, Allenby,' he said, trying to keep his own voice as mild as possible. 'Do not allow yourself to bandy words with such scum as this. Leave him—and the lady—to their fate.'

'Bandy words?' returned Will, fine eyebrows raised. '*I* have not been bandying words. I have barely spoken, and then only to defend a lady's reputation.'

John Allenby lunged at him—to be held back by those around him. Harry Fitzalan, for once aroused from his

usual languid torpor, exclaimed, 'I say, Uncle, not here.
You don't want to create a scandal by brawling at the
Opera, of all places. Not your style, at all.

'Will, old fellow, go and join Beck, I'll help to quieten
Uncle Allenby down. Beck's not your responsibility
now, Uncle, nor cousin Beaucort's either. She's her own
mistress.'

Will did not hear John Allenby's response to that. He
was too busy slipping back into the box where he found
Miss Rowallan engrossed in the action on stage. She
ignored him completely until the soprano's aria had finished when she turned her head to say calmly, 'I hope
that you had a pleasant stroll, Mr Shafto. I fear things
became rather lively in here, but all is quiet now.'

Mrs Grey, who had hitherto said nothing, suddenly
exploded. 'How can you talk such nonsense, Rebecca?
You know perfectly well that Mr John Allenby became
quite impossible, and you were no better—no, you were
worse. The whole theatre was staring at the pair of you.
I wonder at you, Mr Shafto, for leaving Miss Rowallan
to defend herself on her own.'

Miss Rowallan said sharply, 'He withdrew because I
asked him to, Amelia. I did not wish him to be exposed
to the insults of Mr Allenby, a man who calls himself
my uncle, says that he wishes to protect me, and whose
idea of protection is to marry me to Mr Hedley
Beaucourt, who is a penniless cur.'

'Mr Shafto is penniless, too,' responded Mrs Grey
miserably but truthfully, avoiding Will's eye as she
spoke.

'But not a cur. Most emphatically, *not* a cur. I was
informed that you frequent Jackson's rooms in Bond
Street and that you spar with professional prizefighters,
Mr Shafto.'

Oh, Miss Rowallan had employed only the finest to investigate him. Will had visited Gentleman Jackson's gym twice a week until his money had run low, and he still tried to keep himself in trim.

'That is true, Miss Rowallan, but not to the point, I fear. In Mr Allenby's eyes...' he began, only to be interrupted: Miss Rowallan had a fine line in interruptions.

'I am not interested in Mr Allenby's eyes, nor in his behaviour, and neither of them pleases me at all.'

She turned away from them both. 'And now if you would be so kind, let us pay attention to the music and forget what has passed. Cease to fidget, Amelia—and Mr Shafto, pray cease to smile. I cannot imagine what in the world you are finding to be amused about!'

Inexplicably the duns were holding off, or so Josh Wilmot came to tell him the day after the Opera. 'I was even informed that if Mr Will Shafto needed credit it would be supplied at a low interest.'

This was a surprise which Will had not expected. Unless the sight of him in Miss Rowallan's box had reached the duns and he was now considered a good prospect—if he married the lady, that was. Even so, he had to make sure that his friend was telling him the truth. Will never took anything on trust.

'Now, Josh, you are bamming me, surely.'

'No, Will, so if you need money, you have just to say the word.'

Yes, Will needed money, if only to be able to escort Miss Rowallan properly—and visit Jackson's gym again. He did not ask himself why he needed to do the latter, because he did not wish to answer himself correctly. Miss Rowallan had expressed admiration for his dabbling in the Fancy, as the boxing ring was known, and consequently Will was stirred to action again.

But he would not admit why.

He had promised to visit Miss Rowallan in the late afternoon so that they—or rather, she—could plot their next moves. He smiled ruefully to himself. She was firmly in the driving seat where matters between them were concerned, for he had to admit that at present he needed her more than she needed him and it was to his advantage to keep her happy.

But for all her shrewdness, and the hold over him which his poverty gave her, he was already determined that matters would be different once they were married. Oh, he was quite determined not to consummate the marriage, but he was equally determined to exert more power over their life together than she was allowing him in planning their future.

He gave Josh Wilmot *carte blanche* to arrange a further loan from the shark who was so eager to offer him one, secure in the knowledge that Miss Rowallan had promised to pay all his debts.

Consequently, when Will arrived at her home near Hyde Park that afternoon he was in a buoyant mood, ready to admire the lady's impudence and profit from it. He did wonder a little why she detested the Allenbys so much, but doubtless, later, she might tell him.

Miss Rowallan was, he saw immediately, dressed a little more stylishly than usual in a blue walking dress with lace inserts and a lower neck than usual, which allowed him to admire her creamy skin.

He was not to know that earlier that afternoon, as early as custom and good manners would permit, she had visited Lady Leominster, that great hostess and one-time mistress of the Prince Regent, to ask a favour of her.

Lady Leominster had been one of the curious at the Opera who had stared at the spectacle of the supposedly discredited Mr Will Shafto seated in Miss Rowallan's box. She was delighted to receive her privately—a signal honour—for being a great gossip, she was determined to glean something confidential about her visitor's relationship with Mr Shafto—which, of course, she would pass on.

Which was precisely why Miss Rowallan was visiting her. But it was not the only reason.

'So delighted to see you in such spirits, my dear,' Lady Leominster complimented her guest, immediately noting that Miss Rowallan's day wear was so much more voguish than that which she usually ventured out in. Was that Mr Shafto's influence? 'You have a particular reason for such an early visit, perhaps. In what manner may I assist you?'

She was nearly as frank as Miss Rowallan, and equally as devious. Miss Rowallan's smile would have been impressive on a crocodile.

'How like you, my dear Lady Leominster,' she gushed at her intended victim, 'to guess why I am here. I would ask a favour of you. Pray do not hesitate to refuse my request if it seems rather too particular. I shall quite understand.'

Inwardly bursting with curiosity, but outwardly calm, Lady Leominster riposted with, 'Until you make your request, my dear, I cannot know whether you are being too particular or not. I would be only too willing, you may be assured, to assist you, if I deem it politic to do so.'

Miss Rowallan put on a pretty air of diffidence which

would have had Mr Will Shafto grinning had he been there to see anything so unlikely as a diffident Miss Rowallan.

'You have sent me an invitation to your ball this very Friday. I wonder if you would be so good as to allow me to bring a friend along with me. Mrs Grey will be accompanying me, of course.'

'Of course,' echoed Lady Leominster, who thought that she knew what was coming. She had rarely seen Miss Rowallan so youthfully shy. She was plucking at her shawl in the most *distraite* fashion.

Miss Rowallan decided at last to look Lady Leominster in the eye. 'I have recently become acquainted with Mr Will Shafto, and find him a most delightful companion, so knowledgeable and witty. I was astonished to discover that he could converse sensibly of Burke and Tom Paine with me. Now that he is no longer engaged to Miss Sarah Allenby, and is a free man again, I wonder if you would be willing to allow him to escort me on Friday. I think that you would find him as charming as I do.'

After coming out with these last compromising sentences, Miss Rowallan looked down at her lap as though acutely embarrassed at confessing to a *tendre* for Mr Will Shafto. What she was really thinking was: judging by the Lady's expression, I am reeling her in like a fish. It will be all over the *ton* tonight that I am enamoured of Mr Will Shafto to the degree that I am calling in favours for him!

Lady Leominster leaned forward in her chair to say confidentially, 'My dear, I shall be delighted to allow him to escort you. You have been far too behindhand in the matter of enjoying yourself. This is your first season, is it not? I believe that I have seen the gentleman in question on several occasions, but we have never been introduced. That must be remedied on Friday. Discusses Burke and Paine with you, does he? That sounds most impressive! Although I must confess that though I have heard somewhat of Burke, I know nothing of Tom Paine, but no matter.'

She paused, and asked something which seemed to her more to the point than Will's literary preferences.

'Does he dance?'

'Like an angel,' answered Miss Rowallan, who had not the slightest notion of whether Mr Will Shafto danced at all—some gentlemen did not—or whether he was accomplished in the art.

'Splendid, my dear, splendid. He will not lack for partners, nor will you, now that you have chosen to come out of your shell. You will partake of some Madeira before you leave, I trust? We have not, I confess, exactly been bosom bows, seeing that your Allenby connection favours the party of which Leominster does not approve—but we must remedy that.'

'I don't exactly favour my Allenby connection, either' admitted Miss Rowallan shyly, biting her lip, 'so there is a bond between us.'

'Exactly, and here comes Francis with the Madeira. We will drink to you and to Mr Will Shafto. After all, what matters it if he is penniless? You are not, and as a rich man may choose a girl for her looks, why should not you choose a man for his?'

So it was done. Miss Rowallan did not immediately inform Will of her manoeuvres on their behalf until she sent Mrs Grey away so that she and Will might talk confidentially.

'Lady Leominster,' she told him coolly, 'is London's biggest gossip and the news will be all over town by tomorrow that I am in deep water so far as you are concerned.'

Will marvelled at her all over again.

'I had understood that she was a tough nut to crack and rarely offers anyone favours. What nutcrackers did you employ to pierce her shell?'

Miss Rowallan smiled a secret smile. 'Oh, by my manner she thought me an innocent.'

Will began to laugh in spite of himself. 'Now why in the world would she think that?' he wondered.

'Because she sees what she wishes to see,' returned Miss Rowallan, her grey eyes as cold as the sea. 'Most people do, I find.'

Would she never cease to surprise him? 'Now that, Miss Rowallan,' he admitted, 'is true, but I had never met a woman who understood such a harsh truth until I met you.'

For once Miss Rowallan's smile was painful. 'Oh, Mr Shafto, to be an orphan and to be rich beyond the dreams of avarice is to learn many harsh truths about life.' She stopped to turn her face away from him before adding, 'And one learns them early, too.'

For the first time Will felt sympathy for her. Impulsively for him, for he was accustomed to calculate the effect of all his actions before he performed them, he leaned forward to take the hand which had been lying lax in her lap in his.

Why did he wish to comfort her? Comfort the woman who had always been so contemptuously dismissive of him, the man she was buying—as she was contemptuously dismissive of everyone. He did not know: he only knew that he wanted to stroke her pale hand and, by doing so, make her look at him again—with happiness written on her face.

He did not say 'There, there', he did not need to; his stroking fingers told their own story as they gently caressed the back of her hand.

Miss Rowallan slowly turned her head. For a moment of time of which neither of them could gauge the length, nothing was said. Her expression did not alter, nor did Will's. There was nothing sexual in what he was doing. On the contrary, it was similar to the action of a woman trying to soothe a hurt child.

And then, it was over. Miss Rowallan pulled her hand away, and her face, which had softened as Will had seen it soften once before, grew hard again.

'I see that you are a kind man, after all, Mr Shafto,' she told him emotionlessly, slowly withdrawing her cold hand from his warm one. 'But I do not need your kindness. It was not part of the bargain which we made, and which we agreed was to be a purely business one. Pray try to remember that. After all our hard work, I would not wish to cancel it and start again with someone else.'

She was ice, she was stone—as Harry Fitzalan had warned him. Yet the hand which she had spurned felt curiously empty. The fingers with which he had stroked her were suddenly deprived of the comfort which he had experienced in comforting her. Needless to say, this was a strange and new emotion for Will Shafto, too—to feel for another person. So new that he was quite overset.

What, to his eternal surprise, he was suddenly experiencing was an enormous pity for the lonely woman sitting opposite to him. What could have happened to her to stifle all the warmth and pleasant ease which a young woman of her age ought to be enjoying? Did Miss Rebecca Rowallan's *joie de vivre* solely come from putting down those around her as though they were enemies whom she needed to overcome? For a brief time he had felt her pain as though it was his own.

He said nothing of this, only, his voice desolate, 'I shall not forget your wishes in future, Miss Rowallan.' They were back to the beginning of their relationship again: that of a pair of merchants in the market place.

What he could not know was that Miss Rowallan, quite against her will, was remembering the warm sensations which had overcome her when Mr Shafto had first kissed her hand, and later had stroked it. She shook herself mentally. She must be sickening for something: yes, that was it!

Their masks resumed, they continued their conversation in its most practical mode. Will arranged the details of their visit to Lady Leominster's ball: Miss Rowallan informed him of his duties once they were there.

'You must conduct yourself towards me as though I have become the passion of your life,' she told him, 'but you will be discreet in your admiration of me—as I understand you were with Sarah. Should any of your friends—Harry Fitzalan, for instance—attempt to twit you about your sudden *tendre* for me, you will indignantly reject any suggestion that it is my money alone which attracts you. On the contrary, after your experience with Sarah Allenby, you regard it as a drawback.'

The fascinated Will could not stop himself from answering her, a wry smile on his face, 'In other words, I am to lie like a trooper!'

Levity, he found, would keep breaking in, particularly when the contrast between Miss Rowallan's demure appearance and the enormity of what she was constantly saying to him, became too great, so that he was compelled to answer her in kind.

As usual, nothing he could say shook her almost regal calm.

'Just so, Mr Shafto. I am delighted to find that you understand me perfectly. Now, I think that you should leave. We have been alone together quite long enough. Poor Mrs Grey will be quite beside herself—a condition in which she frequently finds herself since being employed by me. It is a great pity that she cannot know the truth of our situation, for it would ease her mind greatly to know that we have not the slightest intention of misbehaving ourselves after the fashion which she supposes.'

'True,' returned Will, rising and bowing. 'I find that our têtes-à-têtes together are of such a nature that all improper thoughts are quite driven from my head.'

Miss Rowallan did not inform him that it was not the condition of Mr Will Shafto's head which might trouble her, but that of quite another part of his anatomy. Such a remark would have been most improper!

And, why, in the name of everything that was commonsensical, should such a disgraceful thought have popped into *her* hitherto most well-ordered and maidenly mind?

'So, it's true, Will Shafto, you devil! You *are* after Miss Moneybags. Old Mother Leominster's been putting it all round town that Beck Rowallan is so smitten with you that she has even asked for you to be invited to her latest thrash so that you might act as her escort. Good luck to you so far as laying your hands on her tin is concerned, but you do have to take her to bed as well, you know.'

It was two mornings later. Will and Harry were in Gentleman Jackson's well-appointed gymnasium at 13,

Bond Street. The walls were decorated with boxing prints designed to show the amateur what was what in the ring. A weighing machine stood in one corner. Will was dismayed to discover that since his last visit he had risen above his best fighting weight.

He had arranged to spar with the Tottenham Tiger; Harry, though, was merely one of a group which had just arrived and which had come to see any fun there might be on offer.

Will made no attempt to defend himself or Miss Rowallan. Instead, he offered his friend a mysterious smile, and continued to allow one of Jackson's orderlies to lace up his boxing gloves whilst Harry roared on.

'Haven't see you here lately, old fellow. Decided to get into trim again before the parson turns you off, are you?'

'Haven't had the time or the tin to patronise Jackson's lately.'

Harry put a finger by his nose. 'Moneylenders ready to fund you now you're so near the Rowallan goldmine, eh? But what will you do if the lady changes her mind?'

Will considered him as though from a great distance, well aware that the men around them were waiting for his answer.

'I don't think that Miss Rowallan changes her mind very often,' was his cryptic reply.

'Aye,' laughed one of his hearers, 'that's her trouble—having a mind.'

This caused a roar of laughter and set everyone's heads nodding in agreement. Will said mildly, 'I think that we ought to respect the ladies by not indulging in crass comment about them in private.'

Many heads nodded. Harry looked as though he might be about to say more, but Jackson's arrival with the Tottenham Tiger in tow brought all gossip to a stop.

The Tiger was a big fellow, not as tall as Will, but broader and heavier. Like all the professional bruisers Jackson employed he had orders to let the gentlemen down easily: they were not employed to rearrange the young men's features.

He knew Will from of old, and knew that in his best fighting form he was one of the few who needed to be treated with respect. Before he touched gloves with him, he said drily, 'Not been training much lately, sir. Bit overweight, I see.'

Will gave a short laugh. 'I've come here to remedy that, Tiger, my friend. Don't hold off, I need the exercise.'

He was a little fitter than he thought. The Tiger needed to be wary, but was still able to pull his gentleman round the room. Jackson stood watching, occasionally saying sharply, 'Keep your guard up, sir.'

As the mock bout ended with Will puffing and blowing rather more than in the old days, Jackson took the trouble to say to him, 'Pity you're a gentleman, sir. I could have made a fighter of you. You'd have gone a long way.'

Privately he believed that Mr Will Shafto had a deal of spirit beneath his easy exterior. Will thought ruefully that if he had known Jackson in his penniless early twenties he might have taken his offer up. Successful bruisers could earn a comfortable living.

On the other hand, unsuccessful ones often ended up as paupers with deformed faces and bodies...

He touched gloves with the Tiger at the end and stepped back, sweating visibly, his white shirt clinging to his torso. Unnoticed by him in the heat of the bout, Hedley Beaucourt had entered the gym and had been watching him with feral eyes, willing the Tiger to plant such a facer on him as would spoil Will's looks for good.

No such luck. One more count against Mr Will Shafto was his athletic prowess. It wasn't fair; if everyone had their rights, fortune-hunters ought to possess no social or physical talents at all. It never occurred to Hedley Beaucourt that both he and his father were also fortune-hunters. They were Beaucourts, and that forgave all.

Consequently when Will, his gloves discarded, made for the small room where customers towelled off and changed into a clean dry shirt after their exertions he found himself face to face with Mr Hedley Beaucourt.

Mr Beaucourt looked him up and down. 'Ah, Shafto,' he said, his lip curling. 'I find you in your proper milieu: a boxing booth. I wonder you never took it up. Not brave enough, eh?'

Will chose not to answer him. He continued steadily on his way. Mr Beaucourt caught him by the shoulder, tried to turn him round, and failed.

'Look at me, damn you. I asked you a question.'

Will wrenched himself free. 'Which I chose not to answer.'

He made to walk on. Mr Beaucourt snarled at his back. 'I suppose that your only bravery is displayed when you're alone with that silly bitch, Beck Rowallan.'

Will's reaction was purely instinctive and went against all the advice which Miss Rowallan poured over him whenever they met.

He swung round, saying, 'This will teach you to insult a good woman,' and struck Hedley Beaucourt in his ugly, leering face. The punch was not thrown with his full power, but it was still strong enough to half-stun his jeering opponent, and throw him back into the arms of those around him.

Sanity returned to Will as Harry Fitzalan and the Tiger pinioned him to prevent him from landing another blow on Mr Beaucourt, who was being helped to his feet by another of Jackson's bruisers.

'You can let go of me,' Will said stiffly. 'I shan't hit him again—unless he mentions her name again, that is.'

For some reason he could not call her Miss Rowallan, something which surprised him nearly as much as his sudden rush of anger on hearing her slandered.

'You shouldn't have hit an unarmed man without warning,' Mr Beaucourt snuffled at him, his handkerchief to his damaged and bleeding nose.

'Unarmed!' Will shot back. 'What arms am I carrying? I wasn't even wearing my gloves. And I warn you, if I hear that you have misnamed the lady again I shall call you out and you can face me when we are both carrying arms. As it is, I demand that you apologise to me or I'll call you out now!'

His inward reaction was not so brave, for he had no doubt that Miss Rowallan was going to be very cross with him when the news reached her that he had been involved in a brawl over her good name. She was likely to call their bargain off immediately. And what if she did…?

Will stopped this line of thought: it was too painful. He concentrated on staring at Mr Beaucourt, who was still whimpering something through his scarlet handkerchief. Harry and the Tiger, convinced that Will was now sane again, had released him.

'I'm waiting,' he said. 'I give you one minute to apologise, and if you don't I shall call you out.'

Mr Beaucourt knew when he was defeated. He snuffled something intelligible.

'Louder,' said Will. 'I can't hear you.'

Mr. Beaucourt looked desperately around him for support. Finding none, he muttered, 'I said that I'm aware that it was wrong of me to mention a lady's name in a place like this.'

'Don't insult Mr Jackson's establishment,' Will returned sternly. 'Simply admit that you were wrong to traduce a lady. And after that be sure that you don't try to blacken her name in public again, or, by God, I'll strike you again.'

Mr Beaucourt took his handkerchief away and babbled something which seemed to suggest that he had learned his lesson. He was not helped by being unhappily aware that, although many present thought that Will had gone a bit too far by striking him so hard, he had asked for it by what he had said of Miss Rowallan.

Honour was satisfied. Will turned away. He had probably dished himself for good—and his hopes for the future as well. And all for a woman who felt nothing for him—as he felt nothing for her.

If so, where had the rage come from?

Will became aware that it was Harry's turn to babble. 'Shouldn't like to get on the wrong side of you, Will. Always thought you were a mild fellow. Just now you looked exactly like the Tiger when he finished off the Tooting Terror, and no mistake.'

'Just leave it, Harry,' Will told him wearily. He was sure that his day of judgement would soon follow. Such a lovely piece of gossip would be all round the town in no time. The second juicy *on dit* about Will Shafto—no, the third—in a week.

What in the world would Miss Rowallan have to say to him when she learned that he had done exactly what she had told him not to do?

Chapter Four

'I thought, Mr Shafto, that I asked you to behave with decorum and discretion. You may imagine my astonishment, nay, shock, when Mrs Grey informed me of what had passed at Mr Jackson's gymnasium. Discreet you were not.'

'She would tell tales,' muttered Will. 'She couldn't wait to sneak to you, I suppose.'

Miss Rowallan serenely ignored him. 'I was not, I must say, sorry to learn that Mr Hedley Beaucourt received a bloody nose, I believe it is called. He has been asking to be rewarded with one for some time. No, what did distress me was that you chose to give it to him after all I have had to say to you.'

She didn't look distressed. On the contrary she was smiling.

'He insulted you. By name,' Will announced, deciding to go on the offensive. 'Before a pack of so-called gentlemen he questioned your honour—and mine. I couldn't let the insult to you pass, the one to me didn't matter.'

Miss Rowallan closed her beautiful eyes and lay back in her chair. She was, Will suddenly noticed, attired in a much more fetching turn-out than usual. Pale amethyst with pearls. Chaste, yet luxurious. Her glossy chestnut hair was dressed less austerely, too. Her tone, on the other hand, remained as austere as ever.

'I suppose,' she said at last, 'it's useless to ask you to be discreet. Gentlemen never are.'

No more than that? Will, who had fully expected that she would give him his *congé*, was a trifle unsettled on learning that she wasn't going to.

'*He* wasn't discreet—so how could I be? Your remarks ought more properly to be addressed to Mr Beaucourt, not to me.'

He expected another cool riposte, instead she asked him earnestly, 'Pray, what is it like at Mr Jackson's, Mr Shafto? What do you do there? Other than knock down offensive fools on my behalf?'

To say that Will was thrown by her rapid change of manner would be to understate matters.

'I work out, and then I spar with one of Mr Jackson's bruis— I mean, boxers. Sometimes with Mr Jackson himself.'

'Work out, Mr Shafto?'

'Exercise,' he said. 'To keep myself in trim. I've not been so much in trim lately.'

Miss Rowallan looked him up and down. Mr Will Shafto was wearing a deep blue jacket, cream trousers, a shirt and cravat of the purest white, and his hair was disposed in a fashionable Brutus cut. He looked a very tulip of fashion.

'Really, Mr Shafto? You do surprise me. You look very much in trim to me.'

Will decided to humour her. 'But I don't look very much in trim to a professional pugilist, Miss Rowallan. My wind is poor, for one thing.'

'Your wind, Mr Shafto?'

'Yes. I begin to huff and puff somewhat when I've been sparring for only a short time. The Tottenham Tiger would make short work of me and no mistake if we were in the ring together.'

'And are you likely to meet the Tottenham Tiger in the ring, Mr Shafto? Is that why your…wind…matters?'

By God, she was teasing him, no doubt of it. Because she had been speaking in her usual measured fashion he had thought that she was serious.

'You're bamming me,' he said, beginning to smile himself.

'So I am. I wondered when you would realise what I was doing. I am to suppose that boxing is one of the great mysteries which men perform in the absence of women, and I was somewhat curious about what it entails.'

'Dear Miss Rowallan,' said Will, unconsciously using an endearment to her for the first time, 'you might be surprised to learn that when boxing matches are held in the deep country—since they are illegal, you understand—a large number of women are often present who halloo on the champion of their choice and cheer each blow he lands.'

'Really, Mr Shafto? Yes, that does surprise me…' she paused '…I think. And now we ought to discuss our visit to Lady Leominster's tomorrow. I must insist that you refrain from knocking any one down for me there. Brawling at Jackson's is one thing—one quite expects it. Engaging in a mill at Leominster House, would, I am sure, be most ill seen.'

'You may depend upon me to behave myself,' Will assured her, relieved that being royally teased was all that he was going to suffer. 'I shall be as solemn as a bishop.'

'See to it, Mr Shafto, see to it, and now I will ring for Mrs Grey and tea. We must both look as grave as a pair of parsons when she arrives. I believe that she thought that I would show you the door, but we are too far along for that, Mr Shafto, are we not?'

The only possible answer was, 'Yes, indeed,' so Mr Shafto made it.

Mrs Grey, by her manner, made it quite plain that she disapproved of both her employer and the man whom she was so unaccountably favouring.

'A rogue,' she had said angrily to her best friend, Mrs Champion, who was Lady Leominster's chief attendant. 'He's nothing but a rogue. He was turned away by the Allenbys because they discovered that he was a penniless fortune-hunter, and now Miss Rowallan has nothing better to do than take him up. I had thought that she was the very acme of common sense, but no. I wonder at her, I really do.'

'She doesn't intend to marry him, surely!' exclaimed Mrs Champion as though she were speaking of Miss Rowallan catching the plague.

'Anything is possible,' admitted Mrs Grey mournfully, 'anything.'

So she glowered balefully at Will when Miss Rowallan was not looking at her, and Will smiled sweetly back at her in return. He did not blame her for her antagonism to him; in her place, he would have felt the same.

He had learned long ago in a hard school that more flies are caught by honey than by gall, as the saying had it, and he might yet win Mrs Grey over if he did not allow her to upset him.

She was still antagonistic, however, when he called for her and Miss Rowallan on Friday evening to escort them to Lady Leominster's ball. They were travelling in Miss Rowallan's carriage: she was well aware that Mr Shafto did not possess one of his own, and would not put him to the expense of hiring one.

'May I compliment you both on your appearance,' Will said after he had settled himself in the carriage opposite to the pair of them. Not was he being insincere. Miss Rowallan, superb in old rose and silver, was a vision of gauze and crêpe adorned with tea-roses made from silk. She was sporting her pearls and a large fan with a small mirror in its heart.

Mrs Grey was modest in pale blue. Her gown was elegance personified in its classic simplicity. Will thought that she must be in her middle thirties. He knew that she was a penniless widow of good family who needed a post with someone such as Miss Rowallan.

He handed them both out of the carriage, making little distinction between her or Miss Rowallan in the civilities which he offered to them. He walked between them up the great staircase at Leominster House to the landing where the Leominsters were receiving their guests.

He was immediately aware that their small party was a centre of interest. Eyes and whispers followed them. Lady Leominster herself made a great point of kissing Miss Rowallan on the cheek and welcoming Will warmly. Mrs Grey received only an indifferent nod.

The great thing, though, as he and Miss Rowallan well knew, was that Lady Leominster's enthusiastic reception of them meant that he would be accepted everywhere. She was a patroness of Almack's and one of society's greatest arbiters: her word was law. Had she turned Mr Will Shafto away, or spoken to him coldly, then it was likely that Miss Rowallan might have changed her mind about their bargain.

Many such as the Allenbys might have reservations about him, but now, provided he behaved with discretion, he was a made man.

'I had not thought him to be so handsome,' was the comment of more than one young lady, as well as many older ones. Miss Sarah Allenby, seated beside the middle-aged Marquess she was going to marry, could not help comparing his gross body and well-worn features with Will's athletic physique and his strikingly handsome face—to her new fiancé's detriment.

'I wonder,' said Mr Allenby to m'lord Marquess of Wingfield, 'that he dare show his face in decent society, but since the Leominster woman has chosen to favour him, then the rest of us are stuck with him, I suppose.'

His face darkened when he saw Will bend down to Miss Rowallan, who was seated on a chair beside him, in order to speak confidentially to her when she had drawn his attention by tapping him with her closed fan. 'The silly chit's run mad to encourage such a base fortune-hunter,' he muttered.

He was foolish enough to say this to Miss Rowallan a little later, when, temporarily deserted by Will—who had been taken off by Lady Leominster to be introduced to her nephew, Colonel Minster—she was consequently sitting alone with Mrs Grey.

She smiled sweetly at him and promptly trumped his ace by asking him if he would explain to her what the difference was between m'lord Wingfield, who was middle-aged and penniless, and was now betrothed to Sarah, and the equally penniless Mr Will Shafto.

'For,' said she demurely, 'the only difference I can see, apart, of course, from the Marquessate, is that Mr

Shafto is a handsome young man, whilst m'lord is an ugly old one! Does fortune-hunting, as well as kissing, go by favour? Does the possession of a title make up for the lack of practically everything else in a man?'

'You forget yourself,' stammered Mr Allenby, purpling with rage. 'There is every difference between them. My only hope for you is that you are merely amusing yourself, and trying to annoy me, by taking him up so fervently—and will later amuse yourself by dropping *him*.'

Miss Rowallan fanned herself vigorously before replying, 'Oh, sir, you know that I never merely amuse myself. That is not my way. And I have not the slightest intention of dropping Mr Shafto. On the contrary, having caught him, I am thinking of taking him up permanently—if he will have me, that is.'

By ill—or possibly by good—luck, Mr Shafto arrived back at this moment, Lady Leominster on his arm. The Lady summed up the situation in a flash. She saw Miss Rowallan's control of the situation, Mr Allenby's jealous rage, and also took in the hovering Mr Hedley Beaucourt, who had been on his way to ask Miss Rowallan to join him on the dance floor.

Stirring any pot which needed it in order to ensure that society had a full complement of scandals and *on dits* to keep it happy was a speciality of hers. Particularly when, as now, she disliked one of her victims. The Allenbys, she considered, with all the benefit of a five-hundred-year-old title behind her, were a collection of parvenus whose money was mainly derived from trade—money which was but two generations away from its original creation, and therefore insufficient time had passed to allow it to be sanctified.

'I am returning Mr Shafto to you,' she carolled at

Miss Rowallan, who had risen and bowed at her approach. 'You told me that he was handsome, you did not tell me that he was charming and clever.'

She turned to Mr Allenby, who was torn between glowering at Will and fawning on the Lady so that his facial expression was, to say the least, peculiar.

'You will, I am sure, agree with me that Miss Rowallan is most happy in her chosen companion to-night. I have been telling her how pleased I am to see that she has at last come out of her shell and is enjoying herself as befits a young lady of her station in life. She could have no better person to assist her in that task than Mr Shafto. They make such a handsome pair, do they not?'

What could Mr Allenby say? Miss Rowallan was smiling at him. Mr Shafto, the subject of more praise from the great ones of his world in one evening than he had received in the whole of his previous life, stood by looking as gravely composed as the bishop whom he had promised Miss Rowallan he would resemble.

He was inwardly amused at the grotesque spectacle of the obsequious snob whom he knew Mr John Allenby to be having to express his pleasure on meeting him and then being compelled to agree that Miss Rowallan could have no better companion.

He mumbled something which Lady Leominster chose to construe as consent, but the moment that she left them, still scattering benediction and imaginary posies around Miss Rowallan and Will, he turned on his heel and walked away.

Miss Rowallan raised her fan in order to laugh behind it, unseen. Her stratagems were working even more successfully than she had expected. It was plain that Lady Leominster had taken one look at Will and succumbed to his charms. Matters were moving along even better than she had dared to hope.

She could see young Mr Hedley Beaucourt hovering in the distance, hoping that Will would go away long enough for him to offer to take her on to the dance floor if he did so.

Will, amused by his roaring social success, but not to the degree that his head was turned, had also seen Mr Beaucourt. He bowed to Miss Rowallan, and as he straightened up, murmured, 'There is a gadfly hovering, Miss Rowallan. Would you care to dance with me so that you may be spared having to refuse him publicly?'

Miss Rowallan handed her fan to Mrs Grey, who was thinking that not only had Miss Rowallan run mad over Mr Will Shafto, but so had the rest of the world. She accepted the fan with a sigh and watched the pair of them make their way to join the quadrille which was about to begin.

It was sadly true that he and Miss Rowallan made a handsome couple. But was he not a rogue? And for all society's sudden endorsement of him, Will had only lived on its fringes before. Surely that acceptance was insufficient reason for Miss Rowallan to decide that she wanted to marry him? No doubt about it, she ought to marry one of her own kind.

The quadrille began. Will and Miss Rowallan bowed to one another before the intricacies of the dance took them away—only to reunite them before they parted again.

In one of its many variations Miss Rowallan met Sarah Allenby, whose fat Marquess was finding it difficult to keep up with the quadrille for all its slow stateliness.

'What are you doing with *him*?' Sarah hissed at her.

'Dancing,' replied Miss Rowallan sweetly.

'You know what I mean,' Sarah hissed at her again when next they met.

'Enjoying his company. You did,' added Miss Rowallan incontrovertibly.

This was one of those statements which does not possess an answer—or not one which can be made with any dignity.

'He was after my money,' Sarah said defiantly.

Miss Rowallan was all composure. 'Yes, I know. He's after mine.'

They parted again. The dance brought them side by side again. Miss Rowallan asked Sarah, her face puzzled, 'Does his title make up for his appearance?'

'I'm sure that I don't know what you mean,' was all she got back.

'Oh, yes, you do. At least my fortune-hunter is handsome and clever. Yours is ugly and stupid.'

This was to say the unsayable, even if it was truthful. Miss Rowallan had learned long ago that the truth is almost invariably unsayable in the kind of formal society to which she belonged. Telling it, as now, first gave her the most exquisite pleasure, and then made her feel sorry for having done so.

Sarah's eyes when next she passed her were full of tears. '*You* don't have relatives and a guardian to tell you what to do. I do. You're lucky.'

'Yes,' agreed Miss Rowallan. 'I'm sorry I twitted you, Sarah.'

But it was too late to repent—it always is.

Next there was Mr Will Shafto to deal with when the dance was over.

'What did you say to Sarah Allenby to distress her?' he asked. 'She was almost in tears.'

Miss Rowallan never lied. Well, hardly ever.

'I was unkind to her.'

Will looked at her. 'You shouldn't be, you know. She was happy with me. I made her laugh. Her Marquess won't. On the contrary, from what I hear of him, he'll make her cry. You should feel sorry for her.'

Miss Rowallan, for once, was almost defensive. 'She threw you over, and allowed her family to treat you cruelly.'

'It wasn't her wish,' Will said. 'She had no choice in the matter. Whilst you, *you* are free to do as you please.'

Not only was it what Sarah had told her, but he was rebuking her and they both knew it. If she chose to take offence… Will shrugged his shoulders.

Miss Rowallan recovered her fan from Mrs Grey and took refuge behind it to digest something which she had not known before. *Her* fortune-hunter was kind.

So the evening passed. Miss Rowallan made a point of confiding in Will behind her fan, and encouraging him to behave as though he were her devoted cavalier. She seemed, Will thought, a little gloomily, as much in command of herself as ever—more so, perhaps.

He was not to know that for the first time he had said something which had pierced the hard shell which Miss Rowallan had erected around her most inward self. She had thought that she was immune to either praise or blame—and most certainly immune to criticism from anyone.

But Will's gentle remarks about poor Sarah's sad condition and, by inference, her own unkindness, had made her uncomfortable, more particularly because she had regretted her remark herself. Such regret was new to her. More than that, he had made her understand that wit, carelessly used, could be too cruel a weapon when wielded against someone as helpless as poor Sarah Allenby.

For the first time for many years, Miss Rowallan examined herself, and did not like what she saw. And it was all Mr Shafto's fault, the rogue whom she had bought with her money, and who was no better than he should be.

Truly, life was strange when a rogue could bring tears into the eyes of a woman who had not cried since she was seventeen years old… Remorse, experienced after a long absence, is an uncomfortable companion. It whispered its sad message in Miss Rowallan's ear throughout the long evening and made it seem even longer.

Towards midnight that new and daring dance, the waltz, was played. Its daring lay in bringing the dancers in close contact with one another for the whole of its duration. That, and the exciting sensations roused in the bosoms of the performers.

For a woman to dance it with a man was to make a certain statement of involvement. Will had just escorted Miss Rowallan back from the supper room when its music began. Neither of them had eaten very much. Somehow in their odd situation it did not seem that it was quite the thing to be seen gorging themselves.

It did not occur to Will that the outwardly proper Miss Rowallan would wish to waltz with him, so he stood gracefully behind her chair and wished the evening were over. His surprise was great when she put a lace-gloved hand on his arm and whispered, 'I would, of all things, wish to dance this with you, Mr Shafto. Pray, I beg of you, invite me, so that all will be proper.'

Proper? For a maiden lady of mature years and so-far impeccable propriety to dance it with a person as dubious as he was? For a moment he was stunned, until he suddenly saw the light. It was simply a part of her campaign to persuade the *beau monde* that they were so smitten with each other that they were prepared to defy convention.

Will was suddenly all gallantry. He bowed low to her and said in a voice loud enough for those around them to hear him, 'My dear Miss Rowallan, will you do me the honour of dancing the waltz with me?'

Surrounded by shaking and disapproving heads, Miss Rowallan rose, handed her fan again to the aghast Mrs Grey, and shyly agreed to do so.

'I should like that of all things,' she whispered demurely, 'if you will not think me overbold for agreeing.'

'No, never,' murmured Will. 'However could I think such a thing of you, so charmingly modest and unforthcoming as you are!'

Considering everything, Miss Rowallan would have liked to kick his shins for making such a two-edged remark: an action which she had not performed since she had so rewarded an impudent boy cousin for trying to take liberties with her when she was fifteen. Instead, she felt compelled to hang her head a little, try not to blush—and walk on to the floor with him.

'I am afraid,' she whispered, 'that I have not performed the waltz with a gentleman before, only with a dancing mistress. You will be patient with me, I trust.'

'Oh, you already know that patience is my middle name,' retorted Will. 'And I also know how quick you are to learn.'

So saying, he took her into his arms, being careful to hold her at some little distance as he whirled her round the floor.

They knew that every avid eye was on them while they quartered the room with such infinite grace that it might have been supposed that they had been dancing together for years.

Was it that which was causing such odd tremors to run through Miss Rowallan's virgin body? The certainty that they were being watched?

Or was it being so near to Mr Will Shafto, so near that she could feel the warmth of him, not only of the strong hands which held her so gently, but of his whole body? She could smell the lemon in his hair dressing, and in the soap with which he had washed himself, as well as the aroma of something subtly masculine, quite unlike any scent which a woman gives off.

A scent which was uniquely male and which had always previously been distasteful to her, but which was now exciting quite another feeling in her breast. Except that it wasn't only Miss Rowallan's breast which was being affected. Her whole body was responding to him.

In all the plans which she had had for Mr Shafto, none of them included feeling any kind of emotion for him other than mild gratitude for his unfailing obedience to her wishes—as now. She chided herself. These new and strange feelings were most untoward and inconvenient and must at all costs be suppressed.

The problem was that, held in this intimate fashion, she was also becoming frighteningly aware of the sheer strength of him. It was as though she had been mercilessly baiting a mild pony only to discover that it was a stallion in his pride which she had been provoking!

This was yet another disturbing thought. Even more disturbing was to discover that, whilst experiencing these new and unwelcome impressions, she was apparently quite capable of performing the waltz without making a mistake—something which she had never accomplished with her instructress! Miss Rowallan was so surprised on realising this that she stumbled—to be kept on her feet by Mr Shafto's strong arms.

'Forgive me,' she quavered, finding herself at a loss with him for the first time in their acquaintance. 'I had not meant to be so clumsy.'

'Do not trouble yourself,' he told her. 'For a novice you are performing quite splendidly. All eyes are upon us.'

'For quite other reasons than our dancing ability, you must admit,' she announced tartly, recovering her balance and her *savoir-faire* at the same moment.

'That, too,' agreed Mr Will Shafto, who was having a few problems of his own now that he had Miss Rowallan in his arms for the first time.

Not only was she lighter on her feet than he had expected her to be, but she was so soft and tender in his arms, all her hard logic and severe self-command having disappeared from the moment that he had led her on to the floor.

Not only that, but she was wearing some subtle perfume which he had not encountered before. It was lightly floral, but with a certain spice added to it. Perhaps it was not a new perfume at all, but was eau-de-Miss Rowallan, as it were, instead of eau-de-toilette.

This thought was so erotic that it had the effect of rousing him, something which he had been firmly convinced that Miss Rowallan could never do! If her feelings for him in the dance were inappropriate and unwanted, Will felt the same about what she was unwittingly doing to him!

For one thing, dressed as he was in skintight breeches, it was a damned inconvenient state to be in. No wonder the waltz was described as sinful if this was what it did to you! He refused to believe that it was Miss Rowallan who was affecting him so strongly. No, it must be the music.

A conclusion which Miss Rowallan had also reached by the time that the dance had ended. They were both relieved that the entertainment which they had been providing was over.

'I should like to sit down now—and perhaps you could arrange for a footman to fetch me a glass of water.' She added in explanation, for one seemed to be needed, 'I have become a little overheated.'

So had Will, but water would not cure him. Not unless someone hurled a bucketful of it over him!

He bowed to her painfully, and thought of waterfalls, cascades of the stuff falling down into a vast pool, of swimming in it, shivering as he did so. This seemed to do the trick, and he tried not to look directly at her, even when he was handing her to her chair, and avoiding the reproachful eyes of Mrs Grey.

The water was duly ordered and arrived in a finely chased crystal glass carried on a silver tray by an obsequious footman. He was accompanied by Lady Leominster all of a-twitter.

'My dear Miss Rowallan, I do hope that this does not mean that you have been overdoing matters on your first major excursion into society. I vow that you and Mr Shafto were the most handsome couple on the floor. *That* is how the waltz should be done, I told Leominster, with airy grace, not in the clodhopping fashion that so many employ.'

Will bowed, amused. It was plain that whoever else disapproved of them, Lady Leominster was completely in his thrall. Miss Rowallan assured her that she was merely a little overheated, the waltz being rather more strenuous than the dances which she was used to.

'True, true,' agreed her ladyship. 'Leominster will have it that we are turning into savages by dancing two and two and not in a group. He says that we shall be performing on our own next—he will have his little joke, you know!'

Her hearers duly obliged her by laughing politely at it. Gratified, she left them, but not before she had made them promise that they would join her and her husband in their box at Drury Lane. 'A week from tonight, my dears.'

She did everything but wink complicitly at them, and if Miss Rowallan had wished not only to display Mr Shafto to the world as her cavalier, but also to have him accepted by society, that wish had been granted in the most public manner possible.

The Allenbys might roar as they like, Mr Hedley Beaucourt and his papa might sulk, Mrs Grey might deplore, but the deed was done. Miss Rebecca Rowallan and Mr Will Shafto were an accepted pair.

Chapter Five

Was he happy? Will did not know. He knew that he ought to be. He had at last achieved the goal which he had set himself. He was marrying wealth, if not high rank, and only he—and Miss Rowallan's senior lawyer, Mr Herriott—knew of the strings attached to his marriage.

Miss Rowallan's lawyers were thrashing out the financial details of the marriage settlement, with Josh Wilmot attending. Josh was surprised by the extent of Miss Rowallan's generosity over Will's allowance, but was not surprised by the conditions which hedged Will about in other ways. He knew nothing of the other settlement, privy only to Mr Herriott, Miss Rowallan and Will, which ensured that the marriage would be one in name only, and would not be consummated.

'You are sure that you wish this?' he had asked both of the parties when he had presented the document for them to sign. Both of them had earnestly assured him that such was their deepest desire. 'There will be no marriage without it,' Miss Rowallan announced firmly.

They had each decided that their sensations during the waltz had been something of an aberration, and had privately resolved that in future they would touch the other as little as possible. Only thus could they keep to their strange bargain.

'You could, of course, break this agreement if you both decided that that was what you wished,' Mr Herriott told them. Neither of them answered him, and he gave a great sigh.

He could understand Miss Rowallan protecting her money and property from Will's possibly predatory hands, but that she should also protect herself from Will's handsome person was quite another thing!

Finally, all the legal matters pertaining to their marriage were arranged—only its timing remained to be decided, and that would be when Miss Rowallan considered that Will had been accepted as her certain and future husband.

They remained the sensation of the Season. They were seen in the Leominsters' box at Drury Lane; they rode together in Hyde Park; visited Astley's Amphitheatre; boated on the Thames near Richmond where Miss Rowallan was exposed to Mr Shafto's athleticism again—and womanfully resisted its attractions.

Every great hostess invited them to their balls and receptions and even Almack's opened its doors to them—the final accolade. At which point Miss Rowallan decided that her campaign was over.

Nothing remained to them but to bring all speculation to an end and to marry, and it was Miss Rowallan who was ready to 'pop the question' as her kitchen staff had it, and not Mr Shafto as they all, quite naturally, supposed.

Will had not seen her for several days—he had business of his own to clear up, he had told her—but when he walked into her drawing-room one sunny afternoon he knew at once that she was about to make an announcement of some kind.

For all that she was a woman whom he told himself firmly possessed no attractions for him, it was wonderful how well he was coming to know her. He wondered uneasily if she was coming to know him after the same fashion. He hoped not.

She had motioned him to a seat opposite to her, sent an unwilling Mrs Grey away and had begun by asking him if they really needed to attend Lady Jersey's ball that evening. He was only too willing to agree that they didn't. Privately, for each did not confide in the other, they were both growing bored with the empty round of the High Season.

Will missed the country which, being penniless, he could no longer afford to live in, and Miss Rowallan missed her pretty home in the Yorkshire Dales and the village where everyone knew her as someone quite different from the cold beauty who adorned the London ballrooms.

There were times when she wondered how Will would fit in with her uneventful rural existence, but at the moment all that concerned her was manoeuvring him into agreeing to her marriage plans.

She had dressed herself with great care in a slightly more frivolous turn-out than usual—something which Will had already noticed. A high-waisted pale-green afternoon dress with cream lace insets, collars and cuffs brought out the highlights in her chestnut hair, and flattered the cool porcelain of her complexion.

Mr Will Shafto would not be able to complain that his future wife did not do him credit so far as her dress sense was concerned. She listened to him gravely as he agreed with her that balls and receptions were vastly overrated affairs.

'Unless, of course,' he ended, 'one is a Member of Parliament, or a patron of the arts, or like the Leominsters ''count coup'', as the North American Indians have it, every time that they arrange a function which outshines everyone else's in splendour.'

'Indeed,' said Miss Rowallan, and then continued without so much as drawing breath, 'I think, Mr Shafto, that it is time that you proposed to me.'

She had surprised him again.

'You do?' was all he managed.

'Oh, yes, indeed. And you must apply for a special licence at once so that we may be married as soon as possible.'

How was it that she so often managed to take his breath, as well as his sense away? Will liked to think that he was as blasé as a man might be, but beside Miss Rowallan he was a mere amateur in the game of over-setting others.

'I am crazed with love for you, you understand, and I am informed that persons in that condition commit the most impulsive acts.'

'They do?' Could one, Will asked himself, ever imagine Miss Rowallan committing any act which could conceivably be described as impulsive? She was surely reason itself, with logic as her goddess.

Miss Rowallan took his stunned silence for consent. 'Also, Mr Shafto, I think that it is time that I addressed you as Will, and that you saluted me as Rebecca.'

Mr Shafto took a small revenge. 'Not Beck, or Becky, then?'

'Indeed, not. I had rather you called me my love, only that seems a little excessive given our circumstances.'

Mr Shafto made an immediate resolution that if he ever wished to annoy Miss Rowallan he would most certainly address her as Beck. This mutinous thought gave him great pleasure.

Aloud he said, 'Perhaps it might be simpler if we called each other nothing at all—other than ''you'' if the occasion were sufficiently intimate.'

Miss Rowallan was not sure whether or not Mr Shafto was serious in proposing this, his face was so straight. She decided to ignore him and said graciously, 'Then that's settled, then.'

To his own surprise Will exclaimed, almost violently, 'No, it damned well is not! I haven't proposed to you, and I refuse to be fobbed off in this fashion. We must at least go through the forms. I may have sold myself to you for some purpose of yours which is obscure to me, but at least grant me some dignity in my servitude.'

He went down on one knee before her, seized her right hand roughly and said in a voice in which chagrin and self-mockery were finely blended, 'My dear Miss Rowallan, before your humble servant expires for thwarted love of you, pray do him the honour of agreeing to his proposal of marriage.'

Now he had her at a disadvantage. Miss Rowallan looked into his eyes, which were level with her own, and replied almost humbly, 'Forgive me if I took things for granted. I lacked tact, I fear.'

'Tact!' Will stood up. 'That is the least of it—Beck. But I forgive you.'

He was aware that he had lost his fine control and that, from being players in a sophisticated comedy, he and Miss Rowallan had become snared in something more dramatic.

He walked over to the window and looked down on

to the street. While they had been talking an organ grinder had set up his machine, had begun to play it, and his monkey had started its melancholy dance. Will knew exactly how the monkey felt. Beck Rowallan, he thought savagely, would make a splendid organ grinder and he her perfect monkey. He swung to face her.

'If you want to call this damned business off, and look for someone else,' he ground out, 'then say so now. I shall quite understand.'

Miss Rowallan was silent. Her expression had not changed. It was as inscrutable as ever. Her hands were lightly clasped together in her lap.

Will said nothing further. His back being to the light meant that his face was in shadow.

'No, Mr Shafto, you may not retreat so easily. We have a bargain, you and I. May I remind you that, without coercion, you have already signed the papers which dispose of your future for the next five years. For you, the bargain is a good one, whilst I am satisfied that in choosing you I have chosen well. No, I will not call this damned business off.'

Will bowed. 'I apologise,' he said stiffly, 'for using such language before you. It was not the act of a gentleman.'

Miss Rowallan's response was a little surprising. 'Oh, I have heard much worse than that, Will, and from a gentleman, too. If I promise not to demean you again, will you sit down so that we may discuss ways and means?'

It was more of an apology from her for her high-handedness than he might have expected, and Will accepted it as graciously as he could.

He resumed his seat, saying wryly, 'My dear Rebecca, our mutual apologies have convinced me that it is possible for us to continue without further acrimony. May I suggest that by uniting to deceive others we may enjoy ourselves in the knowledge that we know something which they don't.'

'Assuredly, Will,' and Beck laughed for the first time. 'I have spent much of my life in that happy situation and am greatly pleased to learn that I have chosen some-one who will enjoy sharing it with me. Now, let us begin to make plans for the marriage which will shortly take place.'

Was he happy? Perhaps not. Will had a Friday face when he reached his rooms again. Gib opened his mouth to comment on it but, for some reason he could not have explained, he forbore.

Will ate an early supper and then retired to his bed-room, to emerge dressed in clothes of a kind worn by clerks and lowly functionaries—respectable but shabby. He had put on a porter's cap with a large peak.

'Thought you didn't need to trouble with all that any more—sir.' The sir was an afterthought.

'Probably not,' returned Will mildly. 'But I have a duty to perform—and the sooner the better.'

'Goin' out by the back way, are you?'

'Can't go by the front in this.' Will was brief.

'Be careful. Wouldn't do to get done over just when you're about to win the tontine of your life, sir.'

'If you mean by that I'm going to marry Miss Rowallan, then say so,' Will riposted.

'Miss Moneybags, then. She don't seem to be making you very happy—with respect, sir.'

'You've never shown me the slightest respect in the past, so don't pretend that you're starting to do so now.'

Will picked up a stick of the sort commonly used in

the country, stout and thick. 'You'll note that I'm taking heed of your warnings.'

Gib plucked Will by the sleeve as he walked out of the room. 'I meant what I said, young master. I know the hard time of it you've had. I don't want you to make it any harder on yourself by marrying this fine lady.'

Will disengaged himself gently. 'Believe me, Gib, if there were any other way of surviving, if it were only myself I had to think of, then my life would be very different. Now let me go, and if you can't give me your blessing, then don't grumble at me, either.'

He carried the memory of his servant's worried face to the shabby street where George Masserene ran a gaming hell for the lowly of London's varied world—who never met, and knew nothing of, its high society. It was up a dark alley and a burly porter stood at the door.

'Evening, Mr. Wilson,' he greeted Will.

'Evening, Jim. House busy tonight?'

'Aye. The master will be pleased to see you.'

The gatekeeper having been acknowledged, Will walked down some steps to find himself in a long low room, brilliantly lit, and filled with people.

Gaming tables were ranged down the middle of it. At the far end, in a poor imitation of the largesse available in London's richest gaming hells, stood a long table full of cheap food, wine and beer. A portly man, smoking a cigar, lounged by the open door of an office.

'Evening, Wilson. Made it this evening, have you? We're busy, as you see, good pickings, and later I've some accounts for you to go over for me.'

Will said, 'I'll run a table for you tonight, sir, but this is the last time I shall be coming. I've found a better, more secure position, a day job as well.'

George Masserene looked unhappy. 'I knew that you

were too good to last, Wilson. What's an honest man
doin' here? I asked myself. If you give the books a last
once-over before you go, I'll add a guinea to your pay.'

Will nodded agreement. No one at Masserene's knew
who he really was. He had been a houseman there for
almost two years, running a gaming table for three nights
a week as well as keeping Masserene's books for him.
He had also stood in on other nights.

When needed, he had acted as a strong man and had
helped the porter to throw out those patrons who had
become obstreperous when they lost. The pay had not
been great but, as he had told an unhappy Gib, every
little helped.

The job also had the advantage that it could be done
at night, and not every night, leaving him free to play
the gentleman and try to make his fortune at other times
of the day. Now that he was to marry Miss Rowallan he
no longer needed this small source of ready money.

He was surprised to find as he sat down to deal from
his first pack of cards that he felt a certain sorrow at
leaving. After all, he gave a good service to Masserene
for his pay, and he was, as George had said, honest. He
sought to defraud neither the punters nor the house, and
in that sense he was almost unique.

It was, he told himself, with some inward sad amusement, exactly the same service as the one he was providing for Miss Rowallan.

Dawn saw him walking home, dog-tired. He had
straightened out all of George's books for him before he
had left, and in return George had added another half-
guinea to his pay. 'If you ever need a job, Wilson,
there's always one for you here. An honest man is a rare
thing to find in London—especially in these quarters.'

This was another cause of sad amusement for a man who was so frequently despised as a barely honest fortune-hunter. What would George have thought if he had asked him to put his testimonial in writing so that he might show it as a proof of his integrity from a man who ran a gaming hell! His good memory and his mathematical ability Will took for granted. Neither of them was of much practical use to a poor gentleman.

He was turning into Duke Street when, by ill-chance, he encountered a party of young bloods on their way home after making a night of it at establishments better regarded than George's—if frequently less honest.

Among them was Harry Fitzalan, half-cut, but still able to stand. Will pulled his cap over his eyes, but even in his fuddled state Harry was acute enough to recognise Will by his body language rather than his face.

'Will?' he croaked. 'It is Will, isn't it? What the deuce are you doing in that get-up?'

Will had no need to answer, for Harry gave a great guffaw and clutched at the lapels of Will's dirty coat.

'No, old fellow,' he choked, 'don't tell me. Had to give Beck Rowallan the slip to get your oats, didn't you? Go somewhere where you weren't known, in case it got back to her. Don't worry, I won't peach on you. Mum's the word and all that. You'd do the same for me, I know.'

His companions had staggered past them. One of them turned round and howled at Harry, 'Don't get left behind, Fitzalan, by arguing with a filthy beggar. Throw him a few pence and have done.'

Harry put an unsteady finger by his nose and winked at Will. 'Here, take this,' he laughed, thrusting a florin into Will's hand. 'I'll not give you away. Neither now nor later.'

'Coming, coming,' he shouted to his cronies, and reeled up the road towards them, leaving Will to laugh ruefully and put his tip into the pocket which held his pay from George.

'All's grist to the poor man's mill,' he told himself. 'Harry will never know how welcome his largesse was to me!'

'It's true, then! He's proposed, and she's accepted. Beck Rowallan, of all people, to marry a pauper. I'd have thought nothing less than a Duke would have done for such a high-nosed piece of work.'

'They say that one of the Royal Dukes did propose, and gained nothing but a dusty answer.'

'Ah, but he doesn't look like Will Shafto when he strips off at Jackson's, does he?' and the pair of male gossips collapsed into knowing laughter.

Conversations such as this—more discreet when the ladies were discussing this unequal match—took place throughout London society when it became known that Beck Rowallan—she was rarely accorded the title of Miss—had accepted her rogue.

Sarah Allenby, already married to her Marquess and regretting it nightly, took a different view of the matter, but no-one asked her for her opinion, least of all her Allenby relatives.

It was fortunate for both parties that neither of them troubled much about what others thought of them—so long as they were being polite to them when they met face to face.

Beck, for so Will always thought of her, had never cared much for the opinions of others, and Will had learned in a hard school to put a brave face on life. Of the two he privately suffered the more—although he was never quite sure of his future wife's true thoughts.

Behind her carapace of hard indifference might beat a suffering heart but, if so, she never gave any sign of it to Will, or to anyone else. Now that the die had been cast, and marriage was near, dining or dancing, riding or boating, at the theatre or the opera, she offered everyone the same composed face which she had always shown them.

Will's trials were perhaps the harder since few ventured to say anything to his supposed beloved, but many of his circle of male friends were not averse to shoving him in the ribs and congratulating him for being such a lucky dog, or, as in Harry Fitzalan's case, commiserating with him yet again for having to get into bed with Beck Rowallan.

'Is the money worth it?' he demanded solemnly of Will at Jackson's one afternoon.

Will had been working out with the Tottenham Tiger and had been fighting him with a rare savagery as though they were truly in the ring together, gloves off and betting on. He turned a face on Harry which Harry had never seen before, so grim and dour it was. There was nothing of equable Will Shafto left in it.

'Cut it out, Harry,' he snarled, 'or I'll challenge *you* to take a turn in the ring with me. The *lady*—' and he dwelt on the word '—is going to be my wife. So that's enough. Don't mention her again unless you can do so with respect.'

Harry blinked at Will. 'Didn't mean any harm, old fellow. Not at all. No.' The prospect of entering the ring with the Will Shafto he had just seen held no attraction for him whatsoever.

Will turned away from Harry, still seething. His own guilt at marrying a woman he did not love, and could never bed, so that his marriage was a hollow sham, rode on his shoulders and was partly responsible for his savagery with Harry.

He worked it off by demanding another bout with the Tiger, who was beginning to wonder what ailed this gentleman. Will should be feeling pleased with life after netting such a golden dolly as Miss Rowallan was, rather than indulging himself in a fit of the dismals.

Afterwards Will felt better, even if he was drenched in sweat for his pains. One of the boys who acted as attendants on the society nobs who patronised Jackson's poured buckets of water over him until, feeling cleansed in soul as well as body, he roared 'Enough!'

Clothed again, he decided to visit his betrothed whom he had avoided for the last few days. They were to be married in a week, and after that he would be compelled to behave, in public at least, as though he were a loving husband.

In prospect this had not seemed difficult, but the nearer the day of reckoning drew, the more Will agonised over how he was going to manage his new life.

He was still agonising when he walked into Beck's drawing-room where he discovered, with some relief, that she already had another visitor.

In the armchair which he usually occupied sat an elderly straight-backed woman, or rather lady, for by her expression and her posture no one would ever call her anything else. She remained seated as Beck rose to greet him, and he responded by bending over her hand and kissing it.

'Will, I'm so happy to see you today. I have someone to whom I wish to introduce you. I don't believe that I have ever spoken to you of my distant relative, my cousin, or rather my aunt, Mrs Petronella Melville.'

Since Beck had never spoken to him of any relatives, distant or near, whom she wished Will to meet, Will could only nod assent and bow to the lady herself who responded by waving a gloved hand at him.

She was very much of the old school, raking Will from head to foot with her stern eyes. He concluded somewhat dismally that there was little doubt that she and Beck were related—they both had the same expression of severe authority.

She pulled off her glove and extended her hand, which Will assumed she wished to have kissed—and gratified her.

'So, you are the fortune-hunter whom my niece has decided to marry,' she barked at him. 'Let me have a good look at you, young man.'

She raised a quizzing glass the better to inspect him. Amused and intrigued, Will was grateful that he was turned out in the fullest fig and that although he had tied his cravat himself at Jackson's—or perhaps because he had—it was a discreetly modest affair, giving no indication that he was a member of the dandy set.

Inspection over, Aunt Petronella lowered her glass. 'Hmm,' she said. 'I see at once how you managed to charm my niece who, until now, I had thought to be the most sensible gal ever to be left in control of her own fate—which ain't saying much, to be sure. I had feared that the odour of loose fish would be strong about your person, but I own that now that I have met you, I am most pleasantly surprised.

'Rebecca tells me that you are a sensible fellow, too, and may be depended on not to fling her fortune away on the gaming tables. Is that true?'

This was barked at him in a sergeant-major's best voice. Will answered her with a lie which was not a lie.

'I assure you, madam, that I never gamble—that is not one of my failings.' Which was a true statement so far as it went—for at George Massarene's Will gambled with the house's money, never his own. Nor did he gamble in his proper person.

'Oh, so you do admit to failings, young man!'

Will bowed again. 'Under God, madam, we are all sinful men and women, and I do not claim to be different from the rest of my kind.'

Aunt Petronella turned to Beck, who was truly relieved at Will's clever and adroit handling of a woman who had a reputation as a dragon, and who, if she did not exactly eat those who displeased her, gave them the edge of a scarifying tongue.

'You are right, my dear. He's clever. Whether he's clever for you—or for himself—is another matter.'

Will answered her immediately. 'Since in a week's time, God willing, we shall be man and wife, which means that in the eyes of God and the law we shall have become one, then my cleverness must be as much for my wife as for myself.'

The old woman rewarded him with a crack of laughter, stood up and put out her hand. 'Let us shake on it, Master Will Shafto. For the moment I am pleased to recognise you, but beware…if I believe that you are exploiting my niece in any way, then you will have a formidable enemy in me.'

And that, thought Will, must be the joke of the year, seeing that in this situation the only person being exploited is myself!

But he said nothing, merely bowed again, sat down and proceeded to enjoy the old woman's forthright conversation. Opposite to him his proposed bride watched him, equally thoughtful. She was beginning to find depths in Mr Will Shafto which she had not believed existed.

At least he had managed to win over her formidable aunt. Beck had not informed her of the coming marriage, believing that she was safely hidden away in her draughty mansion in the Borders. Some interfering busy-body, however, had written her an excited letter giving her all the details of Beck and Will's courtship and their coming marriage.

At which the old lady had immediately ordered her horse and carriages to be harnessed and had set off for Honyngham House, her home on the Thames outside Richmond, to use all her influence with her niece to stop the marriage if she thought that Rebecca had been bamboozled by a bare-faced adventurer.

Instead, here she was smiling at Will and asking him in her usual forthright manner, 'And where, young man, do you and my niece propose to spend your honeymoon?'

Beck forestalled Will's answer by replying brightly, 'Why here, of course, Aunt. Where better?'

'Nonsense,' exclaimed her aunt, banging her stick on the ground. 'Of course you can't stay here! You will wish to be on your own, of that I'm sure, without prying eyes to gape at you.'

Before either Will or Beck could assure her that of all things they wished to remain in London, she said imperiously, 'I have it. I shall come to live here for your first fortnight and the pair of you must go to Honyngham! You will have the country, the river and the trees—and one of the best views in England from Richmond Hill. The situation is ideal. You will be quite

alone, but that does not matter, for I am sure that you
will wish for no one's company but your own.'

Privately appalled, both Will and Beck opened their
mouths to decline this honour, but Aunt Petronella was
having none of it.

'Stuff,' she declared robustly. 'Your modesty does
you both credit, but I know that you will thank me afterwards. For my part, I shall be happy to be able to join
in the Season from such a comfortable lodgement. Say
no more. I shall leave you shortly in order to return to
Honyngham as soon as possible, in order to ensure that
my staff makes everything ready for you.'

How to answer her? Will, his face firmly fixed in an
agreeable expression which bore no relationship to his
true feelings, was as dismayed as Beck at the prospect
of them being imprisoned in the country, unable to get
away from each other, and compelled to pretend to the
old battle-axe who was gazing benevolently at them that
all was for the best in the best of all possible worlds.

She would brook no denial; and since it was to their
joint advantage that the old woman smiled on their
union, they could not refuse to do as she asked. So far
as she was concerned it was a love-match, and everyone
knew that lovers wished to be alone together—particularly when they were first married.

Disillusionment might settle in later, but who cared
for that? She beamed at them, and though neither of
them had uttered a word she announced proudly, 'There,
that's settled. Now let us talk of the details of the marriage ceremony. Do I understand that you propose to be
married from here?'

Beck cursed the gossiping fool who had involved her

aunt in all her doings, but there was nothing for it but
to agree with everything that she said—and contemplate
the prospect of two weeks alone with Mr Will
Shafto—something which she had not bargained for.

Chapter Six

'Have you taken leave of your senses, Petronella? I understand from Rebecca herself that you have given this disgraceful marriage your blessing.'

'Lord love you, John Allenby, I'm only too happy to see the poor girl married to someone. He may be a rogue after her money, but he's also presentable, well spoken, of a good family, and all my instincts inform me that he'll treat her well once they are married. Besides, I believe her fortune has been tied up so tightly by her lawyers that he'll have a devil of a job getting his hands on it.'

'Praise a fair day at night,' snorted John Allenby. 'She could have had anyone, anyone.'

'So she might. She might have made a fool of herself by marrying Hedley Beaucourt, something which you wanted for her, I'm told, and only the deity knows why you wished that—and he ain't telling. No, depend upon it, she has made a good choice. At least the children will be handsome, and that's one blessing.'

John Allenby lifted his eyes to heaven. It had always to be remembered that the old woman was a relic of the last century when manners and language were much coarser. And home truths were her speciality. She was now reproaching him for his niece Sarah's marriage.

'To marry the poor young gal to such an elderly roué was the outside of enough. What were you about, man? And because you were so dead set on acquiring a title, you didn't even tie her money up properly.'

'He wouldn't have married her if we had,' grudgingly admitted the man she was harrying.

'So it *was* his title you wanted. Heaven's above, man, you won't get rid of the stink of trade so easily. It takes more generations than two to wash away *that* odour. She was Mr Shafto's first choice, was she not? And you put a stop to the marriage? God grant that you don't regret what you've done. Young Shafto would have made her a far better husband.'

'You know nothing of him, or the matter,' exclaimed John Allenby, goaded beyond the prudence which dictated that he did not oppose her overmuch lest she leave her considerable fortune away from the family. 'I suppose you'll be at the wedding to lend it some respectability.'

'Wouldn't miss it,' exclaimed Aunt Petronella, banging her stick on the ground to emphasise each word she spoke, 'and you're not to worry about its respectability. The Bishop of Bath and Wells will officiate at the ceremony, and cousin John Ffolliot has promised to be present. Only too happy to see dear Rebecca caught at last. She'd better have married her head groom than no one at all, he told me, spinsterhood being such an unnatural state in his opinion.'

John Allenby closed his eyes and moaned inwardly. John Ffolliot was the Duke of Durness, a man so grand that he scarcely ever condescended to speak to anyone below the rank of Baron. But he was Petronella's cousin by marriage and rumour had it that he had once wished to marry her when he had been penniless Jack Ffolliot, and ten lives stood between him and the title.

Drink, disease, drownings and a carriage accident had carried them all away, but not before Petronella had been married off to a lowly, if rich, Baronet, so he had remained single, surrounded by a changing harem of ladies of easy virtue.

In old age he had got religion, or religion had got him—no one was quite sure which—and now he was as virtuous as he had once been vicious. For him to attend the wedding was to set the last—and greatest—seal on its respectability.

'I think that you have all taken leave of your senses,' was John Allenby's feeble riposte.

Petronella Melville stared at him coldly, and decided to change her will, leaving everything of which she was possessed to Will Shafto, who, whatever anyone else said, she judged to be a man as upright as any penniless gentleman could be.

Good, clever and sensible though her dear Rebecca Rowallan was, it was neither right nor proper that her husband should be condemned to be her permanent pensioner.

She would visit her lawyers the first thing in the morning, and no one, absolutely no one, was to know of her decision.

'A Bishop and a Duke? Have you run mad, Beck? I thought this was to be a simple ceremony.'

'And so it was until that idiot John Allenby wrote to Aunt Petronella to inform her of the marriage. She told me that he did so in order to try to persuade her to bring her influence to bear on me to stop it.

'Instead, it only took one look at you for her to suc-
cumb to your charms. So much so that she wishes this
to be one of the weddings of the year—and is making
sure that it will be. And please don't call me Beck!'

Will groaned. He had thought that they were going to
have a quiet little ceremony, followed by an equally
quiet little marriage. Instead, the whole business was
turning into a version of Greenwich Fair, with only the
tumblers and fire-eaters missing.

It put quite a different complexion on matters and if
he had known this beforehand he would never have
agreed to become entangled with Beck Rowallan at all.
For some reason he could not think of her as Rebecca.

'I'm not happy, Beck. This is turning into a circus.'

'And I'm not happy, either,' exclaimed Rebecca spiritedly. 'What's more, Aunt Petronella is making a great
to-do about you not having invited any of your relatives
to be present.'

'I haven't got any relatives.' Will was equally spirited
if not exactly truthful. He hadn't many and all of them
lived far from London society and he particularly didn't
want any of them to know of this marriage until it was
over.

Worst of all, this whole brouhaha was making him
question not only his behaviour, but Beck's.

'Why?' he asked abruptly. 'Why do you really want
this odd marriage, Beck?'

She closed her eyes, and said, her voice weary, 'Why
can you never remember to call me Rebecca? It's a small
enough request to make.'

Will didn't know, so he couldn't tell her. Later, alone
in his lodgings he concluded that it was the only way
left to him of showing her that she couldn't dominate
him completely. Everything else which she had de-

manded of him, he had agreed to without argument, so that to call her Beck against her will was to bring her down a little, a very little.

'Our first quarrel,' he told her. 'We have been so charmingly agreeable to one another I suppose that it's not surprising that it couldn't last. Most unnatural to be so constantly pleasant, do admit. And you haven't answered my question. Why?'

'You know why. Once I'm married, all the ceaseless bullying from those who think that they have some claim to control me will stop. I shall be safe. And once you are my husband it will be your duty to protect me from those who might wish to exploit me.'

'And who is to protect me, Beck? Tell me that?'

Unconsciously they had drawn nearer and nearer to one another so that very little space lay between them.

'Me—and my money,' she told him coldly and cruelly.

It was Will's turn to close his eyes when he heard this harsh pronouncement.

'And who is to protect *you*, when we are married? Are you not afraid that once the knot is tied I shall play Stony Bowes to your Countess of Strathmore?'

Will was referring to the marriage between Bowes, an adventurer, and the wealthy Countess to whom he had been so charming before marriage, but whom he had brutalised after it.

Beck shook her head. 'No, Will. I had you carefully watched. I know that you are quite unlike Stony Bowes. You would never hurt a woman.'

'Not even if she provoked me?' Will asked her softly. 'As you are doing now?'

He had brought them so close together that they were breast to breast, face to face, their breaths mingling.

Will wondered whether Beck's heart was thumping as hard as his was. He knew from experience that when a man and a woman engaged in violent argument strange consequences often followed. He was experiencing a strange consequence himself!

He wasn't sure whether he wanted to shake her or to overwhelm her with caresses. He wasn't sure which action would make her lose her unshakeable calm, and it was suddenly that which was troubling him, for he wasn't sure of anything.

No one, but no one, should be in such control of themselves. He imagined for one brief moment a Beck Rowallan who had lost her iron self-control. Would it be possible for her to shiver and moan beneath him, begging him to…to…?

Will blinked. He had, quite without willing it, closed his eyes, and now that they were open again he was astonished to discover that Beck and he were closer than ever, that her mouth was quivering and her eyes were slumberous.

Miss Rowallan with slumberous eyes! What a turn-up! Equally as surprising was this sudden lust for her which had him bending his head to kiss her mouth which had become so soft, was no longer firm, straight and forbidding.

He was going to kiss her, he was going to…he was going to do nothing, for there was a knock on the door so imperious that they sprang apart, staring at one another.

'Aunt Petronella!' exclaimed Beck, who did not know whether she was pleased or sorry at this haughty interruption. Something decidedly odd had been going on between her and Will. Something which she had not foreseen. 'It's Aunt Petronella. Only she would hammer on a door like that. If I don't answer her, she will be in without further warning.'

So she was. Her eyes gleamed and her mouth twitched before she said, her voice triumphant as she correctly read the expression on both their faces, 'Ah, love birds at last, I see. I thought that you were never going to get down to it!'

'Really, Aunt!' exclaimed Beck, for once at some loss to express herself with her usual logical clarity. 'What a thing to say!'

'Come, come, Beck,' said Will smoothly, not prepared to let an occasion pass which would enable him to catch his beloved on the hop as she had so often caught him. 'No need to deny what was so obvious. We were discussing our future together,' he explained, 'and matters became a little…confidential, didn't they, my love?'

He spoke as though they had been caught grappling together on the floor like a housemaid and a footman, fumed Beck inwardly. She opened her mouth to say something scathing but, catching the gleam in Will's eye and reading it correctly, she grasped that to do so might land her in further trouble from his ready tongue.

Besides, the old lady was so pleased to see her behaving like a woman passionately in love with her soon-to-be husband that it would be unkind to disillusion her—especially when that was the impression which she had been trying to create.

Beck simpered—what else could she do? Will almost choked at the sight—and at the same time felt a strange relief. She obviously loved the outrageous old woman—and here he had been thinking that she loved no one but Beck Rowallan.

Perhaps there was hope for both of them in this unequal marriage.

If so, Beck took pains to disillusion him as soon as Aunt Petronella left them alone again.

'Do not think that because it was necessary for us not to distress my aunt that anything has changed in the arrangement which I made with you, Mr Shafto. It hasn't.'

So, she was punishing him by not calling him Will.

'No, indeed,' he returned obligingly, 'and pray do not reproach me for following your orders. I was merely trying to persuade your aunt that this was truly the love match which you wish the world to believe it is.'

Beck interrupted him angrily. 'That is enough, sir. Do not try to bam me. You know perfectly well what you were about.'

It was disconcerting her mightily that Will was suddenly no longer her passive slave, but was choosing to wrongfoot and discomfort her at every turn. She had given a hostage to fortune which she had not intended when she had begun this masquerade and Will was showing her that, perfect gentleman though he might be, he was not above teasing her in situations in which she could not answer him without betraying their true relationship.

Of course, he had to behave like a passionate lover—for was not that the play which she had written for them? And despite her brave words it was too late to retreat. They were within a few days of the wedding.

Will saw the signs of a small surrender on her face, and pressed home his advantage. 'I trust,' he said, 'that you will allow me to escort you to Rundell and Bridges tomorrow. I wish to buy you a ring to mark our betrothal.'

It was truly the day on which Beck's tact was in abeyance. 'From the Court jewellers,' she exclaimed. 'Can you afford to do so? Perhaps—'

'If you are going to offer to lend me money to buy the ring,' Will announced through gritted teeth, 'then pray refrain. I have but little with which to indulge you—and myself—but that little is mine—and honestly earned.'

He was referring to the money which George Masserene had paid him before he had left his employment, but he could not say so. Beck realised her error at once and, wrongfooted again, began to apologise.

'Think nothing of it,' retorted Will, a trifle bitterly. 'It is quite understandable, given how much you are already endowing me with, that you should suppose I needed the money to buy you something which you could display with pride. I fear that what I might purchase would be too small and trifling, so perhaps we had better forget the matter.'

'No!' Beck's reply was rapid and heartfelt. She offered him a flag of truce at once. 'I assure you that that was not my reason for making such an offer. On the contrary, I shall now treasure any gift from you the more because it was truly you who have given it to me.'

It would be churlish to refuse her—and Will thought ruefully that, under the circumstances of their marriage, he had no excuse for displaying hurt pride.

'Very well,' he said. 'Tomorrow afternoon. I shall call for you at three.'

'Or,' Beck said, thinking to save him the expense of a cab, 'we could meet at the jewellers, and after that you could walk me home.'

Honour satisfied and hurt feelings forgotten, the following afternoon she and Will spent half an hour at the jewellers in Bond Street. The ring he chose for her was small but exquisite: a plain gold band with a small pearl set in it. And if the assistant who served them thought that it was an extremely modest present for a woman of such wealth, nothing he said betrayed the fact.

Instead he remarked as Will slipped the ring on Beck's finger, 'On madam's hand the ring possesses a chaste simplicity which far outshines a more gaudy offering.'

Beck held her hand up as he spoke and, as though regretting her ungraciousness of the day before, came out with the most spontaneous remark which she had ever made to Will. A remark which carried in its utterance the ring of truth.

'I am compelled to agree with you. Good taste and modesty frequently go hand in hand.'

The look which Will gave her carried its own reward. For the first time the pair of them experienced a little, a very little, of the emotion which a genuine pair of lovers might have felt.

But as, arm in arm, she and Will walked away from the jewellers, they were confronted by a shadow from his past...

George Masserene, feeling more successful than he had done for years, was walking along Bond Street. He was well aware that his shabby gentility ill accorded with the splendour of the men and women of London society around him.

As Will and Beck were jointly bowed out of Rundell and Bridges he first registered them only as a pair of well-dressed lovers, or perhaps a husband and wife who had been indulging themselves. It was only when he was almost upon them that he remarked on the man's extraordinary likeness to his former employee, Wilson.

The nearer he got, the greater the likeness grew, until, on reaching them, he exclaimed, 'Why, Wilson, it is Wilson, is it not? I never thought to meet *you* here.'

Will had only one wish—that the heavens might open and swallow him up. He could see the avid curiosity on George's face, and could only imagine what Beck must be thinking.

He gave a light laugh, half-turned towards Beck and said, his face as serious as he could make it, 'My dear, allow me to introduce to you an acquaintance of mine, Mr George Masserene, with whom I recently completed some useful business transactions. I must present to you, George, my future wife, Miss Rebecca Rowallan. We are to be married in a few days.'

Beck curtsied, George bowed. Will continued desperately, 'I am sure, George, that you now understand why I cried off recently, and will not, for the present, be able to collaborate with you in any further ventures. My time is otherwise occupied.'

George Masserene was no fool. He had also heard tell of Miss Rebecca Rowallan and her fortune, and knew immediately that to reveal that Wilson—if that was his name, for he had seen Will wince when he had first spoken—would certainly not relish it being known that the 'business' of which he had spoken was his work as a professional gambler in a lowly gaming hell.

Better than that, he also thought that he knew that he might be able to benefit financially from this fortunate encounter, for surely Wilson would not wish his future bride to know how lowly a fortune-hunter he was.

Nor, it was to be assumed, would he wish his wealthy bride to know that he had been using another name.

George wished he knew what his real name was. He was unaware that Miss Rowallan would not care tuppence if she did learn of his involvement with George, or of his assumption of another name. For it was precisely because of his financial desperation that, to put it bluntly, she had bought him.

'Business transactions?' asked Beck sweetly. She had not for one moment been deceived by the scaly pair of rogues doing their deceptive dance around her. 'You interest me, Mr Masserene. Exactly what kind of business transactions? If a humble female may so ask?'

She looked anything but a humble female as she came out with this dangerous question.

George, whose imagination was not a lively one, looked wildly at Will, his mouth open. Will duly obliged by remarking airily, 'Oh, George and I have been plunging on the Stock Exchange, my love, in enterprises connected with the current war. My investment was modest—it allowed me to buy your ring—but George here is a devil of a fellow and netted much more, having risked more, of course.'

George, offered a lifeline, closed his mouth and murmured his assent to this unlikely statement. It would not pay him at the moment to give Will away.

Beck continued her pinpricking game, and offered him yet another lifeline—deliberately, for it amused her to play the pair of them as a picador might play with two lively, but confused, bulls.

'I am so happy to learn that my dear Mr Shafto has had such a useful partner. You must invite me to your counting house some time soon, Mr Masserene. I have never been inside one.'

She tapped Mr Shafto lightly on the arm and reproached him prettily. 'I wish you had told me of this before, Will. You know how interested I am in all matters financial! Pray arrange it soon, I beg of you.'

Oh, yes, Mr Will Shafto knew how interested his beloved was in money matters. He bared his teeth in a desperate grin at George, who, having been handed Wilson's real name on a plate—which was a plus—now had a minus to consider: he had no counting house. How the devil was Will Shafto going to wriggle out of that one?

And which was his real name? Wilson or Shafto?

Mr Will Shafto could, it appeared, wriggle out of anything. He clapped George on the shoulder, exclaiming, 'Yes, we must arrange it as soon as possible, old fellow—after you come back from your expedition to the north.'

Even for a rogue and consort of rogues like George Masserene, this latest bout of invention from Will was a little rich. He almost blurted out, 'What journey to the north?' but something in Will's steely eye stopped him.

That, and the sudden belief that the listening Miss Rebecca Rowallan might not be the total simpleton that she was pretending to be. George knew men and women, and knew that beneath their trappings—or lack of them—rich and poor were made of much the same stuff. He also knew from hard experience that women were by no means the fools which most men supposed them to be.

Did Wilson—or Will Shafto—know the true nature of the woman who was clinging to his arm so prettily? George never let the grass grow beneath his feet. He smelled danger. It was time to take his leave.

'I shall write to you, Shafto, when I return, giving you the latest news of our northern ventures,' he announced in his bluffest manner.

He bowed to Beck. 'Delighted to have made your acquaintance, madam. You're a lucky dog, Shafto, but I suppose you know that. I bid you both good day.' He strode away from them, whistling to himself.

Will heaved an inward sigh of relief at his departure. He was too forward, for Beck said in her best slightly mocking fashion, 'Do you consider yourself a lucky dog, Wilson? That was the name he called you by, I believe, before I kindly supplied him with your true one, was it not?'

'Now, Beck,' Will began.

'No, no,' she replied, laughing. 'Do not try to offer me an explanation of your involvement with Mr. Masserene, which I know before you make it will be as untrue as all the flim-flam with which you and he have just been trying to deceive me. I must admit, though, you make a more plausible liar than your friend.'

'He is not my friend,' Will offered loftily, 'merely a business acquaintance.'

'In a relationship in which he was most certainly your superior, judging by the tone which he adopted towards you before he grasped that you were not Wilson, and that I was a rich heiress, not some barque of frailty whom you were entertaining for the afternoon.'

Goaded, Will riposted, 'You ought not to speak of barques of frailty, Beck, even if you know what they are.'

Beck stopped, took her hand from his arm, faced him and in the most earnest voice which she had yet used to him, said, 'Will, I have not the slightest desire to know all the details of your life before we reached our agreement, so you need not make up any more Banbury tales to explain who and what that dubious gentleman was to you.

'As for visiting his counting house, I am sure by his expression when you spoke of it that it does not exist, so we shall certainly not be visiting it. If he tries to blackmail you by threatening to reveal to me all your secrets if you do not pay money over to him, you may tell him to go to the devil because nothing that he might say of you would surprise me.'

There would come a day when Mrs Will Shafto would bitterly regret this confident statement, but at the time it was simply one more nail in the coffin of Will's disappearing independence.

He shook his head, and said nothing. What he thought was that he must never underestimate the woman whom he was to marry. More than that, Will had recently begun to feel a little tenderness for her, but she had trampled that untoward emotion to death beneath her elegantly shod feet as they walked along Piccadilly in the wake of George Masserene.

Chapter Seven

A quiet wedding! Well, Aunt Petronella had certainly knocked that idea on the head. Instead of a discreet little ceremony in the small room off the Grand Salon at Beck's home, a large crowd was gathered in the Grand Salon itself.

Most notable of all were the Bishop and the Duke of Durness who had come from his country home in Kent to, as he put it, 'bless the nuptials of my dear Petronella's niece.'

From the way in which he was carrying on, thought Will sardonically, it might have been thought that it was his nuptials with the aunt, rather than Will's with her niece, that were being celebrated.

The Allenbys were there in full force, again at the insistence of Aunt Petronella. 'You must not make too many enemies, child—you never know when you might want them to be your friends,' being her aunt's robust comment when Beck had demurred at the mere idea of inviting any one of them.

Will's supporters and relations were conspicuous by their absence. He had toyed with the wry notion of inviting George, but tempting though that notion was, he thought that it might be going a touch too far.

In the event he invited Harry Fitzalan and his crony Gilly Thornton, with whom Will had occasionally sparred at Jackson's, together with Josiah Wilmot with whom he had been at Oxford for a year when he was sixteen.

'Have you no relatives, young man?' Aunt Petronella had asked him severely, waving her stick at him like the wicked fairy in *Sleeping Beauty*.

'They all live in the north, madam, and the notice has been far too short for them to be able to attend.'

There was nothing that even Beck's indomitable aunt could say to that, so she said nothing.

Will did not inform her of the other reason why they were not present: that they would find the cost of visiting London beyond them. He had written to those nearest to him, saying that he was well, but had said nothing of his marriage. He would try to explain that later, at a more favourable date—if such a date ever arrived, that was.

Both Beck, quietly, and Aunt Petronella, noisily, had separately confirmed that Mr Will Shafto was truly the Mr. William Shafto of Shafto Hall in Northumberland through the good offices of Josiah Wilmot.

Josiah could scarce believe Will's good luck in bringing this match off. He looked around the brilliant company with awe: cringing before both the Bishop and the Duke.

'Have you told them at home of your grand marriage?' he whispered urgently to Will as they stood waiting for Beck to walk through the great double doors of the salon to be united with Will.

'No,' Will whispered back, equally urgently, 'and you are not to inform them, either.'

'But they will want to know why you are suddenly so flush—'

'That's all arranged,' Will whispered back, praying that no one was overhearing this intimate exchange. 'They believe that I have made money on the Stock Exchange. Now, leave it, Josh. My bride is almost with us.'

Sure enough, there she was. Josh gazed at her, awe-struck. He had not believed that Beck Rowallan could look so beautiful when dressed with such charming simplicity.

She was wearing a classic high-waisted cream dress, with little in the way of frills and furbelows to ruin the purity of its line. A silver fillet was threaded through her hair. It was adorned only with a small posy of lilies of the valley made from silk.

Another silver fillet which bound her slender waist was also decorated with silk lilies of the valley. Her only jewellery was a rope of small pearls, a slender silver bracelet, and the modest ring which Will had bought for her.

So why did she look so completely altogether as Harry Fitzalan put it later? For the first time Harry actually envied Will, the lucky dog who was going to climb into bed with such a stunner. Why, she had lost that cold, forbidding expression which was enough to freeze a fellow. Her mouth was so soft it quivered, her eyes shone as though tears lay behind them, and as she entered the room she blushed the most delicate rosy-pink.

She's like a camellia, a very camellia, thought Harry, who had never before considered himself to be poetically inclined.

He was not the only person to be shocked by Beck's appearance. The bridegroom, who had believed that he could carry off this occasion without feeling anything but a mild inward amusement that he was getting married in such state to someone for whom he felt nothing, was surprised to discover that the sight of his bride was reviving in him all those untoward feelings which he thought Beck's recent coldness to him had suppressed.

How did she expect him to hold off, not to make her his true wife—to put it vulgarly, to bed her—when she turned up looking like that? 'Like that' being the exact image of the loving and tender woman whom Will Shafto would most like to have had for a wife, but had given up all hope that he ever would.

Good God! One might almost think that she was shy! Beck Rowallan shy? What an impossible thought. Either she was a consummate actress or the mere fact of getting married had created in her all the appropriate feelings for such an occasion.

Beck, as she entered, saw Will standing there, waiting for her, turned out immaculately in black silk, all his clothes perfect, and all of them fitting him perfectly. She felt her mouth quiver. For the first time the enormity of what she was about to do struck her. The man waiting for her, his face and body as perfect as his clothes, would, in a few short minutes, be her husband.

What had she done?

What was she doing?

She could not, would not, allow any man to touch her, either in love, or in hate, but the dreadful truth, a truth which she had been pushing to the back of her mind ever since she had first met him, was that Will was the only man whom she had ever met who possessed the power to make her forget her vows of eternal chastity.

No, she would not forget them, for he was nothing but a rogue. Had he not as coldbloodedly accepted her bargain as she had coldbloodedly proposed it? He was her rogue, Rebecca Rowallan's rogue; she must never forget that. A rogue who had never told her the truth about himself or his origins or the devious tricks he had got up to before he had proposed to Sarah Allenby, and, when that failed, had allowed himself to be bought by herself.

Ah, but had she told the truth about herself to him? And if she had not, did not that make her his equal in deceit?

All this while she processed down the room to face the Bishop, the smiling Duke, Aunt Petronella nodding her head approvingly, Harry Fitzalan staring at her, his mouth agape, the witless fool, and finally, Will himself who extended a hand to her.

For one dreadful moment when she took it Beck wanted to run. To run out of the room, to rush upstairs in order to jump into her chaste bed and pull the covers over her head and pretend she was still little Beck Rowallan who had yet to grow up and find how wicked the world was.

The moment passed. She gave Will a cool smile. He offered her a warm one: both, in their different ways were equally false. The Bishop started to read the marriage service in that special clerical voice all priests use, and the service began.

Neither of the principals was ever, for their different reasons, to remember much about it. The one thing which Will recalled was the phrase in the ceremony about marriage meaning forsaking all others, since it made him feel uncomfortable.

Beck lost everything. She moved in a dream, spoke

in a dream, and looked like a dream of loveliness. So much so that afterwards everyone there, like Harry, agreed that they had never before known how beautiful she was.

'Love,' bellowed the Duke when Aunt Petronella murmured her surprise in his ear at the wedding breakfast which followed the ceremony. 'Love always does that to a young woman, and to a feller, too. Depend upon it, this is a love match whatever anyone might think. Handsomest pair I ever saw, and no mistake. Worth marrying a fortune-hunter to get a feller who looked like that, I dare say.'

His bluff words floated out over the heads of all the guests. If anyone had thought that such home truths might visibly overset the bridegroom they were quite mistook, as Harry said later when reporting on how Will was 'turned off', as the slang saying had it.

Will laughed aloud, immediately raised his glass to the Duke and offered to toast him, 'For having the courage to say aloud what others were only thinking,' he told the Duke later when the meal was over.

'An honest rogue, I like that,' exclaimed the Duke. 'Look after her, my boy. My Peter'—he meant Aunt Petronella—'says that she's a deal more sensitive than she thinks she is. And no wonder when one knows what she went through when she was only a young lass—but no doubt she's told you of that.'

'No doubt,' echoed the amused Will, who had not the slightest idea of what the Duke was talking about, but was stowing away in his good memory what he had just heard.

'Enough!' commanded the Duke, who like many people was happy to speak his mind himself, but frequently counselled others against doing so. 'Here comes your good lady and she must not know that we have been talking of her. Wouldn't do. Strong minded, Peter says.'

Beck didn't look strong-minded. She looked as quietly modest and shy as a new young bride ought. And so Will told her.

'For the moment, yes,' she replied. 'I had no notion that I should feel quite so overwhelmed. I suspected that I might be—a little, perhaps—which was why I wanted a small and quiet ceremony.'

'All those prying eyes making one feel like an animal in a cage at Greenwich Fair,' offered Will.

'Exactly.' Beck had not expected to find him so perceptive. She was beginning to grasp that there was more to Will than his reputation, and the bargain he had agreed with her, might suggest.

They were given no time for further confidences which was, Will reflected, perhaps a pity. Instead they were torn apart by distant relatives who wished to speak to her of their mutual past and Will wandered off. For the first time he understood at what a disadvantage having none of his family present had put him. It left him very much the odd man out.

He walked over to a window embrasure and looked out at the garden, golden in the noonday sun. He was hidden by the curtains and so overheard something not meant for his ears. John Allenby was talking to a female Allenby cousin.

'Well,' he said, his voice heavy, 'it's done, for good or ill. I cannot but think it ill that she should marry a landless penniless man.'

'And of no family—or so I have heard say.'

'Then whoever told you that heard wrong. There's nothing odd about his family. He's Shafto, of Shafto Hall, no doubt of it. But his father lost everything gambling—hence the fortune-hunting. He's the last of his line, and there are, I understand, no near relatives. Someone said that his mother died not long after his father—and since she's not here I suppose that must be the truth. What I still don't understand is why Beck, who is supposed to be strong-minded, was so determined to marry him.'

'His looks?' ventured the cousin.

'If it were anyone but Beck I might agree with you. No, she's the coldest of cold fish. She's been so ever since Paul died. Now, if he'd lived she wouldn't be in a position to hand over the Rowallan fortune to a ne'er-do-well, for being the son he'd have inherited everything. Oh, she'd have had a nice little dowry, but nothing more. Not enough to tempt this fellow, I'll be bound.'

Will heard no more. They had evidently moved away. He abandoned his unsought and unwilling role of eavesdropper, moving through the crowd of smiling well-wishers. He suddenly wanted to find his bride. A bride who had possessed an elder brother of whom she had said nothing. But then, he hadn't told her everything, either.

What would he say to her when he found her? He didn't know. Something? Nothing?

He met Harry Fitzalan, who had an Allenby girl clinging to his arm and who greeted him with, 'Looking for Beck, old fellow? I think that she went down there with that old aunt of hers.' He pointed through the open double doors which led to the grand staircase.

'Probably getting into her duds to leave for Honyngham, you lucky dog. Never thought I'd say that.'

On an impulse Will followed Harry's pointing finger and made for the staircase himself. To do so he had to pass the small drawing-room whose door stood slightly open. He was almost by it when he heard, coming through it, muffled sobbing.

Beck? Surely not. It couldn't be Beck crying. But all the same Will was suddenly overcome with dreadful guilt. He couldn't think what for, except that if it were Beck crying it almost certainly had something to do with himself, and he ought to try to do something about it.

He pushed the door completely open and walked in. 'Beck?' he murmured. 'Beck? Is that you?'

Out of sight of the door, but visible when he walked further into the room, a large armchair stood by the fire-place. A woman was huddled in it, her face pressed into the cushions.

By her pale blue silk dress and her golden curls she was plainly not Beck—and therefore no business of his. Prudence dictated retreat, so Will retreated.

Too late. The woman reared up and turned a tear-stained face towards him, to show him Sarah Allenby, or rather, the Marchioness of Wingfield, as she now was.

All her pink and white prettiness had quite disappeared. Her face was blotched and stained with the marks of heavy crying. She had, during the wedding ceremony, been wearing a blue silk shawl, but that had fallen away to reveal that her upper arms were covered in bruises.

She took one look at Will before he could remove himself, and ran forward to fling herself into his arms. 'Oh, Will, oh, Will,' she sobbed into his chest, ruining his cravat and marking his elegant waistcoat.

'How could you have married her, of all people, so soon after we were parted, when you knew how much I loved you? Why did I not refuse to give you up? Why did I consent instead to marry that…monster?'

Will tried to disengage himself, but failed. He nobly refrained from pointing out that despite her great love for him, she had married her Marquess before he had so much as proposed to Beck. Unfortunately, the more he tried to hold her off, the more she clung to him, her sobbing becoming hysteria, her little shrieks becoming big ones.

The only way in which he could escape from her boa-constrictor grip was to knock her out with the kind of blow which he would have handed an opponent at Jackson's gym, an act which was quite beyond Will.

At the very moment when her shrieks were at their loudest and her struggles with him became frantic, the door opened and in came the Marquess of Wingfield looking for his wife.

To find her in Will's arms.

'You strumpet,' he howled, a word which Will had never before heard used except in a bad play. 'I've been looking for you everywhere in order to leave, and what do I find? That you're betraying me with Beck Rowallan's bridegroom. Wait until I get you home, m'lady, and you'll soon learn what it is to try to cuckold me. I shall give you such a lesson as you'll not forget.'

Will registered with wry amusement that Wingfield was not threatening him. He obviously knew of his physical prowess. Still trying to detach himself, Will said, as coolly as he could over Sarah's shoulder, 'By the state of your wife's arms and neck, Wingfield, you've already given your wife one more lesson than you should have done. You're a fool to think that I would try to deceive you with her on my wedding day.'

The Marquess ignored all of Will's rebuttal except that referring to his name. 'Hey, what's that? Did you call me Wingfield? Address your betters by their proper style, man. Just because you've tricked Beck Rowallan into marriage doesn't give you leave to be familiar with your superiors.'

Sarah, showing signs of recovery, and beginning to grasp that she had put Will at some disadvantage, stepped back, snuffling gently, and tried to appeal to her husband who ignored her.

Will was content to say, 'My superiors? Where are they, Wingfield? I'll not admit anyone to be that who strikes a woman.'

'Been bleating to him, have you, m'lady? I'll give you something to bleat for.'

'No, no,' cried Sarah. 'I didn't, I didn't. He guessed, that's all. It wasn't Will's fault.'

'I've a mind to call you out, Shafto—see if I don't.'

By now, to Will's horror, some of the guests, attracted by the noise, were finding their way into the room, to gaze entranced at the spectacle of the bridegroom being caught with another woman before he'd as much as gone on his honeymoon.

The Marquess swung on the newcomers who included the Duke of Durness.

'I found him alone with my wife—you may guess why—and he refused to address me properly when I taxed him with it.'

'Which offence was the greater?' asked the Duke politely. 'Bein' alone with your wife, or not calling you m'lord? It might affect the sentence we agree on for the offender.'

The Marquess glared at the Duke as though he could kill him. His silence gave Sarah her opportunity.

'There was no assignation, Duke. I was alone here for quite some time, feeling a trifle overset, when Mr Shafto came looking for his wife. I was asking him for comfort when my husband came in and misunderstood matters.'

'Is that true, Mr Shafto?' asked the Duke, who had obviously appointed himself judge and jury.

Will agreed that it was the truth. He could see John Allenby staring inimically at him.

The Marquess bellowed, 'He lies, damn him.'

The Duke stared at him. 'You are a trifle offensive, sir—even if you were being wronged, which I doubt. Lady Wingfield, pray approach me.'

Sarah, shaking, her face pale, did so.

The Duke said to her kindly, 'I do not wish to distress you, my dear, but you said that you had been crying for some time before Mr Shafto came in. Now I saw Mr Shafto leave the Grand Salon only a few minutes ago, and I would have followed him immediately, only I was detained.'

He took her face in his hand and tipped it towards him. 'I know what a crying woman looks like, and you have plainly been crying for quite some time—which is not the conduct of a woman who has arranged an assignation.'

He turned to the Marquess who was glowering at him.

'I fear that you misunderstood matters, Wingfield, which does not surprise me; you were never known for the sharpness of your wits. I suggest that you apologise to both injured parties if you wish to remain *persona grata* in any circles I frequent.'

This, Will and the others, understood to mean that the Marquess faced social extinction if he failed to comply with the Duke's order.

Grudgingly he did so.

'Now go home,' the Duke said, 'and comfort your wife, who appears to be more distressed than a new wife

should be. Shafto, you will take my arm and allow me
to escort you to the Grand Salon where I believe that
your wife will shortly be arriving, ready for you to take
her to Honyngham.'

Sarah threw an agonised glance at Will before she
followed her crestfallen husband out of the room; a
glance which the old Duke saw. Will was beginning to
understand how shrewd he was and how little escaped
him.

'You were lucky there, m'boy,' he told Will, not low-
ering his voice as he walked him along, and caring little
that Sarah's Allenby relations were all around them.

'A flighty piece, always in the boughs, that one. None
the less, you'd have made her a better husband than the
brute she's been saddled with. You're much better off
with Beck, you know. Not only is she richer, but she's
a sound head and a good heart—if you can fight your
way through the armour she wears to find it.'

Will hardly knew how to take this last statement. He
was profoundly grateful to the old man for rescuing him
from the predicament into which he had fallen through
Sarah's ill-judged claim on his sympathy. On the other
hand, he did not wish to antagonise Beck's relatives
more than he had already done by marrying her.

'You do me too much honour, sir,' he managed.

The Duke snorted. 'Not at all, m'boy. Just telling the
truth as I see it. Never could stand the man, gave me
great pleasure to put him down. Ah, I see Beck's already
waiting for you.'

So she was. She was wearing pale green silk now, and
a bonnet of a deeper green which was adorned with
cream ribbons. To Will's astonishment the look she
threw him was an agonised one, a look which asked for
support.

However, when she spoke it was to employ her usual sharp manner to him. 'Goodness, Will, what was all the commotion about?'

Before he could answer her the Duke replied in stentorian tones, 'Never mind that, now, Beck.' He had adopted Will's nickname for her. 'All over, and your groom will tell you about it on the way to Honyngham—if he isn't employing his time in a more enjoyable fashion!' He rewarded them both with a giant wink.

'Haven't been to a wedding for years, so don't know the form. Peter tells me that I ought to throw rice over you, but damn that for a tale. Uncomfortable business sitting on rice. Off with you both,' he suddenly roared, 'and leave us to drink to your health until the moon comes up.'

'Now, Jack,' said Aunt Petronella who had suddenly materialised and was now busily playing the good fairy. 'Leave the young things alone. They don't need an old bachelor like you to tell them what's what.'

'And whose fault was it that I'm an old bachelor, eh, Peter? Should have run away with me, but too late now, water under the bridge.'

He leaned forward and gave Beck a smacking kiss on the cheek. 'Making up for lost time,' he said, and pushed Will at her.

'Blessings on you both,' he called after them to the amusement of the crowd of wedding guests who were just beginning to grasp what a true eccentric the Duke was.

'All the same,' Beck whispered in Will's ear when they walked through the great front door to the carriage waiting to take them to Honyngham, 'I really do insist that you tell me what you and Sarah Wingfield were about. Most odd that you and she should somehow be compromised on our wedding day.'

'You heard the Duke, my dear,' Will whispered back climbing into the carriage after her. 'Later, when we are well away, you shall have all the details of my supposed misdemeanour. Can you honestly believe that I should play the fool on our wedding day? Considering that you know how much I stand to lose by it.'

'True,' nodded Beck. 'But why is it that I have the oddest notion that you have frequently sailed close to the wind in the past—so why not in the present?'

'Well, I was never in the present with you before, Beck, and that being so, any desire I have to sail close to any wind, north, south, east or west, has completely left me, knowing how much you would deplore any such thing—you being the soul of straightforward truthfulness yourself in all your dealings with everyone.'

There was a terrible silence in the carriage. Will wondered whether he had gone too far. But his bride surprised him yet again.

She began to laugh, softly, before burying her face in the small lacy muff which Mrs Grey had given her in exchange for the wedding bouquet she had been carrying before she left for Honyngham.

'Oh, Will, you constantly surprise me! Every time I think that I have begun to know you, you do or say something which betrays that I don't.'

'Then, if I assure you that in the matter of poor Sarah I was completely innocent…' He paused.

'I shall believe you,' Beck returned. 'And why poor Sarah?' So Beck did not know everything. And this was something which she ought to know.

'He is already beating her,' Will said grimly.

'No!' Beck's face was white. She caught her breath. 'Can that really be true? So soon?'

For some reason the words 'so soon' annoyed Will profoundly.

'What can you mean by ''so soon'', Beck? Are you implying that after a decent interval it would be quite proper for Wingfield to set about his wife? Are you wondering whether or not you might have to fight me off?'

Beck's face grew paler still. 'Of course not. I knew that he had a reputation as a brute, but I had hoped that Sarah being so young and pretty after a fashion which men admire, unlike myself, he might have held off.'

'Held off?' Will shook his head, bemused. 'I saw the marks of his displeasure on her arms, Beck. And another thing, what can you mean by comparing yourself unfavourably with Sarah? Surely you must be aware that although your looks are quite unlike hers, many would think yours were superior.'

'Oh, please, Will.' Beck's voice was as frosty as she could make it. 'There is no need for you to curry favour with me by showering me with pointless flattery. You are not, after all, either in love with me, or my true husband. I know only too well that I do not in the least resemble what most men like.'

Could she possibly be speaking the truth? There was that in her voice which said that she was. Did she really not know how beautiful she was, after a fashion which made Sarah look pallid and characterless by comparison?

Evidently not, for Beck began speaking again. 'You will do as I ask, I am sure, and not raise the subject again. I am well aware that it is stupid of me to be pained by empty flattery, but since I am, and since we must live together in some amity, I must ask you to respect my wishes.'

Will looked out of the window rather than look at his wife. How had she come to this pass? To think of herself as a plain woman, when she was a beautiful one? Was this the explanation of her ruthless approach to life which had resulted in her arranging for herself a cold-blooded marriage of convenience—something which most women strove to avoid? But not Rebecca Rowallan, now Beck Shafto, who unaccountably thought herself to be plain.

The Arcadian scenery of the Thames valley streamed by the coach window. The day had begun as a grey one, but once the sun had burned through, it had become both fine and fair. Would the sun in Beck's life ever dissolve the illusions under which she was living?

More to the point, could a man who had married her for his own ends forget himself and help her to find the happiness which was so obviously eluding her?

No! How could he, her self-confessed rogue, ever pretend that he could save her when he could not save himself?

But there was nothing to say that he could not try, was there?

Chapter Eight

Honyngham was beautiful. The house, all mellow rose and gold brick, stood back from the River Thames, but its gardens ran down to it. Will and Beck's rooms overlooked the river and a small quay where boats were moored.

Inside the house all was elegance and comfort. For one desperate moment when he was ushered into the entrance hall Will had found himself wishing that Beck was truly his wife and that they were going upstairs to consummate their marriage as soon as possible.

He checked himself. What was he thinking of? After all, it was surely only pity which he felt for Beck—and perhaps a touch of lust. Certainly not love, he told himself firmly, only to ask himself uneasily a little later when he looked out towards the river whether he was deceiving himself over that, in the same manner in which Beck was deceiving herself over her looks.

Because, at this very moment, he was wondering how he was going to spend the next fortnight alone with her without touching her! When he had first met her, she had been so cool and distant, so totally unlike the kind of woman he had always desired, that it had been easy to contemplate living with her in a loveless, unconsummated marriage.

No longer! The more he knew of her the more she had begun to attract him. Even her coldness, her severity, now seemed a challenge: a challenge to find the true woman beneath her austere façade.

Will shrugged his shoulders and began to turn away from the window. What he ought to be thinking of was how grateful he was to Fate that it had brought him a way out of the hell in which he had been living…

Two days ago, with the marriage settlements signed and all the financial details arranged, without telling Beck, he had gone to Coutts Bank, where each quarter she had arranged for a handsome sum of money to be paid into an account specially opened for him. It was his pay for agreeing to do as she wished and would ensure that he was able to present himself to the world as a monied man.

The clerk who had dealt with him had been all subservience. For some reason he had assumed that Will wished to transfer his account from whichever bank he used into this new one.

Will had rapidly disillusioned him.

'Indeed, no,' he had smiled. 'What I wish to arrange is something quite different. I have here a piece of paper with the address of a bank in a northern town and the name of a solicitor who holds an account there. I am authorising you to pay into his account each quarter sixty percent of the sum which will be placed in my name. I have given him the authority to transfer this money to the owner of a small estate which he manages, and I have here a letter from him accepting this duty and a copy of the agreement between us which will prove to you that this transaction is above board.'

The clerk read both the letter and the document. He looked closely at the name of the person to whom Will was acting as a benefactor and raised his eyebrows superciliously when he had done so.

Will leaned forward and took him negligently by his cravat, tightening his hand so that the clerk began to choke and splutter.

'Little man,' he said, 'you will not question what I wish to do with my money. You will carry out my orders—which are no business of yours—so long as my business is honest. Your bank claims total confidentiality for all its transactions, and if I discover that my confidence has been breached, I shall not hesitate to demand an interview with Mr Coutts himself.'

He paused, looking coldly at the clerk's purpling face.

'On second thoughts, you will take me to him now. That should ensure that my affairs are not gossiped of.'

He released the clerk who gasped at him, 'No need for that, sir. You may rest assured…'

'No, *you* will rest assured that you will take me to Mr Coutts. At once.'

It was done, and Will signed the banker's orders in Mr Coutts's presence. Mr Coutts made no demur about his somewhat odd request, and told Will that his business would remain confidential between the three of them.

Which did not prevent him, once Will had left, from picking up the papers before him and trying to make an educated guess at exactly what the fortunate Mr Will Shafto, who was marrying a great heiress, was about. He wondered briefly whether the new Mrs Will Shafto was aware of what her husband was doing with his princely allowance, before he returned to the task of running England's richest private bank…

Back in the present, Will shrugged again before taking

one last look through the window. There, strolling along a gravel path which ran between two formal lawns, was his new wife. She had changed from her travelling dress into a simple pale grey gown with a Puritanic linen collar and cuffs. She was carrying a white lace parasol to shield her face from the sun and looked the picture of idle contentment.

Once she gazed up at the windows. Will stepped back so that she should not see him: it had not been his intention to spy on her. Rather he would join her.

Rapidly he ran down the stairs, shocked a little by his desire to be with her, and by the thought of how difficult it was going to be to keep his hands off her now that they were truly alone.

Beck watched Will walk from the house. He was still wearing his wedding clothes, and splendid he looked in them. He was smiling.

He was her husband! Her husband!

Beck wanted to run, to hide, anything rather than be with him. Alone. She had not bargained for this. She did not know whether he frightened her, or attracted her. The two sensations were so mixed together that all she could think to do was to assume her frostiest face and manner.

'You are in a hurry, sir.'

'Always, on my wedding day.'

She did not want to be reminded of that, Will saw, glumly.

'You are remembering our agreement, I trust?'

'How could I forget it?' Will riposted. 'It is written on my heart.'

'As it is written on mine.'

'Have you a heart, madam wife, for anything to be written on it?'

'My heart is no concern of yours, sir.'

So it was still war, even on their wedding day. Beck's eyes shot ice at him, not fire. Will was not to know that the icicles were an armour she had assumed in order to hold him off, for with him she was starting to find that her emotions were starting to rule her, and not her reason—which would never do.

He smiled at her again, though. Faint heart never won fair lady, the old saying had it, and whatever Will was, he was not faint-hearted. Had he been so he would have gone under long ago; the cruel world would have rolled over him and left him dead.

But he was not dead, he was very much alive. He had married a woman in cold blood, and now he wanted her in hot blood.

If Beck's plans were beginning to go awry in the face of their mutual attraction, so were Will's. It was no longer a question of a cold woman employing a hard rogue to play a trick on the world and, that trick played, then part.

The little god of love, Dan Cupid, who posed before them in stone in the middle of a bed of roses, his bow held high, its arrow missing since it was in flight, had taken a hand in the game.

The missing arrow had found not one target, but two, and the question was whether the pair of lovers who were walking by him could tear his arrow from their heart and ignore its potent message.

As though he were trying—and failing—Will pointed to the statue. 'There's a thing,' he said. 'His bow is empty; the arrow has gone to pierce the heart of someone fortunate. Who could that someone be, Beck?'

The look he turned on her was frank and free. If the arrow had pierced her heart, as he was trying to suggest, then so did that look. Answer him as that wounded heart told her, and she was lost.

Reason prevailed. 'Fortunate, or unfortunate, perhaps? Not all who love are happy. The songs that are sung of it tell of pain and suffering as much as fulfilment. Best perhaps not to heed Cupid—or the arrow.'

'"'Tis better to have loved and lost,"' quoted Will, '"than never to have loved at all."'

'Oh, Shakespeare,' shrugged Beck dismissively, picking up the allusion. 'But can one trust poets?'

'Can one trust anyone?' countered Will. 'I think that perhaps we might trust…' he paused '…our hearts. I believe that that is what poets trust.'

'How foolish of them,' retorted Beck. 'The only safe thing to trust is our reason.'

Although the day was warm, Will shivered. Beck's tone was so implacable.

'What happened to you, Beck,' he asked her, 'to make you so unfeeling? I do not believe that you were born that way.'

She turned away from him, and stared past the smiling Cupid towards the house and the rising hills beyond, away from the river—and from Will.

'And you, Will? Why, being a rogue, are you yet so sentimental? Does not that make it difficult for you to succeed as a rogue?'

She had twice used the derogatory word rogue to hurt him, to keep him at a distance, Will was sure. Strangely, on another's lips the word might have wounded him, but hearing it from Beck failed to move him.

He laughed a little. 'Which shows, madam wife, how little you know of being a rogue! Sentiment, not true feeling, is one of our stock-in-trades. If I were, at this

moment, being a rogue with you we should not be trad-
ing ideas, but I should be doing—this.'

Suddenly he swung towards her, took the parasol from
her hands and tossed it away before taking her in his
arms, and then laying his head on her startled breast.

'Oh, my heart's darling, see how you move me! I have
only to be near you to forget everything.' He took her
hand and pressed it to his chest. 'Feel how my heart
beats—and know that it beats only for you. Lie with me,
Beck, here under Apollo's chariot, the sun, and let us
celebrate our love in the lists of Hymen now that we are
married.'

Slowly, slowly, he began to lower her to the ground,
murmuring the while, 'This, my sweet, is what you were
made for. Let me love you, or condemn me to die, slain
by the power of your eyes.'

Beck was overwhelmed by him, his masculine scent,
the feeling of his powerful body, the strength of the arms
which encircled her. She gasped—but not to refuse him.
The fear which always consumed her whenever she was
as near as this to a man had gone, as though it had never
existed.

Without warning, Will briskly lifted her away from
him, to stand free of her, murmuring, 'You see what I
mean by a rogue's sentimentality, Beck? As good as a
play, was it not? The lists of Hymen, indeed! See how
a seducer chooses his words.'

What he did not tell her was how difficult it had been
for him to release her: that his honeyed sentences had
begun to affect him as well as her, that from mockery
he had found himself moving on to true passion. Only
the knowledge that this was not the time or the place to
overcome her—for afterwards she would have thought

that he had tricked her into submission to him—had stopped him from turning pretence into reality.

Will now knew that he wanted Beck to come to him freely and willingly, offering herself to him, rather than being half-coerced against her will.

As it was, Beck stared at him, her lips quivering. 'Oh, Will, you must not do that again. You were breaking all the rules to which we agreed before marriage.'

What really shocked her was to find how desolate she felt once Will had released her. It was as though the sun had gone in and the world was full of shadows again. Worse than that, she felt angry with him: for one glorious moment she had believed that he truly meant what he was saying to her. Only when the sense of excitement they had created was past had she become aware of their shoddiness.

On the other hand, what would a man who truly loved her say?

This particular man was picking up her parasol and handing it back to her. She was thanking him mechanically, and wondering how she was going to struggle through the next fortnight without accidentally committing herself to someone whom she ought to despise, seeing that she had chosen him for his mercenary nature.

No matter. She had spent the last eight years successfully living her solitary independent life, so sharing it for a short space with Will without giving way to him ought to be easy enough. But would it be? For the gods themselves must be laughing at her as they slowly broke down the barriers of fear and distaste for all men which she had erected around herself since she was seventeen years old.

Will Shafto was busy thinking the same thing about the gods—with a slight difference. If he truly loved her, then he must be resigned to sacrificing his love for her when this masquerade was over. The penniless wretch that he was must still retain enough honour not to hold on to the rich heiress, who would be sure to believe that he did so only because of her money, not because he loved her.

Unless, of course, he could persuade her otherwise.

Supper that evening set the pattern of their days together. They sat at each end of a long table with half a dozen servants waiting on them. Later they sat opposite to one another in a pretty drawing-room. Will read a book—one of the late Tobias Smollett's picaresque tales whose heroes somewhat resembled himself in the uncertain nature of their lives.

Beck embroidered. She had left Mrs Grey behind, so she was not there to act as a buffer. After a time she laid her embroidery down and began to play the pianoforte which stood at one end of the room.

She had been well taught and was a skilled executant. Listening to her, Will admitted morosely that she excelled in everything she attempted—and wondered why the knowledge of her many talents did not make her happy. That she was not truly happy, he was sure.

Shortly after ten o'clock, true to the resolution she had made earlier, Beck excused herself and retired to her room. This was the only time she had spoken to him since their conversation in the garden.

Loneliness encompassed Will. It had walked with him since his father's death when he had discovered that all that was left of a once-great fortune was a neglected house and the few acres of farmland around it.

Almost he was tempted to drink himself into oblivion, but since his father's ruin had partly been brought about by the bottle, as always, he resisted the temptation. Finally he went upstairs to his own room to be ministered to by Gib. Lying awake until the small hours, he wondered wryly what the servants at Honyngham were going to make of his strange marriage.

A week later when matters between himself and Beck had not changed, he found out. He was being helped to dress for the day by Gib, who had been eyeing him satirically for some days.

He was tying Will's cravat, and was taking a long time about it. At last he stood back, apparently to admire his handiwork, but when he began to speak it was of something quite different.

'They are laying bets in the servants' hall as to when, if ever, you intend to bed the missis,' he said bluntly. 'If you do know the date you could perhaps tell me—I wouldn't mind winning a few bob.'

'I wouldn't dream of it,' Will told him. 'It's neither their business, nor yours for that matter.'

'When I heard you were marrying her,' Gib continued, ignoring what Will had to say—a common habit of his, 'I wasn't exactly up in the boughs since I thought her a cold piece. I never thought that you were a cold piece, too. They allows as how you must be, but I said no, it wasn't your habit to go overmuch with the muslin sort, but you were a true man for all that. Don't fancy her now you're married, is that it?'

'Why,' said Will in exasperation, 'do I continue to employ a servant who speaks to me as though he were the master, not I? Tell me that.'

Gib was succinct. 'Because I remind you of better days when you were a hopeful lad and I wore a pretty uniform and you travelled in a chaise with the Shafto

arms on the door. Will she buy you a chaise with your
arms on it, d'you think? Not worthwhile having married
her if she don't. I'm supposing you wed her for her
money, but what I don't understand, nor the staff here
neither, is why *she* married you, if it weren't to get a
man in her bed, seeing as how that's all you're bringing
her. A bad bargain she's made of it, I must say—which
ain't her reputation.'

This earthy analysis of the state of his marriage would
have set Will laughing if it had been made about anyone
but himself. As it was he frowned, told Gib to hold his
tongue, and determined to speak to Beck. It would not
do to have all the servants in London gossiping about
their strange marriage.

It had been remiss of both of them not to arrange their
affairs so that such gossip could be avoided. He must
speak to Beck at once, and insist that as soon as possible
they do something to scotch it.

Beck broke her fast late that morning, and came into
the dining room looking pale. Will watched her drink
coffee before beginning his campaign, once he had ordered the servants attending them to leave the room.

'Madam and I can manage quite well without you,'
he had finished.

When they were alone Beck looked at him over the
rim of her coffee cup.

'Why did you do that, Will?'

'Because I wish to speak to you immediately about
something important. Our conduct towards one another
has become the gossip of the servants' hall.'

'Oh, is that all?'

This cavalier answer had Will springing to his feet
and walking the length of the long table to where she
sat staring coldly at him.

'All, madam wife, all? The servants are placing bets as to the date when we, to put it politely, consummate our marriage. They are well aware by our behaviour to one another, and by all the other evidence, that we have yet not done so. If you wish us to be the talk of the town, then so be it. Rest assured, however, that if we do nothing to silence them, then the next thing will be that your friends and enemies will be placing similar bets at White's. Do you really want that? The scandal would be enormous.'

Beck blushed. She put down her coffee cup before saying, 'You are telling me the truth, Will? This is not some ploy to get me into your bed?'

Will, tantalised for the past week by her nearness, enraged by his inability to do anything about it, and by her refusal to take him seriously, bent down and hissed at her, 'What in the world should make you think that I want you in my bed? No, I am simply asking you to join me in some masquerade, some pantomime to silence the gossips, by enabling someone in the servant's hall to win his or her bet and end the matter. We should have considered this possibility before we came to Honyngham and taken steps to avoid it.'

He straightened up and said savagely, 'On the other hand, if you don't mind your name being bandied about town and being the subject of lewd jokes in the clubs, then we can continue as we are.'

Beck had never seen Will truly angry before. He had always been equable, half mocking, at the worst, or stoically resigned. To her astonishment she found his anger exciting, even if a little frightening.

'You are right,' she said. 'I had forgotten the servants. And, of course, they would say nothing to me. Was it Gib?'

'Yes, it was Gib,' returned Will. 'He was trying to warn me in his rough way, and I shall not listen to any criticism of him from you about his role in the matter.'

'No, of course not.' Beck's tone was placatory. 'What do you suggest we do?'

'To begin with, Beck, you could try talking to me when the servants are with us. The occasional ''dear'', or ''my love'', would help, together with some of the small talk which newly married couples engage in such as, ''Shall we go for a walk, my love?'', or, ''It is a fine day, let us go riding and take a picnic with us.'' Even, ''I have a mind to retire early, if it pleases you.'''

Beck coloured. 'I have been so busy holding you off I quite forgot how it would seem to outsiders.'

'Servants are not outsiders, Beck, they are insiders. They know more about us than we do. Try to remember that tonight when we walk up to bed together hand in hand, and you come to my room instead of shutting yourself in your own. And there is no need to trouble yourself about holding me off. I can hold myself off quite well.'

Will had not meant to be so savage with her, but the frustrations of the last week, nay, the last month were beginning to tell on him. Before that he had led a chaste life for some time because loveless affairs were not to his taste. If this put a strain on the young and athletic man he was, then so be it, but he had not bargained for the effect on him of having Beck constantly in the same room and sleeping under the same roof.

Gratifyingly she looked suitably chastised. Well, it would do madam good to learn that she was capable of making mistakes. It would also do her good to listen to him for a change.

Will had become aware, as a result of his hard life

over the last few years, of the reality which lay behind the glittering surface of the life of the *ton*. He knew that the fortunate few were sustained by an army of servants and flunkies of all kinds, who possessed few illusions about their masters, however outwardly servile they were to them in public.

And not only servants. There was also an army of people who swept the streets, who kept life safe and comfortable for Beck and her kind; who provided their pleasures, dressed them, ran the gaming hells, shops, theatres and the brothels which filled London.

Beck knew nothing of this. It was not her fault: it was the circumstances of her upbringing which ensured her ignorance. But since he had become penniless, Will had learned how hard life was for the many. He did not question the reasons for this—he was no reforming radical—but he simply knew that it was so and must be endured. It made him kind to Gib and able to understand George Masserene.

Nor must he be unkind to Beck, even if her face remained as stoic as ever, as though nothing said or done to her could distress her, for by her behaviour she was a victim, too.

'Come,' he said, smiling, and pulling her chair back for her to continue her breakfast. 'Let us be friends if we cannot be lovers or man and wife, and plan our campaign to confuse our silent watchers.'

It was an olive branch and Beck accepted it. She was beginning to learn that there was more to Will than a handsome face and a good body, and that if he was a rogue he was nevertheless a complex one, not simple as she had once thought.

But her next worry was how to face the coming night when, willy-nilly, they would be thrown together.

Inevitably supper was a fraught meal. For all her outward calm Mrs Will Shafto pecked at her food like an overfed bird, and Mr Will Shafto, who was usually a hearty trencherman, ate little more.

Bland-faced servants, grinning behind their servile masks wondered what, as the butler said afterwards in the servants' hall, 'was a-goin' on. More like they was goin' to an execution than to bed.' He noted 'that the master drank more than usual whilst the missis drank nothing at all.'

Gib said nothing, not even when the under-footman reported excitedly that 'they was a-goin' up to bed together, so they was, and he kissed her outside her bedroom door, whispered in her ear, and then, holding her hand, led her into his room.'

'Tonight's the night, then,' chortled the butler, 'seein' as how she told her maid she wouldn't need her this evening.'

'Guess who's a-goin' to undress her, then?' sniggered the youngest footman, to be silenced by the butler who believed that all the best jokes should be his.

'None of that now, Wattie!'

'When do I get my winnings?' asked the pantry boy, who had bet on this night being the night.

'Tomorrow, lad, tomorrow,' the butler told him. 'They might change their minds—who knows? The bedchamber lass will tell us in the morning what was up the night before.'

This last sally had the whole kitchen staff in convulsions of mirth so loud that it was a wonder that it did not reach the master bedroom where Will sat in one chair, and Beck in another on the other side of the room, both of them fully clothed.

'Be reasonable, Beck,' Will was saying. 'You will

have to get into the bed with me, and we shall have to provide some evidence that we were in it together.'

He gave a short, nervous laugh. To his surprise he was finding this charade as disturbing as Beck did. Any notion he might have had that the pair of them would put the bed to its proper purpose was being rapidly dismissed by the sight of his wife's intractable expression. She sat in her chair as though she were waiting to be tried for a capital offence.

Reluctantly Beck rose. Earlier in the day she had carried into Will's room her night rail and dressing-gown, as well as her toilet water, a towel, slippers, and a little cap for her hair. She picked them up, looked woefully in his direction, and said, 'I shall change in your dressing room, of course, as you will.'

Will bowed. 'Of course,' he echoed.

But even as she spoke there was a knock on the bedroom door, and then, without waiting for Will's command, Gib walked in.

'Oh, sorry, sir, madam, forgive me.' He rewarded them both with a greasy, knowing smile before he left, Will's reproaches for his intrusion ringing in his ears.

Astonishingly, Beck began to laugh, and if there was hysteria in it, what of that? You could never, Will thought bemusedly, forecast how she would react to anything. Wiping her eyes, she said, 'Properly caught. That ought to silence the servants' hall.'

'Not immediately,' returned Will, whose spirits had risen remarkably in response to Beck's surprising acceptance of Gib's entrance. He must remember to tip him later. 'On the contrary, I should imagine that the whole place is abuzz by now. After all, they've been waiting for this for a week.'

He didn't add, 'As I have done.' But he thought it.

Beck suddenly reverted to her normal manner. The sight fascinated Will. It was as though a shutter had dropped. All the liveliness, the spontaneity of the true Beck whom Will believed hibernated behind her usual, frosty exterior disappeared in an instant.

Perhaps he would not need to tip Gib after all, was his melancholy conclusion. Like a sculptor chipping a beautiful statue out of a shapeless block of stone, he needed to find some lever, some tool which would enable him to free Beck from her self-imposed isolation.

She disappeared into the dressing-room without further ado, leaving Will to throw himself into a chair and gaze at the painted ceiling where two Cupids disported themselves above Venus and Mars, who were preparing to enjoy themselves in a way forbidden to him. His only consolation was that, fixed forever in paint, they had gone as far as they would ever go.

Which might also apply to him where Beck was concerned!

She emerged some little time later, demurely apparelled in a dressing-gown which revealed nothing. She might as well have been wearing a sack.

Will grimaced and, in his turn, retreated. Beck sat in the distant chair again; the one which was furthest from the intimidating bed. What would she do when he came back into the bedroom in his night rail?

More to the point, what would he do?

Involuntarily Beck began to shiver.

Time was doing strange things. First it moved so quickly that it left her gasping, and then so slowly that that, too, was disturbing, for it left her too much time to think.

As now when, despite herself, she was waiting to see what Will looked like when his splendid clothes were gone. The thought shocked her: she blinked and re-proached herself for such unseemly internal behaviour. He would, of course, do as she had done, and put on a dressing-gown which would muffle him, rather than, as his day clothes did, show off his splendid physique.

She was wrong.

When, at last, he came into the room again he was carrying his dressing-gown, and was wearing a white linen nightgown with a pie-frill collar which stood up around what Beck could plainly see was his newly-shaven face. His hair had fallen into unruly curls since Gib was not there to dress it. His feet were bare.

They were beautiful feet, long and shapely. Beck could not help herself; she stared at them. They made her feel quite odd. Now why should that be? Feet were feet, after all. Nothing exciting about them. Except that Will's feet were exciting her.

Unlike his face at which she dare not look. She looked instead at the dressing gown he was not wearing.

Will saw the look. He threw the gown on the bed.

'In case anyone else bursts in on us in order to find how far gone we are, it is better that we are not muffled up as though we were about to set off for a walk in the snow.'

'You mean that I am to take off my dressing-gown, too?' asked Beck, betraying agitation for the first time.

'Is that too great a sacrifice?' mocked Will gently. 'When you first approached me, did you not realise that it would inevitably and eventually come to this?'

By her face she had not.

'Oh, the world is coarse,' Will told her. 'It demands proof. It pushes its dirty fingers into our affairs. One thing that I did not say earlier was that it is essential that your enemies do not know the true state of affairs—they might use it against you.'

Now, as he well knew, this was pushing matters a little, but if he were to succeed, then push he must. Standing there, the light of the candle around her head like the halo of some saint in a Renaissance painting, Beck was temptation itself.

The odd thing about her was that she was so unaware of her powers of attraction. She truly believed the contrary, so truly that it would be difficult for any man to convince her otherwise.

'Beck,' he said as gently as he could, for he did not wish to frighten her. 'You must take off your dressing-gown and get into bed, and I will lie on top of it, on the counterpane. I promise not to touch you. When morning comes, while you are in the dressing-room, I will get into bed and make it look as though we spent the night there together. You understand me.'

Beck nodded, her face wry. She said hesitantly, for she could never have imagined before this night that she would mention such a thing to a man, 'Since I am virgin, and we are supposed to have consummated the marriage...' She let the sentence die out, for she saw by Will's face that he understood her.

'Yes,' he said. 'I know that this is not the Middle Ages, but we must provide visible proof of our marriage for the servants to cackle over. Never fear, I'll think of something before they come to examine the bed.'

Deviousness was his middle name, thought Beck, a trifle ungratefully, but she did as he had bid her, took off her dressing-gown and climbed into the big bed. She was careful to leave him plenty of room to lie by her on the prettily worked bedspread.

Will waited until she was comfortable before stretching out a hand to extinguish the one candle by the bed which he had left burning. Beck said urgently, 'No, not yet.'

She did not wish to be in the dark with him.

He nodded agreement before lying down beside her, his hands behind his head. Beck held her breath for a moment. Her tension must have shown for, looking at the ceiling Will murmured, 'Don't worry, Beck, I shan't jump on you. It's not my way.'

Of course, the real truth must be that she didn't tempt him, thought Beck resentfully. It was truly strange that part of her was frightened that he might try to seduce her now that they were sharing a bedroom, and the other part felt insulted if he didn't!

'Yes, I know.' She spoke in her usual crisp and matter-of-fact voice. So matter of fact that Will felt challenged. He reared up on one elbow and leaned over her, teasing her by saying naughtily, 'Don't be too sure of me, Beck. I might be trying to deceive you.'

He received his punishment straightaway. Beck reared up immediately, catching him in the face with the top of her head as she did so. Will let out an anguished 'Oof,' and reared back in his turn, putting a protective hand to his nose.

To Beck's horror, it came away covered in blood.

'Oh, God, Beck,' exclaimed Will, throwing himself back on the pillow as though he had been dealt a mortal injury. 'You've tapped my claret—which is more than Gentleman Jackson ever did!'

'No! Oh, Will, forgive me, I never meant to hurt you,' and then, 'Will, what on earth are you doing?' for he was sitting up again, leaning forward and rubbing his bleeding nose on the undersheet beside her.

'Splendid, Beck, couldn't be better. Sit on it and mark

your nightgown.' He leaned back again, laughing heartily.

Beck stared at him, and then understanding struck. 'Oh, yes. How fortunate. One of our worries quite solved.'

'At the expense of my nose,' said Will, closing his eyes and looking wounded, 'I have proved you virgin. That should make everyone in the servants' hall doubly happy. Firstly because it is visible proof of your innocence, and secondly because it is solid evidence of my manly prowess in the marriage bed. No man or woman could ask for more.'

This came out in such a self-satisfied fashion as though he had truly achieved what a husband ought to achieve on his wedding night that Beck, despite her misgivings about the situation in which she found herself, began to laugh.

'So happy my damaged nose amuses you, madam wife,' moaned Will provokingly.

'Not so damaged,' returned Beck briskly. 'It's stopped bleeding already.' Forgetting that she had promised herself not to move too close to him, she leaned forward to examine it. 'It doesn't seem to be swollen.'

The opportunity was too good to miss. Will caught her by the chin, and said, his blue eyes gleaming, 'Kiss it better, then?'

He had adopted a child's attitude and voice as he spoke, which had the effect of disarming Beck completely.

'Oh, you are ridiculous,' she said, laughing, momentarily forgetting all her fear of him, something which Will saw and immediately took advantage of.

He put his left arm around her shoulders and kissed the tip of her nose as delicately as he could, before withdrawing a little, and murmuring, 'Like that would be nice.'

Beck froze in his encircling arm, offering him the eyes and bodily stance of a trapped deer.

'No,' she told him. 'No, that was not in the bargain.'

'Not?' he queried his head on one side, mischief riding on his face.

Beck was in two minds again. One part of her wished to give way to him, the other, the stronger part, was afraid to do so. The ugly past reared its equally ugly head, and told her No.

'You know that it wasn't, Will. I made myself quite plain.'

'Now, that,' Will told her, releasing her, 'would be difficult. I never saw a woman who looked less plain.'

Beck, leaning back on her pillows, answered him fiercely. 'You are not to try to bam me, sir. I know what I am.'

'Wouldn't dream of bamming you,' retorted Will, 'and you do not know yourself—as I hope to prove one day.'

She gave him her back, safer so, for the sight of his tender, mocking face might yet undo her. 'Go to sleep, Will. We have done our duty and need not fear the morning.'

Will blew out the candle—to which Beck made no objection this time—saying to himself, 'No, Beck, I have not done my duty by you this time, but one day I promise you that I will.'

He rolled on to his back, believing that sleep would be long in coming, as did Beck, lying so tantalisingly near to him, but, to their mutual but not expressed surprise, sleep came quickly to them both.

Shared laughter had anaesthetised Beck, and relieved the tensions which Will suffered, and even their dreams were pleasant—although neither he nor she remembered much of them the following morning.

Chapter Nine

'Didn't bed her, did you, sir? For all that the pantry boy was s'posed to have won his bet.'

'Damn you, Gib, as I warned you at Honyngham, it's no affair of yours what my wife and I do.'

'Told your Pa I'd look after you just afore he died, din't I? Don't like to see you making a fool of yourself, sir, with that cold piece. My duty to your Pa to tell you so.'

'And damn you again, Gib, for putting your duty to a man who squandered a fortune, and left me and mine up the River Tick, before your duty to me. I'll thank you to be silent.'

They were back in London in Beck's mansion, the so-called honeymoon over and, for once, Will was being harsh with his servant. That Gib was right in what he said was one more irritant to a man who was beginning to regret the unequal bargain which he had made, whatever he was gaining by it.

Gib opened his mouth to say more, but was silenced by Will taking him by the shoulders and pushing him out of his bedroom. 'Not another word, Gib, or I shall lose my temper.'

'Niver knew as 'ow you'd got one 'til you married 'er,' grumbled Gib below his breath, safer so.

Oh, the rest of the servants might think that, at last, all was well between Mr and Mrs Shafto, but Gib knew that it wasn't. That haughty piece wasn't doing right by Master Will, that she wasn't, and if he didn't tell him so, who would?

Home truths from Gib were no new thing for Will. He had gone to sleep that night at Honyngham hoping that, come morning, there might be no need to trick anyone again, particularly his sharp-eyed servant.

Alas, he had awoken to find that Beck had risen from her bed and was sitting in an armchair facing him, in the armour of her dressing-gown and a frozen face. He had sighed and, sitting up, tried to coax her back into the better humour of the previous night by saying, 'Come back to bed, Beck. More comfortable than an armchair, I do assure you.'

She had shaken her head at him. 'No, Will. We only shared a bed last night to prevent gossip. The deed being done, we can go on as we were before.'

'You see no need to change your mind, then?'

Will looked so appealing, sitting there, his curls in a tangle, so strongly resembling a large choirboy in his white shirt with its frilly collar that Beck thought that one might almost expect him to begin singing a hymn—if it were not for that certain look in his eye.

Oh, how tempting that look was! How Beck resisted it she never knew. She told herself sternly to remember that he was her rogue, nothing more, there to do her bidding, and her bidding had not changed from the day she had first met him. Her face, as well as her voice, told him so.

Will knew when he was beaten. He would live to fight

another day—or night, and so he had reluctantly come to some sort of accommodation with Beck which allowed them to present to the world a façade of married love.

At least at Honyngham they had been on their own, and if there had been no excitement in their long days, then neither had there been any need to deceive an audience, but returning to London and its distractions had again altered the unsteady balance between them.

Gib's forthrightness that morning had upset Will more than he would have thought possible. Trying to wriggle himself into his fashionably tight breeches and jacket without his valet's assistance didn't help his temper overmuch, nor did the knowledge that he faced an afternoon visiting Beck's friends and relations.

After that he—and Beck—faced another ordeal for they were to spend the evening at Durness House where they would both be on show. Not a happy thought, given the Duke's propensity to generate a near riot either in his home or out of it.

No one, however, could have guessed at the contrary passions which were assailing both the Shaftos by looking at them as they ascended the stairs at Durness House off Piccadilly.

'Whatever else,' exclaimed Emily Cowper, to her lover, Henry Temple, Lord Palmerston, 'they make a handsome pair. Why did she marry him, though?'

'Probably for that very reason,' he drawled. His own nickname was Cupid, and he knew all the stratagems of the game of love.

He frowned as Will and Beck walked by them. 'Something wrong there,' he opined. 'God knows what. If it's scandalous we shall soon know.'

'D'you think so?' Emily Cowper turned to follow Will and Beck with avid eyes. 'Heard something, have you?'

'No,' he returned. 'Sense it, somehow. Tell you what, she's the odder one, not him. He's from a good family, they say, but no money. Perhaps that's what she wanted in exchange for her pile of tin.'

This shrewd remark set Emily laughing, until an old friend greeted her and the Shaftos were temporarily forgotten in an exchange of even livelier *on dits* about the affairs of the notorious Lord Byron who was also present. The Duke had naturally made sure that society's most scandalous member was present to give his guests something to talk about.

'And,' as Emily remarked cattily to Lady Jersey, 'I suppose we ought to be grateful that Lord Byron is spending his days this year in chasing women, rather than making revolutionary speeches in the House of Lords on behalf of the Luddites. It's bad enough that we are fighting the result of that kind of sentimentality in Europe without risking it here.'

'Really,' returned Sally Jersey vaguely, 'but pray enlighten me, who are the Luddites?'

Emily rolled her pretty eyes to heaven and informed Sally that they were handloom weavers who had lost their living because the Midlands manufacturers had introduced more efficient machines which needed less men to work them. Many of them lived on Lord Byron's estates near Newstead in Nottinghamshire. Sally was yawning before she had finished.

'Oh, that!' she said inelegantly. 'Why waste time on that? Tell me, is the extremely handsome man with Beck Rowallan the fortune-hunter she has just married? If so, I can quite understand why she did!' She raised an eyeglass to inspect him more closely.

'I shall ask Durness to introduce him to me at once,' and off she went to bully her host who, nothing loath, did just as she asked.

Will and Beck were both well aware of the gossip which they excited. Fortunately the Duke's patronage prevented it from becoming too malicious. He shook Will by the hand ostentatiously and gave Beck a smacking kiss. It always had to be remembered that he had learned his manners in the rougher days of the eighteenth century.

After that he peered at them through a magnifying glass at the end of a long silver chain to examine them more critically. 'Peaky,' he said to Beck. 'You look peaky, don't she, Peter? Married life being too much for you, hey?'

He punctuated this outrageous remark by giving Will a hard shove in the ribs. Aunt Petronella, who was acting as his hostess, thus addressed, announced forcefully, 'Really, Durness, you must remember that this is 1813, not 1778. That was not at all the thing to say.'

'No?' he queried. 'Just wanted to remind young Shafto here not to overdo things. No harm in that, surely?'

Will was amused to notice that his usually composed wife had flushed scarlet, and that those waiting their turn to be received by the Duke were tittering behind their hands.

On the whole, given their situation, the Duke was doing him and Beck a kindness in spreading the notion that they were so much in love that they couldn't keep their hands off one another.

'I shall take heed of your advice, Duke,' he said solemnly, 'and see that Mrs Shafto gets plenty of rest.'

'But not in bed, eh?' cackled the Duke, shoving Will

in the ribs again, and causing Aunt Petronella to close her eyes in horror. 'But more of that later. There's a lot of fools waiting behind you that I have to waste my time doing the pretty to. Where in the world did you find them all, Peter? Never mind, must do my duty, I suppose. Honour of a Durness and all that. Mind you take notice of what I say, young Shafto.'

It was their *congé*. Will took his wife by the arm and led her away, followed by amused eyes. 'Splendid,' he whispered to Beck, 'absolutely splendid. If I'd paid him to say all that about us, he couldn't have done better.'

'Really, Will,' Beck whispered back, agitated for once. 'How can you talk so? He's made a raree show of us for the rest of the evening.'

'Precisely. We need do or say nothing ourselves from now on. The Duke has pronounced. He has told the world that I am a satyr and you are my helpless nymph.'

He put his head on one side to examine her. 'By the way, Beck, he has the right of it. You do look a bit peaky. Why is that, d'you think? Is there something lacking in your life which I could perhaps supply—thus adding a little veracity to the Duke's despatch to the nation about our marriage?'

How did Will manage to tickle the sense of humour which Beck possessed but which she had spent so many years suppressing? For, despite all her splendid resolutions not to allow him to affect or influence her in any way, Beck found herself laughing.

This was happening too often. She was about to tell him so, sternly, when, unfortunately she looked squarely at him and caught his dancing eyes—which set her off again into the helpless giggles which she thought she had left behind with her schooldays.

'Do confess, Beck. Given everything, is it not the

most splendid joke? That we shall be considered by everyone to be the exact opposite of what we are! Smile, my love. Look at me adoringly. Yes, just like that. Now raise your fan and hide your blushing face whilst I try to lead us towards a cooling drink which will help us to damp down our unruly passions.'

The trouble with Beck, thought Will, is that she hasn't enjoyed herself properly for years. One day, I shall find out why, and perhaps that will help me to breach the wall of ice which she has built around herself.

In the meantime, the more often I make her laugh, the more likely she is to give way to the unruly passion in which the Duke thinks I am already indulging—and what a day that will be.

In lieu of that, he fed Beck lemonade and ices, and it was perhaps a pity that whilst he was doing so Sarah Wingfield came up to them and stared at Will with great melancholy eyes.

The spasm of annoyance which ran through Beck as Sarah said mournfully to Will, 'I trust that my husband's foolishness towards you will not be allowed to spoil my friendship with you—and Cousin Rebecca, of course,' owed everything to unacknowledged jealousy and nothing to sweet reason.

Unacknowledged, because she did not care enough for Will—did she?—to be jealous of those females who sought to make some claim on his time and his attention. Particularly when, like Sarah, they hung on his every word and fluttered their eyes and their fans at him in an unspoken invitation to him.

She pre-empted Will's reply by saying briskly, 'Of course not, cousin. It is not your fault that your husband is a mannerless boor. On the other hand, it is hardly wise of you to spend overmuch time with us in public. Better by far to pay us an afternoon visit when he is otherwise engaged.'

Sarah's agreement was rapid. 'Oh, indeed, cousin. I will remember that. It is kind of you both to show me so much consideration. I bid you adieu.' She walked away before her husband could arrive to vent his displeasure on seeing her with the Shaftos.

'That was kind of you, Beck,' Will said, watching Sarah walk away from them. He was remembering the earlier occasion when Sarah had felt the edge of Beck's tongue.

'She looks so ill,' said Beck simply. 'I used to be jealous of her, she took life so lightly, but no longer. How could they marry her to that old roué?'

Instead of you was the unspoken end of her last sentence.

Will pondered a moment on Time's whirligig. One moment he had been down and Sarah had been up, but now the positions were reversed. No time to think of that, though. Beck must have her reward for taking pity on her cousin, so he suggested that she join him on the floor in the waltz.

Their appearance there gave the Duke another opportunity to crow at Aunt Petronella. 'Look at the lovebirds, Peter, and don't you try to tell me that Beck feels nothing for him. Just look at the face on her.'

Aunt Petronella, who had been worrying that her niece did not truly display what the poet called 'the lineaments of satisfied desire', was compelled to agree with him. Will was swinging his wife around the room with her eyes closed and her mouth smiling, so perhaps Beck was not so cold, after all.

Something which Beck was ruefully conceding herself. One of these days she was going to find herself giving way to Will—and what would that lead to? The kind of grief and shame which she had suffered once before when she had allowed her heart to rule her head.

Nevertheless it was pleasant to be in his arms while the music played and, later to know that she was being escorted by the room's most handsome man. Although, of course, the admirers of Lord Byron, who had leaned against the wall whilst the waltz was being danced, disapproving of it mightily—for the very reasons that Will was enjoying it—would have disputed that.

For Will it was becoming sweet torture to hold Beck in the dance and to know that that was all that was allowed to him. That later that night—or rather in the early morning—they would part outside her bedroom door to spend yet another night in their lonely beds…

'I've been thinking, Will.'

Beck had just walked into the study off the library where Will sat at a large desk writing a letter. He stopped when she came in, and had she not been so intent on what she had to say to him she would have noticed that he unobtrusively turned his writing paper over before rising to greet her.

He decided not to tell her that she thought too much. Instead he smiled and asked pleasantly, 'What is it, my dear?'

'Do you wish to stay in London much longer? The Season will shortly be ending, but I do not think that I wish to be in at its death. Something you once said leads me to believe that you prefer life in the country to the town. If so, why should we not go north to Inglebury next week? You do have some country clothes, but if not, then you could be outfitted suitably when we reach Yorkshire. The best cloth is made there, I'm told.'

Will carried out some quick calculations in his head. Yes, he probably had enough of his allowance left to be able to make himself as splendid as Beck's husband ought to be. She had already asked him why he had not used it to buy himself a curricle and pair, and he had been suitably evasive. He could scarcely tell her the truth about how he spent the majority of his allowance.

'To your ancestral home?' he queried.

He had not meant to mock her, but Beck perhaps thought that he had, for she replied quickly, 'Hardly ancestral! My grandfather, a successful millowner, who brought his only son up to be a gentleman, acquired it cheaply from a failed landowner. Does that qualify as ancestral?'

Will thought a moment. He had not realised that Beck felt defensive about her origins. He said, to amuse as much as to support her, 'My ancestral home was built by a freebooting pirate in the reign of Good Queen Bess. I'm not sure whether, in the great sum of things, that makes him better or worse than your grandfather. On the other hand, my own father threw away everything which came down to him from those times, except the house itself and a few acres around it.'

It was the first time that he had told Beck much about his origins. He wondered why he had done so and regretted it a little: the less she knew of him the better, given their temporary situation.

She said, and he thought that she meant it, 'We ought to visit it one day, perhaps.'

'Before we part?' he reminded her. 'It would take a fortune to restore it. I think not.' There were reasons why he did not want her there.

She made no answer other than, 'Then we are agreed.

We leave shortly—as soon as we have settled our affairs here.'

Will nodded.

Beck paused a moment, as if to say something more, decided not to, and giving him one of her rare smiles, left him to finish his letter.

To do what? To go where?

The semi-detached life they were living meant that they went their own ways—except when they going out into society. Will decided that when he had finished his letter he would take himself off to Jackson's and vent his frustration there on whoever was in attendance that day.

The Tiger, his friend, was absent: the Tooting Terror was present instead. His face, raddled with the effects of heavy drinking, lit up when he saw Will.

'Come for a mill?' he asked. He would dearly like to have the fine gentleman before him in the ring, stripped to the waist, without his gloves, and without having to show him the deference which Jackson expected of his employees. That would be a turn-up for the coddled beau who thought he knew what being a prizefighter meant. The Tiger was too gentle with him.

For his part, Will knew and resented the Terror's attitude to him, which was very different from that of the Tottenham Tiger. He was adept at reading the true feelings of the men and women around him, and the Terror's annoyance with him oozed from his every pore.

'Yes,' Will said. Marking the Terror's face might make up for the frustrations of his daily life. This was unfair of him, he knew, but he was also shrewd enough to be aware that he thought this way because of the Terror's barely hidden opinion of him.

'Fight with your shirt off?' asked the Terror. Now this was against the rules, but Jackson was absent at the Races that day and what the eye doesn't see the heart doesn't grieve, was always the Terror's motto.

'Why not?' Will shrugged.

'And bare knuckles, no gloves?'

'Why not?' said Will again, suddenly recklessness itself.

'Fight to the first knock down, eh—as though there was money in it?'

'Have you lost your mind, Shafto?' hissed Gilly Thornton who was one of the watchers, as Will agreed to this also. 'He'll kill you.'

'He can try,' Will shot back pulling his shirt over his head to reveal a heavily muscled torso which even had the Terror blinking a little.

The bout which followed was long and bloody. Will thought afterwards that he must have been mad to agree to it for his hands, without the gloves, were soon red raw, the knuckles damaged.

Harry Fitzalan, who had arrived just after it began, stood open-mouthed when he entered at the sight of Will mixing it, bare-knuckled, in the ring with the Terror.

'What the devil's going on?' he asked, and, 'Who's Will's second?'

'Only fighting to the first knock down so he don't need one,' answered Gilly, who had earlier queried Will's sanity, but now was more than a little awed that Will was still standing.

The Terror, Will soon discovered, was by no means the Tiger's equal, but he was a professional, up to every trick of the trade, and at first Will found that even to stay on his feet was almost too much for him. But the longer the bout lasted the more the Terror began to puff and blow, whilst Will, on the contrary, was in prime condition.

Thus at its beginning the Terror often had Will on the ropes, but the longer it lasted the more the balance of the fight began to change—until suddenly Will saw an opening.

He took it, to send the Terror crashing like a lightning-struck tree to the ground—and not before time, for his torso was showing the marks of the Terror's fists, and his knuckles were cut as the consequence of the blows he had been landing on the Terror.

'Mill over,' roared Harry, diving into the ring to throw a towel around Will's bruised and sweating shoulders. 'What the devil did you think you were up to, Will?'

'He annoyed me,' retorted Will inadequately, wondering like Harry what had got into him. He had little time for further thought, for suddenly Jackson himself—back early from the Races—was in the gym, his face like thunder. He had not seen the end of the bout, which had broken all the rules he had made for his patrons' safety, and he immediately assumed from the state of Will's face and body that he had been the loser.

'That's it,' he shouted furiously at the Terror. 'You know better than that, man. You'll not work for me again. You know perfectly well that you have to treat my gentlemen with respect, not maul them and knock them down.'

'No,' said Harry urgently. 'Will won the mill, not the Terror.'

Jackson stared at him. 'What? Never say so! I knew you were useful, Mr Shafto, but not as useful as that. But no matter. Rules are rules.'

This time it was Will who shouted 'No.' He could see the Terror's agonised face at the prospect of losing his means of making a living. 'It was my fault. I provoked him. You mustn't turn him away. He couldn't refuse a gentleman.'

Gilly Thornton, who had watched what had happened from the start, would have protested that this was untrue, but caught Will's fierce eye on him, and said nothing.

Jackson looked keenly at both men. At the Terror, bested by an amateur. At Will, who had shown more raw pluck than he would ever have expected of him.

'That's the truth?'

Both men nodded. Jackson knew that they were lying. He hesitated for a moment, then said shortly to the Terror, 'So be it. But if you ever do that again, man, I'll have you out in the street in five minutes. And you, Mr Shafto, you ought to know better.'

Will gave a painful cracked smile of pure delight. 'So I ought. As a cure for the blue devils, it might seem a bit extreme—but it worked.'

He walked over to where his coat lay and fetched a guinea from his pocket and handed it to the Terror.

'That's for the damage I did to your pride, not your body,' he said. 'We should never have agreed to do what we did, but men are men the world over, whatever their rank, as Mr Jackson well knows.'

The only thing which worried him was what Beck would say when she saw his bruised face and his damaged knuckles.

He needn't have troubled himself. She gave a wry smile when she met him in the entrance hall, catching him as he was trying to sneak upstairs in order to repair a little of the damage.

'There is an old saying,' she remarked sweetly as he gave her her wry smile back. '"Boys will be boys", so

I ought not to be surprised that men will be men. And I won't ask what you have been getting up to. I might not like the answer.'

'I took on the Tooting Terror, bare-knuckled.' Will had rapidly decided that with Beck honesty was usually the best policy.

Her eyebrows rose. 'Did you, indeed? Was that wise? He seems to have had a burning desire to rearrange your features.'

Will's smile was sardonic. 'So he did. Unfortunately, it was his features which came off second-best.'

There was something in his voice which Beck did not like. 'Why, Will, whatever possessed you? I shall never understand why men feel the need to fight and struggle with one another. He might have done you a serious hurt.'

'Well, he didn't.' Will was brusque. 'And now, if you will allow, I should like to go to my room to repair what damage he did do to me.'

It was the first time he had been brutally short with her. A mixture of sexual frustration and the punishment which the Terror's fists had inflicted on him, were taking a heavy toll.

Beck made a move in his direction as he walked by her…and then withdrew. She wanted to comfort him, for she sensed by his posture that he was in pain and needed comforting, but the habit of a lifetime was too strong.

Had she not retreated, had she followed her deepest, truest feelings, everything between them might have changed immediately and completely, for Will, as well as she, was vulnerable that night.

But, alas, the moment was lost. Before she could make another move he was up the stairs and walking to his room, calling for Gib—who was to add his reproaches to Beck's as he tried to relieve his master's aches and pains.

Nothing, though, could relieve Will's aching heart—or Beck's.

Chapter Ten

'Going home, are you?' commented Aunt Petronella. 'I would have thought you might see the Season out.'

'We decided against it.'

'You mean that you did,' replied Aunt Petronella bluntly. 'Durness will have it that you're a pair of love-birds, but I know better. He's a good young man, Rebecca. Why did you marry him if you were only going to torment him?'

Beck rose and walked to the window. 'I don't understand you, Aunt.'

'And *I* don't understand *you*, Rebecca Shafto. I thought at Durness's ball that you and he had come to an understanding. But I'm certain that you haven't, even though he puts a brave face on things. Your face is as cold as it ever was—which also tells a story.'

The old lady was too shrewd for her own, or anyone else's, good. A home truth about Will might silence her.

'Suppose I told you that he married me for my money?'

Her aunt snorted. 'Well, of course he did. He wasn't in a position to marry you if you hadn't any. It doesn't prevent him from loving you—and that's a bonus I am beginning to believe that you don't deserve.'

'And if I told you that he frequents Jackson's gym more than I consider wise?'

'Well, that's natural. Working off his frustrations, I suppose. In any case, you surely cannot wish that you had married a namby-pamby. Unless, of course, you wanted to run him ragged—as you have done everyone else connected with you.'

Beck closed her eyes. She opened them again to think that she and her aunt were birds of a feather. Birds who spoke their own mind and to the devil with everyone else.

'You forget that I was run ragged first,' she returned quietly, staring out of the window to see Will riding up the drive, Gib behind him in the undistinguished livery which was all that he would consent to wear.

'No, I haven't. But you can't live in the past forever. Let it go, Rebecca, before you allow it to destroy you—and him. I was a fool to let Durness slip away from me all those years ago. Don't you do the same.'

Will was dismounting, exchanging a joke with Gib and the groom who had come running up to lead his horse away. He had recovered some of his old jauntiness during the week which had followed the fight. Beck wished that she could feel jaunty. Perhaps if they went north together, away from the distractions of the town, they might come to know one another better.

She told her aunt so. Her aunt's reply was as brisk as ever. 'Only if you learn to value him—as I think that he values you. The more fool he.'

She stopped as Will entered. He bowed to Aunt Petronella, who rose and crossed the room to kiss him on the cheek as he did so.

Startled, he put up a hand to stroke the spot she had honoured. 'Goodness, Aunt, whatever would the Duke say if he knew that you were making love to me.'

'That it was time that someone did, I suppose,' was her dry answer. 'Do you really wish to go north with Rebecca in the middle of the Season?'

Will glanced over to his wife, who had resumed staring out of the window. So, Aunt Petronella was at outs with her, and by her first remark might be understanding far too much. Friendly Beck had changed to harsh Rebecca.

'If that is what she wishes and will make her happy, yes.'

Aunt Petronella sighed and was dry again. 'That will have to do, I suppose. Come and say goodbye to me before you leave—if you have time.'

'We go in a week,' Will said, for Beck remained silent, 'but we shall honour your request.'

'Good—and now I must leave you. The love-birds, as Durness insists on calling you, will want to be alone.'

'Now, what,' asked Will when she had gone, 'did your aunt mean by saying that in such a disbelieving fashion?'

'She knows,' replied Beck wearily, 'or has guessed, how matters truly stand between us, and she is reproaching me, not you, and is right to do so. But never fear. She will not talk.'

'Well, that's a relief.' Will was frank. He had decided not to oppose Beck over visiting her home, even if it did mean that he would lose Gib.

On being told that they were to travel to Inglebury in the near future, Gib had announced hardily, 'Well, that's that, then. I'll leave you to her. My brother-in-law has offered me a job as a man of all work whilst he looks after his thriving butcher's shop in Islington. I'll not go north again unless it's to Shafto Hall.'

'You'd leave me, Gib, would you? I need you—you're my last link to the old days.'

'No, you don't, Master Will. You've to make your own way now, and hanging on to me ain't helping you to do it. Oh, you've had a hard time, and getting your missis to see sense might be even harder—but you have to try.'

Nothing Will could say would move him. So, one of the servants in the second coach which would go north—the first holding Will and Beck—would be the young man, John Carter, whom Gib had already secretly trained to succeed him.

Beck, who rarely complained, was complaining. Her voice as she did so was as stoically calm as ever. 'I grow weary of this everlasting rain, and although I am not frightened of thunder, I cannot say that I like it.'

Even as she spoke a flash of lightning, followed by a crackling roll of thunder, lit up their carriage: the afternoon had grown nearly as dark as night.

Will leaned forward to offer comfort if it were necessary, but, as ever, Beck stared calmly at him. Only a slight quiver of the lips showed him that she was more disturbed by the storm raging overhead than she would ever admit. It seemed to have been with them ever since they had left London.

As though the weather had become their enemy, it had been raining hard and blowing a gale when Mr and Mrs Shafto had finally set off for Inglebury. Any hope that matters might improve as they left the supposedly warm south was dispelled by every cruel mile they travelled.

In good weather Will would have enjoyed seeing a

part of England which he had never previously visited, but heavy rain and unseasonable gales continued to make the journey miserable. It was as though the very heavens were weeping on their behalf.

Afterwards Will was to remember thinking that on this journey their marriage had almost reached breaking point; a belief reinforced by Beck's coldness towards him both in the coach and at every inn at which they stopped.

Beck was thinking the same thing. Her coldness was actually a form of defence, for she was fearful that if she once showed any sign of her growing affection for Will, she would be lost. She dare not call it love—for Beck Shafto could not love, could she?

They were making for Inglebury by way of Leicester and Nottingham before taking a post road north not far from Mansfield and Newstead Abbey, Lord Byron's home. Beck had taken this route many times before and preferred it to the Great North Road, which meant that she had to travel across country to her home by poor byways after Newark had been reached in order to avoid going out of her way through Lincoln.

When they reached Nottingham, Will had needed to find a coachman to replace their own who had fallen ill. His replacement was a surly, shabby fellow, one Job Cooper, but since he was the only man available he would have to do.

'After all,' Will had said to Beck when at last they set off again, having spent two nights in the city, not one, 'we are hardly likely to wish to converse with him overmuch, so his lack of manners is no great matter.'

'Nor his unwashed appearance,' added Beck, thinking of her own steady, well-mannered John in his spotless livery whom they had perforce left behind to follow them to Inglebury once he had recovered.

This latest storm, which had driven even Beck to voice her unhappiness, had begun to rage when the road took them through Sherwood Forest. Beck had told Will that, whilst it was not as good as the Great North Road, this stretch of it was better than most that they would travel over before they reached Inglebury. He was not finding it so.

'Might it not be wise to stop at The Hutt?' Will suggested as they jolted over yet another rut. The Hutt was a well-known hostelry on the Mansfield Road which the innkeeper had recommended to them if the weather became so bad that they felt that they could not go on.

Beck shook her head. 'The sooner that we are home the better. The storms cannot last much longer, I hope.'

'Nor will the coach if this goes on,' muttered Will. The road had become so bad that the coach had more than once been on the point of overturning. 'I thought that you said that this was a good road, Beck. It doesn't seem so. This is the roughest ride I have ever had.'

'It was in good condition when I came south in the spring,' Beck returned. She leaned forward to look out of the window—to discover that the darkness was not only due to the storm. They were travelling through a dense part of the forest which she had never seen before, on a road which was merely a track, and covered in ruts and great pools of water...

She turned a pale face on Will. 'We are not on the right road at all. We are on something not much better than a track to a farm! Somehow we have taken a wrong turning. We must tell the coachman so.'

Will swore beneath his breath, pulled down the window, and tried to shout to the coachman to tell him that they were on the wrong road and by some means should turn back. His efforts to make himself heard were made difficult by the noise of the rain, the frequent rolls of thunder, and the gusts of wind which carried his words away.

Either the coachman could not hear him, or more likely chose not to, for he continued driving down what was plainly an increasingly dangerous path.

Cursing again, Will looked back down the way they had come—to see no sign of their companion coach. Either it had broken down, or it had taken the right turn whilst theirs had taken the wrong one.

Neither supposition was attractive!

Will, his head and shoulders drenched, pulled himself back into the coach. He thought Beck was brave enough to hear the unpalatable truth.

'I believe that our coachman can hear me, but he chooses not to answer. I am sure that you are right and that we have lost our way. Our second carriage is not with us.'

He saw Beck's face pale. She said, still steady, 'Is there nothing that we can do?'

Will shook his head. 'Not until he chooses to stop. What troubles me is his refusal to answer. Neither of us liked the look of the fellow, but the landlord swore that he knew the route to Mansfield and from thence to Inglebury.'

'Perhaps he has lost his way in the rain,' Beck offered bravely.

Before Will could answer her the coach gave a lurch even more dangerous than before. So dangerous that it fell off the track altogether, to lodge slowly against one of the giant trees which bordered it.

Beck and Will slid sideways on to the floor. Beck

landed on top of him. Will held her gently for a moment before he released her. He could feel her trembling.

'What now?' she asked him, still in the same cold steady voice.

Even from Beck, Will had expected hysterics, re- proaches, or tears. He had never admired her more. He was not given long to do so for the door was wrenched open by their driver.

'Out wi' the pair on you,' he shouted at them.

'What, in this rain?' Will said, staring at the pitiless face the other offered them.

'Won't hurt you. We 'ave to stand it often enough. Do as you're bid, and you'll not come to harm.'

To reinforce what he was saying he was waving a blunderbuss at them.

'What is it?' asked Beck. She was behind Will and could not see that the coachman was armed. 'He cannot really mean us to get out into the rain, dressed as we are.' She was wearing a light muslin dress, a cashmere shawl, for the day was cold, and white kid slippers.

'Oh, but I do!' shouted the coachman, grinning evilly. Seizing Will by the shoulder he pulled him out, and then, whilst Will was gaining his balance, he leaned forward to perform the same office for Beck.

Once they were both out in the open and shivering in the pouring rain, they became aware that the coachman was not alone. He had brought them to a clearing in the forest. Facing them, standing in front of some rude huts and hovels was a silent band of ragged men, women and children. The men and boys were armed, either with iron-tipped staves or large hammers, or with ancient muskets which still looked lethal.

'Wh-wh-what?' stammered Beck, clutching at Will's hand, not sure which she liked least: that she was rapidly being soaked to the skin, or that she and Will were the target of the malevolent glares of the tattered crowd before them.

It was as though time had suddenly stopped and she and Will were the centrepiece of a ghastly tableau—a sensation which Will was also sharing.

And then it was over. Time started again. Their coachman shouted at the watching crowd, 'It's yours, my pretties. All yours. The coach alone will keep you in firewood for weeks, and there's money and clothes for you to share among you.'

In a second Beck and Will were engulfed by a crowd of screaming men and women who flung them aside to get at the treasures before them. Beck was hurled into the mud, but not before a skeletal woman had pulled the shawl from her shoulders.

Will, better able to protect himself, helped her to her feet as the looting of their coach began. Beck, her face a distorted mask of fear and cold combined, suddenly remembered the footman who had ridden behind them.

'Giles,' she cried at the coachman who had stayed behind to see that they did not run off, although where they could have run to was difficult to imagine. 'Giles, what have you done with Giles?'

'A knock on the head at the last stop disposed of him. We drove on without him. And now, behave yourselves. Don't try to run away. You're deep in Sherwood, and every man and woman's prey.'

His speech, Will noted, was more educated than that of the ragged looters. A large woman, stronger than the rest, had found the trunks holding their clothes in the boot at the back of the coach. She had lugged them on to the muddy ground and was throwing bonnets, petticoats, elegant Paris gowns, shawls and light kid shoes to the women around her.

One of the men had forced open Will's trunk and was holding up his fine shirts for admiration. To Will's surprise it was not a free-for-all: impromptu leaders were busy sharing out the finery so that no one was left without something.

One haggard woman, wearing Beck's best bonnet above her grimy rags, ran up to shake her fist at them and screamed something incomprehensible in a broad Nottinghamshire dialect at Beck and Will before she hurried back lest she lose her share of the loot.

Will's pistol and his fowling piece were swiftly discovered—but there was no sharing there. The coachman, who seemed to be their leader, was presented with them.

The coach was stripped of everything: even the cushions were thrown out to be carried triumphantly away by running boys. The numerous leather straps, both inside and outside the coach, were cut free and handed out. The coach doors were ripped from their hinges and two men ran with them through the trees towards distant hovels, barely visible in the pouring rain.

The brass lamps were carefully removed and placed in a large sack. Will was later told that they were taken off to be sold at Mansfield market. One blessing was that the cases containing Beck's jewellery were in the other coach under Mrs Grey's care. It had presumably fallen behind them, taken the right road, and no one would be aware that they had disappeared until Mansfield was reached.

'Watch, my beauties,' gloated the coachman, 'and see how the things which you take for granted are treasured by those who go without them.'

Neither Will nor Beck could speak—Beck because

fear had her in its grip, and Will because he did not deem it politic. Besides, he was too busy wondering desperately if there was anything which he could do to save them from the dangerous predicament in which they found themselves.

He felt Beck tug at his sleeve when the coachman's attention was drawn away from them. He was busy organising a party of men armed with hatchets who were arguing about how best to cut up the carcass of the coach for firewood. Its wheels had already been removed, and were being stripped by a brawny man with the muscles and appearance of a blacksmith.

'Will,' she whispered, 'who are these men and women? I had no notion that such wretched creatures existed in England.'

'They are,' he told her, 'framebreakers, that is handloom weavers who have lost the means of making a living because the new machines have made the ones they own out of date. The manufacturers can make more money by installing the new ones—thus putting them out of work. They are known as Luddites when they band together to smash the new machines and attack the manufacturers who have robbed them of their livelihood.'

Beck, like Sally Jersey at the Duke of Durness's reception, was about to ask him why they were called Luddites and why they were living in the forest when the coachman, having settled the dispute over the destruction of the coach, returned and overheard them.

'You can stop mumbling between yourselves. I'll not have you plotting and planning.'

To Will's horror, Beck, who had begun to accept her plight, was now ready to argue with her captor in her usual brisk fashion. 'We are not fools. We weren't plotting and planning anything, or trying to run away—a more stupid suggestion I have never heard. I asked my husband if he knew who you are and why you have attacked and robbed us. He said you were Luddites.'

Will's relief was great when their captor, instead of rebuking Beck, appeared on the contrary to admire her spirit.

She was wet to the skin, her hair had come loose and water was dripping from it on to her shoulders. She was standing ankle-deep in mud, had watched her clothes and other possessions shared out among a pack of women whom she must regard as harpies and was still able to stare haughtily at him.

'Why, missis, you're a pluck'd 'un, so you are. Well, time will tell if you'll still be as proud-stomached when you've lived among us for a few days while we decide what to do with you.' He gave an odd laugh. 'Captain Ned Ludd's our leader, missis—or so some say.'

Beck could not be the only one showing gallantry. Will said in his most winning manner, 'Once this rain stops you could take us back to where the forest track began and set us on the way to Mansfield. Someone would be sure to see us and offer us assistance.'

The coachman thrust his face into Will's. 'D'ye take me for a fool, Mester Whativer-your-name-is? And then you'd go to the authorities, so you would, and lead them here.'

'I could promise not to.' Will was still trying to use his charm on the monster before him.

'And what would your promise be worth, mester? Word of a gentleman, you would say, but I'm not a gentleman, so most like you wouldn't keep your word to me. No, here you stay, until our man comes from Nottingham to advise us on what to do wi' you.'

One of the brawnier man carrying a large hatchet on his shoulder came up to them, saying to the coachman, 'I vote to cut their throats straightway. Dead men don't talk, Job.'

'Aye and those who make them dead most often hang, Jem.'

'I'll take that risk, Job.'

'It's not just you taking that risk, it's all on us what would suffer. No, wait until Mester Henson comes. 'Twas him what gave me the wink about the coach. The lady here is passing rich, he said.'

'Then 'ow about demanding a ransom for 'em?' Jem was eager to make the most of their captives. He surveyed the ruin of Beck's clothes and appearance, and said doubtfully, 'She don't look rich to me.'

'Use your noddle, Jem. We'd niver get away wi' that. They'd have the sojers on us like lightning, so they would. No, best this way, Henson said, seein' as how they'll have disappeared mysterious-like, with none to guess where they are, so there'll be none to track us down.'

'They'll blame Ned Ludd most like—and they'll be right,' sniggered Jem, before walking away to join a bedraggled woman and two dirty children who were loaded down with loot.

Beck had begun to shiver uncontrollably from a combination of the cold, the rain and the shock of their capture. Will, forgetting all prudence, said impatiently, 'How long are you going to keep us standing in the pouring rain before you allow us to shelter? My wife is not dressed for this weather. She is shaking with cold and has not eaten since breakfast. Common humanity should make you show a little pity for her.'

'Oh, aye,' retorted Job. 'A little rain won't harm

her—and as for missing her food, why, that means she'll be the same as all the women and bairns here. We live on short commons and no mistake.

'But not tomorrow—tomorrow we go to Mansfield market with the guineas from your coach and buy us enough for a feast day. 'Twon't hurt your missis to go without today—and perhaps tomorrow. Cool her temper down most like.'

Before Will could stop her Beck burst out with, 'Oh, no, it won't cool my temper down. I'm sorry for your women and children, but it is not my fault that they are starving.'

'No?' Job raised his brows. 'Is that so, missis? Why, Mester Henson allows as how your grand-daddy began life as a millowner in Yorkshire. Tell me, how many men and women starved so that he might make his fortune?'

'None,' said Beck spiritedly. 'He was a merciful master. But even if he weren't, it is no reason for you to leave me standing in the rain.'

By the end of this forthright defence she could scarcely speak for shivering. Job stared at her in admiration and horror mixed. 'I'll say one thing for you, lass, you're not the mardy sort. Does she speak like this to you, mester?' he asked Will. 'If she did, and she were mine, I'd take a stick to her, so I would.'

'Would you now?' said Will solemnly. 'Best not tell her so!'

To Beck's indignation both men laughed together companionably, shaking their heads over the vagaries of women, their class differences temporarily forgotten.

But only temporarily.

Job shook his head at them both. ''Tis true that you're

passing wet. You can shelter in old Mother Cayless's hut for the time being.'

He looked around him. 'Bob,' he called to a man who was busy sawing the panels of their coach into pieces suitable for the fire, 'take them to Ma Cayless's. They can shelter there for the time being.'

Bob, still sawing, shouted back, 'She'll not be best pleased when she comes back from birthing Lizzie Orton's babby to find them cluttering up t'place.'

'Then she'll have to lump it, won't she?' Job roared at him.

With sad amusement Will noted that Job's democratic beliefs disappeared when it came to managing the affairs of the landless men and women of the forest. Like Beck he allowed his tongue to run away with him.

'You're not taking a vote on it, then?' he enquired politely as Bob led him and Beck towards the largest of the makeshift dwellings in the small clearing. 'Just issuing an order?'

Job glared suspiciously at him. 'Makin' fun of me, are you, mester?'

'Not at all.' Will was still reckless. 'I just wanted to see revolutionary radicalism in action. Jacobin beliefs have always interested me.'

He thought Job was about to strike him. Then his captor threw his head back and laughed.

'By Gow, Bob, we've snared a right pair here and no mistake! You're well matched with your shrew of a wife for all your mild looks, mester. I wish you joy of one another. Get a move on, Bob, I want to be out of the rain meself. And Bob, you can have the Mester's fine coat for your pains.'

Ma Cayless's hut consisted of one room and was dark and smelly. There was an empty primitive fireplace at one end, but no chimney. The smoke from the fire when it was lit could only find vent through a hole in the thatched roof. The floor was a dirt one on which a straw palliasse rested, with a battered trunk at its bottom which presumably held its owner's clothes.

Two stools, another small table and a wash-stand holding a cracked china bowl, a jug, and a candlestick were ranged along one wall. A bigger table on which stood some rough crockery and a knife, fork and spoon stood in the middle of the room and made up the tally of the room's furniture.

Daylight came in through the open door: there were no windows. It was apparent that anyone living in the hut carried on most of their business out of doors.

Will walked over to the table and picked up the knife. It was so blunt it would scarce cut butter, and would be of no use to a man and a woman seeking some sort of weapon to help them escape.

Beck sat herself down on one of the stools after looking around the room for some clean cloth with which to dry herself. In vain: a piece of ragged towelling was thrown down by the hearth next to a small pail holding coals and wood obviously cut from the surrounding trees. Alas, it was black with grime. Beck stared at it and shuddered.

Not only was the interior of the hut dark, but it was also cold. Will was relatively warmly dressed, even though he had lost his coat and was only in his shirt-sleeves. His breeches protected him, and he still had his boots so that he was by no means as wet as poor Beck in her thin muslin gown and her light kid slippers.

But he wasn't to keep his boots for long, nor Beck her slippers. He had scarcely had time to seat himself on the stool by Beck before Job came in with a fresh demand.

'Off wi' your shoes and boots, the both on you. You'll not be able to run far wi' out 'em. Besides, I've a mind for a good pair of boots and we're much of a size.'

Briefly Will considered suggesting that they fight one another for them, but rejected the idea immediately. He was in no position to bargain about anything, and he must do nothing to make Beck's situation any more uncomfortable than it already was. He must protect her as well as he could.

So it was goodbye to boots and slippers. Beck looked ruefully at her feet in their torn stockings, and tried to offer some consolation to Will.

'If we were to escape, it might be easier for us in the mud without slippers or boots. On the other hand, since we have no notion where we are, it would be difficult to know exactly in which direction to go if we did manage to get away.'

Will stared at her, bemused. She never ceased to surprise him. When he had first met her he had thought of her as a simple bully, but he might have known that there was nothing simple about Beck. Her stiff-backed, stiff-necked attitude to life was sustaining her now. The raw courage of her staggered him. She might be wrong about how easy it was to walk without shoes, but at least she had given the matter some thought.

'How do you propose that we escape, Beck?'

She shook her head, and said, 'I don't know. I shall have to think about it. Do you have any useful suggestions to make, Will?'

'At the moment, no. To begin with, Job will have undoubtedly put a guard outside the hut. All the men we have seen so far are armed in one way or another. We have, as you said, no idea where we are, other than that we are somewhere in Sherwood Forest, between Mansfield and Nottingham, perhaps not far from Newstead, Lord Byron's home. It is likely that these are not the only squatters in the Forest—even if the others aren't Luddites.'

Whilst he was speaking Beck had risen from her stool and walked to the door to peer out into the rain which had slacked a little. He heard her talking to someone— the guard, no doubt. He closed his eyes. Whatever would she do next? Her fearlessness, admirable though it might be, was dangerous given their situation.

He opened his eyes to find that she had returned. 'You were quite right, Will. There is a guard outside. I asked him where we were and he said hell. I told him that, all things considered, that was a good answer. He told me that I talked too much.'

'And so you do,' retorted the goaded Will. 'I don't think that you understand the danger we are in.'

She traded him glare for glare. 'Of course I do. But I refuse to sit down and wail about it. That would not benefit either of us. Tell me, when do you think that Mrs Grey and the others in the second coach will realise that we are missing?'

Will thought for a moment before answering. 'Not when they reach Mansfield, unfortunately. They will assume that they have fallen a long way behind us and that, arriving there early, we continued our journey to Chesterfield without changing our horses. When they find that we never reached Chesterfield they will probably think that we lost our way, and, to avoid the storm, stayed overnight somewhere else before making for Chesterfield.

'I'm afraid that it's highly likely that it will be midday

tomorrow before they grasp that we have disappeared. And even then they may carry on to Inglebury, believing that we have simply gone ahead of them at full speed.'

For the first time Beck's brave front shivered a little. 'Never say so, Will. But, of course, you are right.'

Will had been honest with her because he thought that she was courageous enough to be told the truth. He cursed himself a little, and then as she firmed her mouth, and blinked at him before resuming her stoic face, he knew that he had done the right thing.

'I'll think about possible escape, Beck, I promise you, but don't be too hopeful.'

'They hate us, don't they?' she said simply. 'Because we are rich. That is what frightens me. You called them Luddites. I had heard of framebreakers, and even of Luddites—but why that particular name?'

'They are supposed to have a secret leader named Captain Ned Ludd—but it's very likely that he's a myth like Robin Hood, who also roamed Sherwood as an outlaw in the reign of Richard I. They have settled in the Forest as squatters because they have lost their homes. Lord Byron made a speech about them in the House of Lords asking that they be helped, but we are in the middle of a major war and authority sees them as expensive nuisances.'

Not for the first time Will surprised Beck by the depth of his knowledge. He was also behaving as she would expect him to. If she had not moaned and wailed and complained, neither had he. Like her he was weighing up their options, and if they did not seem too hopeful he was not allowing that fact to daunt him over much.

'But they have little children,' she said sadly, 'and no money to feed them—which is why they robbed us. I pity them, Will. Do you find that odd of me? Of course,

I cannot condone what they have done to us, but I can understand why they did it. In their place I should do the same.'

And that was true Beck, and it was why he loved her. Here, in this miserable hovel, as she sat opposite to him, drenched, her delicate beauty extinguished, her spirit was as unextinguished as ever. Will fiercely asked God not to allow her to be treated after a fashion which would extinguish it forever.

'We must not do anything stupid,' he said at last, 'for that would be worse than doing nothing.' Something with which Beck wholeheartedly agreed. She told him so.

He came over to her and took her hands in his. 'That's my brave girl. You must not be too brave, too foolhardy. You understand me?'

Yes, she did, and told him so. Moved by everything which had happened to them and her stoic acceptance of it, Will took her in his arms to comfort her. For the first time Beck offered him no resistance. At last they stood heart to heart, breast to breast, as a man and wife should. Will stooped a little to join his lips to hers...

And then a harsh voice broke in on them.

'Ain't Job Cooper got owt better to do than use me 'ome as a prison for you, and make me share Janet Thurman's dirty hut?'

It was Ma Cayless, come to lament the loss of what was hers, and to reproach them for being the cause of her losing it.

Their improbable moment of rapport was broken. Improbable because neither of them could have foreseen that they might come together as captives held in a squalid hut deep in a dense forest far from everything that they knew and loved.

Chapter Eleven

'I never thought a hunk of black bread and cheese and a tin mug of water would taste so sweet,' Beck told Will, as she tore ravenously at the bread, forgetting her manners in her hunger.

'That's because we haven't eaten for nearly twelve hours,' said Will who was also enjoying his harsh fare, being more used to it.

They were sitting in the open doorway. The rain had stopped and a weak sun, almost on the point of setting, had come out. Their captors were enjoying a better meal. They had roasted joints of venison, cut from a deer which one of them had killed with his ancient musket. Several rabbits and some pigeons made up their bill of fare. They had not feasted so well for months.

The scent of their cooking was making Beck's mouth water. They had not been offered any of the meat, for as Job had said earlier, 'Do you both good to starve a bit—as we often have to.'

'You know that you could be hanged or transported for poaching the deer—and the rabbits,' Will had said quietly when Job had given them their short commons on one tin plate.

'What's that to us, mester, when we'd starve else? Sherwood Forest and its animals should belong to all on us, not just the lucky few. You be the thieves, not us.'

Will had no wish to debate political morality with their captors. He thought wryly that he had lived for many years on a knife edge where, if he made a mistake, he would descend into the underworld of poverty in which so many lived. Marriage to Beck had saved him from that, but the people around him had no such means of escape.

Shortly before their evening meal was ready to eat the men who had been sent to Mansfield to buy ale returned with several barrels of it. They broached it immediately and began to drink heavily. The clearing rang with their noise. Will took Beck by the hand and led her back into the hut, shutting the door on the saturnalia outside.

'Safer so,' he said. 'Pray God they leave us alone.'

Some of the more reckless, flown with drink, wished to have some fun with their captives, but Job had insisted that they should not be harmed or unduly harassed until Mester Henson came from Nottingham to advise on how they should be dealt with. After much grumbling they unwillingly gave in to his wishes.

Inside the hut Beck said sharply, 'I hope that they saved some of the money to buy food for the children and have not spent it all on drink.'

'For God's sake, don't tell them so,' ordered Will. 'We must try to placate them, not annoy them.'

He was so agitated that when he took her by the hand and said, 'Promise me, Beck, that in future you will say as little as possible,' she nodded her agreement.

'But it goes against the grain, Will,' she said earnestly, 'now that I have seen the poor children who have been living on short commons for so long.'

Her concern for the little ones showed Will another side of her. Because she was so astringent in speech and manner he had often wondered what sort of mother she would make, but he now knew that she would be a loving one.

When Ma Cayless had finally arrived to disturb them Beck had seen at once that the woman was tired after long attendance on a difficult birth and had made no sharp answer to her, but had, surprisingly, apologised for their presence in her home. Which, considering that they were only in her hut at all because they had been ordered there, Will thought was a bit rich.

He watched Beck busy herself about the squalid room. She wet her handkerchief and tried to clean herself a little. She made no open objection when she had to leave the hut to answer the call of nature in some nearby greenery, even though one of the sharp-faced women insisted on going with her lest she take the opportunity to try to run away.

When darkness fell she lit the one candle, and came to sit by him on the stool, saying gravely, 'I fear that we shall have to share the palliasse, Will, there is nothing for it.'

'Is that an invitation, Beck,' he asked her, 'and if so, to what?'

'To sleep,' she returned with all her normal austerity of speech. 'What else! I am tired to the bone, and I suspect that you are, too.'

'Yes,' he agreed gravely. He could scarcely tell her that, tired though he was, the sight of her as she quietly accepted her fate without complaint was rousing him more than she had ever done when she had been dressed in her finery and in command of all around her.

She was a woman in a thousand, and she was his wife.

Come what may, he would protect her, and she might, he feared, soon need his protection. Sheltered as she had been all her life, it had apparently not occurred to her that rape was a definite possibility—a possibility that did not bear thinking of.

More than one of the men had eyed her delicate beauty—still visible beneath her mistreatment—with lustful eyes.

They lay down at last on the bed of straw in the corner of the hut. Hunger and exhaustion claimed them both. Once, Will put out a hand to take Beck's as they lay side by side, and she hung on to it as though it were a lifeline.

Her small hand was cold in his warm one. After a little time he felt her begin to shiver uncontrollably. Will rose on his elbow, and asked, 'Beck, what is it? Are you ill?'

She was silent. He wondered if she had heard him. Presently she answered him in a whisper. 'Not ill, but I'm so cold. I can't seem to get warm. My dress is still damp, and my feet...' Her voice trailed off.

Love, lust and pity fought for dominance in Will. He moved towards her. 'Let me put my arms around you and try to warm you, Beck. I promise not to do anything untoward.'

He thought that she was going to say 'no' in her usual vigorous fashion, but suddenly she gave a little cry and turned in his direction so that he was able to draw her to him and hold her close. To his secret delight she lay on his chest as sweetly and confidingly as a little bird.

'Put your feet between my legs, Beck. Yes, like that. If that doesn't warm them, nothing will.'

He had made the offer although he believed that she might certainly refuse him, but she did not. Instead she did as he had bid her, and they lay entwined together like an old married couple.

She could have no notion of how her nearness, and her growing warmth, were beginning to affect him. He told his treacherous body to behave itself. Only a brute would force himself on her after the awful experiences of the day. But exhaustion claimed her and Will felt Beck's breathing alter as she slowly fell asleep. Her trust humbled him. He kissed her damp hair gently, and wondered whether sleep would come to him as easily as it had come to her.

Outside the noise of the impromptu celebration continued for a little longer, to be followed by the sound of owls hooting. Inside, Beck held close to him as though in the aftermath of love, Will at last fell asleep.

'Where am I?'

Beck had woken up to find herself being held in someone's arms.

Will! It was Will who had his arms around her as though he would never let her go. What in the world had happened last night?

Had he? Had she? Had they?

She asked herself Where am I? again because she was certainly not in any bed or bedroom she had ever been in before. Painful memory flooded back. She sat up and looked wildly around the ill-furnished hovel.

No, they had not...most definitely not. Her last memory was of Will holding her in his arms to warm her, and the comfort which that had given her. He had behaved like a perfect gentleman, exactly as she would have wished him to do.

So why did a tiny *frisson* of disappointment shoot through her?

Beck looked down at him, to find him still sleeping. In the semi-dark of the hut—for someone had opened the door a little, doubtless to check that they were still there and had not, by some magic, escaped—his sleeping face looked stern and strong. It resembled not at all Will's usual amiable and smiling mask. Which was the true man? Or was he, like most humans, composed of many parts, as Beck knew herself to be?

The dark stubble on his chin reminded her that Will usually shaved twice a day and had not been able to the night before. Without her willing it, her hand crept out to stroke his jaw, to feel there not smoothness, but strength. Even as her fingertips touched his face he gave a great sigh—and woke.

Like lightning his hand shot out to grasp hers fiercely. 'Who's that?' he muttered, sitting up and opening his eyes to find Beck's near to his own.

'Oh, it's you, Beck. I feared—I don't know what I feared. Did you sleep at all?'

Beck withdrew, claiming her hand back, wondering what mad impulse had led her to wish to caress him while he slept.

'Surprisingly I did. I suppose that I was tired.'

'Exhausted, rather.' Will rose, yawned and stretched. His fine shirt was rumpled and dirty; his buff-coloured breeches also bore the marks of rain and mud. Beck wondered ruefully what she looked like: she rapidly concluded that in the great sum of things it did not matter.

She rose herself. Her whole body ached after a night spent on an uncomfortable bed quite unlike any in which she had slept before. Like Will she stretched—which might be unladylike but made her feel better.

'I'm hungry,' she said. She could never remember having felt so hungry before.

'Not surprising,' said Will, 'since it's more than twenty-four hours since we last ate a decent meal. But it would be policy to starve us. Firstly because going without food would make us feel low, and secondly because we should be too weak to run away.'

'Run!' exclaimed Beck, walking to the door to find that the day was turning fine and that yesterday's rain seemed to have disappeared. 'At the moment I feel that a brisk walk would be beyond me.'

She stretched out a shoeless foot. To her horror the sunlight revealed great holes in her stockings. While she was lamenting their ruin the door was pushed further open without so much as a 'by your leave', and another tin plate was thrust at her.

'Breakfast,' growled the slatternly woman who had brought it. 'And there's a jug of water outside.'

Breakfast! Both Will and Beck stared disbelievingly at several slices of black bread and a small hunk of elderly cheese.

'I shall never complain about my food again,' sighed Beck as she devoured the meagre fare before her. 'Can this be what these poor folk have been living on?'

'Yes,' said Will. 'At the best of times their diet is not a rich one, to say the least. But these last few years it has declined even further. Unless they poached the game in these parts—which if they were caught would mean that they would hang—or ambushed and looted the wagons carrying grain to the surrounding villages, they would starve to death.'

Beck shuddered. 'Never say so.' For the first time in her comfortable life she was being brought up against the stark realities of the world of the very poor. Realities of which Will was well aware.

'It follows,' he said soberly, 'that we must say and do

nothing to annoy them. Our very lives may depend on it.'

Beck tried to remember this as the day wore on. They were allowed out into the open, but it was plain that they were being given little chance to escape. Curious eyes followed them everywhere. In the late afternoon one of the grimy children, a little girl, ran up to Beck to show her her rag doll.

Beck was seated at the time on a large branch of one of the trees which the Luddites had cut down, either to provide firewood or to build the huts. The child handed her toy to Beck, looking up at her as she did so and saying 'Pretty lady.'

Beck wasn't sure whether the little girl meant by this the doll or herself. She felt far from pretty, and though the doll bore little resemblance to the splendid ones which she had once owned, she dutifully admired it. Its hair was made from coarse brown thread and its eyes were small black boot buttons.

She had scarcely taken it from the child and begun to rock and sing to it when the child's mother, a woman who might once have been pretty before starvation had left its mark on her, darted up and snatched it from her.

'Leave the kid be,' she said, as though Beck had been trying to kidnap her little one. 'She's nowt to do wi' you.'

The little girl put her finger in her mouth and, pointing at Beck, said again, 'Pretty lady.'

Her mother shook the little girl hard, took her by the hand and ran her into one of the huts as though Beck had the plague, but not before shouting, 'And so she should be, she's allus had enough to eat. Well, she knows now what it's like to go wi'out.'

Which was true enough. Beck's stomach was making distressful noises, and it was little consolation that Will's was in the same case.

Job came up to them where they sat watching their captors gnaw greedily at the cold meat left over from the previous evening's feast. They were eating white bread and butter with it: delicacies bought with the money looted from the coach. Beck and Will had been gifted with black bread again.

Job eyed Beck with insolent admiration. 'Aye,' he said, in imitation of the little girl, 'you was pretty yesterday, missis. Not so pretty today, p'raps, but you'll do.' He turned his attention to Will. 'You look a little less dapper today, too, mester.'

Will nodded. 'True. What concerns me is what you propose to do with us. You can scarcely wish to keep us here permanently. If you let us go, we could promise not to betray where, or who you are. Our lives would be a good exchange for the coach and its contents.'

Job shook his head, 'That's not for me to say. The man from Nottingham runs matters for us. He should be here by tomorrow—and then we'll see. Until then you'll have to hold yer hosses.'

'Have you done this before?' asked Will, apparently innocently.

Job guffawed. 'That would be telling.' He rewarded Beck with another leer which set her shivering again, and had Will clenching his fists impotently. He knew that she was in real danger, but guessed that Job would not touch either of them until 'the man from Nottingham' arrived.

In later years both of them remembered the grim week which they spent with the Luddites as having seemed

endless. For Will, the worst aspect of it was the enforced
inactivity as the days went by without the master of their
fate arriving. His beard grew, and Beck, to her great
surprise, found that it made him look more handsome
than ever, like a rakish pirate in an old oil painting.

In the privacy of their hut he astonished Beck by going through a series of exercises. He filled the pail with
stones and earth and lifted it above his head. He performed simple gymnastic tricks which he had learned at
Gentleman Jackson's salon. Out in the open he amused
her and their captors by jumping up to grasp a tree
branch with both hands in order to carry out a series of
acrobatic exercises of the kind which Beck had seen performed in a circus—and this despite only being sustained by their meagre fair.

Not so meagre after the first few days. Because they
behaved themselves, although Beck was hard put not to
use her sharp tongue on their captors, they were given
more to eat. Venison scraps, and a few early plums
filched from the orchard of a local farmer, arrived on
the tin plate together with the occasional slice of buttered
wheaten bread as well as the inevitable cheese.

'Don't want you falling sick, so's we have to look
after you,' announced Job ungraciously.

Beck earned their respect by picking up the little girl
who had called her 'Pretty Lady' when she fell over in
front of her and grazed her knee badly. She promptly
bound the cut with a strip from her cotton under-
petticoat. Slowly some of the women began to talk to
her when they realised that she was no complaining and
idle fine lady, but instead uncomplainingly did her share
of work in the impromptu camp.

At night she and Will lay companionably on their
straw bed, talking as though they had been friends for

years. Beck discovered that Will had an excellent memory and could quote whole chunks of poetry and drama, imitating Kemble and his fellow actors. He did not tell Beck that he had spent one summer before he came to London earning a little money by joining a company of strolling players.

Night by night, they drew nearer and nearer to one another, both physically and mentally. Beck was beginning to lose her obvious fear of men so that Will could only hope that, here in the forest, far from civilisation and the stiff formalities of society, he might achieve what he could not have done in the town. Make Beck his true wife.

And then, one morning, as Beck sat before their hut, mending a tear in the little girl's only frock, there was a great commotion.

The 'man from Nottingham' had arrived.

Chapter Twelve

Will had had no real notion of what the Luddites' leader might look like. If asked, he would have said that he supposed him to be both large and imposing in order to be able to control the unruly mob which had captured them. Instead he turned out to be a small man with a thin clever face, dressed like a superior clerk.

One thing was plain: he had never starved, and Will noted that his boots were good and that the horse he rode was not an inferior nag. Everyone ran up to greet him and to ask for the latest news. Had the government decided to give way and help them?

The newcomer shook his head and said shortly, 'As you might expect, they are offering us nothing.'

This brought a torrent of angry words from Job and shouts and curses from the rest. The newcomer said nothing more, simply dismounted and taking Job by the arm led him away, speaking to him earnestly and privately.

During their discussion Job frequently looked over to where Beck sat, with Will standing by her protectively. Will was left in no doubt that he and Beck were the principal subjects of their urgent consultation. Presently, their conference over, Job called for everyone's attention. 'The Mester wishes to speak to you all.'

This brought cheers and cries of 'Hush' until 'the Mester', as Job named him, stood on a stool so that all might see and hear him before he began to address them in a speech which would have had them rioting in the streets had they been in a town and not in the depths of a forest.

'Brothers and sisters' he called them as he reminded them of their grievances, of their helplessness, and of the need for them to make ready for the great day when, like the French, they would rise in revolt, execute the tyrant king and all the representatives of 'old corruption', by which he meant the Government.

Will had seen and heard radicals speak before, but seldom one who looked so mild and was so effective a demagogue. He had seen prints of the French Revolutionary Robespierre, and read his speeches, and was reminded irresistibly of him. The Luddites' leader was both clever and cunning and this was the man who was to determine his and Beck's fate!

Every now and then the Mester stopped to allow his audience to cheer him—particularly when he promised them that the day would come when they would rise against their oppressors, loot and fire Nottingham Castle and the homes of the rich so that they might be the ones who would dine off silver plate, sleep between silk sheets and rule in the place of their former masters.

Beck's face grew paler as he spoke. And when, his speech over, he walked towards them through the ragged throng who shook his hand, clapped him on the back, and if they were women, kissed him, she clutched at Will's hand for support.

He grasped it tightly and said, his voice earnest, 'Go into the hut, Beck. I wish to talk to this man alone.'

'No, Will. I do not wish…'

He took both her hands and looked deep into her eyes. 'Beck, when we were married you swore to love, honour and obey me. So far you have done none of these things. This is the first time I have asked you to obey me, and I have good reasons for doing so. I promise to tell you all that passes between us. Now, do as I ask, for my only wish is to protect you.'

Beck's lip quivered. He looked so stern and harsh, not like Will at all. She relinquished his hand and replied, meekly for her, 'Very well, Will, but you must take care, too.'

'That I promise you.' He bent down and kissed her. 'Do this for me, Beck.'

He watched her walk into the hut before turning to face what might be their doom. The man before him said coolly, 'I gather Job has been foolish enough to tell you my name.'

'If you are Gravenor Henson,' replied Will, equally cool, 'yes.'

Henson smiled. 'You must understand that that makes matters a little more difficult to resolve.'

'So I would think. I remember your name as one of the so-called moderate leaders of the framework knitters who gave evidence before Parliament recently.'

Henson's thin eyebrows rose. 'Do you, indeed, Mr Shafto? Then you will grasp why it might not be politic for me to allow you to be released. Ned Ludd is an invention, but I am not. My life would be in your hands if we freed you.'

'As mine is in yours,' replied Will. 'And you hold all the best cards in this game.'

'A great change for you, I do admit,' agreed Henson smoothly, 'seeing that in the past you and your kind have always controlled the lives of these poor hard-working folk around you—and precious little you allowed them in return for keeping you in idleness.'

'You mistake, Mr Henson.' Will's voice was firm and steady. 'I am not a mine owner, a manufacturer, nor yet a gentleman who is the lord of thousands of acres and the poor labourers who work them. I have never ex- ploited anybody.'

Henson laughed in his face. 'That's as maybe, and so speaks the fine gentleman whom, I am informed, married a rich woman for her money. You've never done an honest day's work in your life, have you, sir?'

The sir came out derisively. Will refused to be set down although Henson's accusations stung cruelly be- cause they were partly true.

'This is beside the point. I would wish to relieve the sufferings of my wife. At least allow her to be returned to her home and friends even at the expense of doing your worst with me.'

Henson said, 'I do believe you mean that, Mr Shafto. But I have two problems so far as your wife is con- cerned. Job has taken a fancy to her. Indeed, if it were not that he is more frightened of me than of the law, he would already have killed you and taken your wife as his doxy. He says that she is a spirited piece whom it would be a pleasure to tame. Also, if we freed your wife, as a spirited piece she would run straight to the author- ities and inform on all of us.

'Now Job has already asked me to grant him your wife and your death, but I confess that it goes against my principles to agree to what he wishes. I find rape and murder distasteful. On the other hand, alive and free you are both a danger to us all.'

'We could promise not to inform on you,' Will offered. 'I would give you my word as a gentleman to say nothing, and I know that my wife would agree. She has been distressed by the sight of the starving women and children and would not wish to do anything further to hurt them.'

Henson continued as though Will had not spoken. 'A further problem is that it would not be wise for me to overrule Job too often. You see my dilemma, Mr Shafto, I am sure. Now, I have a solution which would have the merit of giving you a chance of freedom and also of providing a little entertainment for these poor folk here. I think that I can persuade Job to agree to what I wish. I wonder if you would be so willing?'

What in the world could the man be proposing? Could he trust a fellow who ranted of revolution one moment, and in the next assured one of his dislike of rape and murder? Truly, he would be another Robespierre if the English Revolution ever came. On the other hand it would be wise to hear what he had to offer.

'In the old days of chivalry, Mr Shafto, I am told that a knight would cheerfully fight anyone or anything on behalf of his lady. Now, we cannot stage a tournament or a joust, but we could arrange it so that you could take part in a prizefight against one of our local bruisers. I am told that gentlemen of your kidney engage in a little amateur boxing to stave off boredom in your idleness.

'If you were so fortunate as to defeat the champion of my folk then we could engage to let you and your wife go free on promise of your silence. On the other hand, if you lost, then I would regretfully be compelled to hand your wife over to Job and you to your execu-

tioners. Which would also be the consequence if you
refused to fight for your lady.

'The choice is yours, Mr Shafto.'

Will's head was whirling. He managed to say, 'But if
I were to win, could I trust you to keep your promise?
And if we are to have a boxing match why should I not
fight Job?'

'Ah, Mr Shafto, but as you are your lady's champion,
so is our bruiser, Job's. That makes you equal.'

'And I have not eaten properly this last week.'

'A misfortune, I agree, but we could put the match
off for two days and fatten you up a little. As for trusting
us—that is your problem, not mine.'

Will put out his hand. 'Then let us shake on it. But
what my wife will have to say about this does not bear
thinking of.'

Henson became almost human. He grinned. 'Being a
spirited piece, a great deal, I dare say.'

Which, as Will knew, was exactly what followed.

'So that was why you wanted me out of the way, Will.
So that you could engage in some hare-brained piece of
gentlemanly piff-paff. I don't want to become Job's
doxy at the expense of your life. I would rather die with
you.'

'You are, like Henson and all his crew, assuming that
this yokel will beat me. He's probably some over-
muscled blacksmith who knows nothing of the Fancy.
And I had no notion that Henson would propose anything so unlikely.'

'And if he is a proper bruiser, Will, what then?'

He kissed her. 'Then we go down fighting.'

Beck said sternly, 'I shall slit my wrists with a bodkin,
Will, if you lose…or…or…something, rather than allow
that odious man to lay a finger on me.'

'So, you will let me fight?'

What could she say to him but, 'I believe that we are doomed either way, so I agree that we do not wish them to think that we are cowardly lackwits.'

'And they are going to fatten me up for two days to make the fight fairer.'

Beck's look at him was a stern one. 'Was that the bribe they offered you, Will, in order to get their fun?'

'Good God,' exploded Will, and then he saw that, improbably, given everything, she was quizzing him. Her gallantry in the face of death and dishonour never ceased to amaze him.

Nevertheless his principal worry was what might happen to her if he lost to Henson and Job's champion and she was left alone to fight her own battles. In the meantime, all that he could do was prepare for the coming match—and pray that he won and Henson kept his word…

One consequence of Will's extra food was that he slept more easily until the morning of the day of the fight when he woke with the dawn. He left the hut to find that most of the men and women had risen, too. Like them he washed his face and hands in the nearby stream.

His beard had grown mightily, giving him the stern look which Beck had remarked on. He would be fighting bare-knuckled and bare-chested. Henson had sent two men to collect the bruiser and bring him and his supporters to the forest.

Their man was from Hucknall, Job had told Will, grinning; his name was Black Jack, and he had some reputation already and hoped soon to be able to go to London to try his luck there.

So Will's opponent was no lumbering over-muscled blacksmith, but a young fellow of his own age who would undoubtedly have some professional skills. It was to be hoped that he was no better than the Tooting Terror or he would have a real struggle on his hands.

The fight would last more than one round, too, and Will had never engaged in a long one. He wondered what advice Jackson would give him. Usually, even among folk as poor as the Luddites, vigorous betting on a prizefight's outcome took place, but none of them gave Will a chance so no money was being wagered.

Except by one little man, Charley Norton, always known as Charley Wag, who had been a tailor in Mansfield until he had lost his job and taken refuge in the forest when his money ran out. He had been a second to one of the fighters from Nottingham who had made their name in London and he had kept a beady eye on Will's acrobatics.

After the fight had been announced he had sidled up to Will one afternoon and asked him to make a muscle with his arm. Will had obliged him and the little man had whispered in his croaking voice, 'I allows as 'ow you might be useful in the ring, young feller. I knows a fighter when I see 'im. You've got the look.'

Will laughed shortly. 'I'm a gentleman amateur, that's all.' He wanted his opponent to underrate him.

'Aye, so you says. But I'll 'ave a little money on you all the same.'

Charley Wag must have been waiting for him that morning for he came up to Will saying confidentially, 'You'll want seconds, young sir. I'll stand in for one, and Bill Pyke will be the other. Not that he's bet on you. He reckons as how he's too fly for that. Time will tell, says I.'

Will nodded and yawned. Time was speeding up for him. He had noticed that before in his life: that when one dreaded something time went rapidly whilst desired events in the future were slow in coming.

'This man, Black Jack,' he asked, 'has he arrived yet?'

'Aye, last night. Mester Henson brought him. He stands to win a deal of blunt if he beats you, else he'd not have come.'

By blunt he meant money. Will knew all the cant of boxing, and that because he was a gentleman he would be mocked by the spectators as a *nib sprig*, a gentleman amateur, ready to be slaughtered by any bruiser who cared to take him on.

'I'll find you a pair of shoes,' Wag offered. 'You can't fight barefoot. Jack knows all the tricks—he'd jump on your toes and break 'em, no doubt about it. And you'd best watch that haymaker right of his, it's like a hammer and done for mor'n one man. Nigh killed his last opponent, that he did.'

Beck arrived in time to hear this last cheerful piece of news delivered in Wag's sepulchral voice.

'No,' she said in her most determined mode. 'No, if that's the case I shan't agree to this, Will.'

'Too late,' he told her, 'and Charley Wag is only trying to help me, not frighten me.'

Beck was acid. 'Well, he certainly frightened me!' But she said no more, for she could see that Will was not to be moved.

The fight was to be held in the afternoon, and from early morning folk from the surrounding villages streamed in. Only the gentry were missing, for the mill was being kept a secret from them. The Luddites were supported by villagers who lived near to Sherwood Forest, which meant that the authorities were never able to find their hiding places, nor would anyone inform on them.

Wag and his friends erected an impromptu ring in one of the forest's clearings, using tree branches rather than the usual posts. Beck noted wryly that the so-called ring was actually a square. It was big enough to hold the boxers, their seconds and two umpires, one of whom was Henson.

'To see fair play,' he told Will.

Black Jack, surrounded by his supporters was introduced to Will just before the mill began, Will having only Charley Wag and Bill Pyke on his side. Jack was all that Will feared that he might be. He was Will's equal in height and weight and looked like the blacksmith's assistant he had been before he became a member of the Fancy.

He thrust a giant fist at Will and, grinning insolently, tried to crush Will's hand with it. 'May the best man win,' he growled after such a fashion that Will knew that Jack considered himself to be that man and that the fight was already won.

Charley Wag, officious and delighted to be at the centre of things, helped Will strip off his once-fine shirt, now dirty and stained, and laced on to his feet a pair of light shoes which fitted him well enough. Any fear that Will might have felt at what he was about to do was banished by the knowledge that Jack was only fighting for money. He was fighting for Beck's honour and for his life, and therefore must not lose. But if he did, he must lose with honour for that was all that would be left for him.

Jack, readied by his seconds, narrowed his eyes a little when he saw Will's torso which was not that of an effete dandy. He had come to the forest believing that he was

going to earn his blunt easily. He still knew that he
would win, but perhaps not quite so painlessly as he had
thought.

Everyone in the large crowd was eager for the match
to begin. Everyone but Beck. Will had told her to stay
away, but Job was having none of that. She was to stand
by his side, at the very edge of the ring, and watch her
husband being hammered. Every blow he suffered would
tell her that she would soon be in Job's bed.

He took a grim pleasure in explaining the rules of the
Fancy to her. There was no set number of rounds to a
boxing match. A round lasted until they wrestled each
other to the ground, when both men retired to be looked
after by their seconds. If either of them was not ready
to fight again in a stipulated time, then he was deemed
to have lost. If at any time his seconds declared he was
not fit to continue, he had lost.

If the opponents were roughly equal the match could
thus be a long one. 'And the longer it goes on, the worse
your man will suffer,' Job told her gleefully.

'Then I shan't watch,' announced Beck defiantly, putting her hands before her eyes.

Job tore them away. 'Oh, yes, you will, missis! Do
that again and I'll give you such a blow as you won't
forget in a hurry.' Nothing for it but to do as he bid her.
Beck was torn in two. If Will won, then they would be
free again—if Henson kept his word. But at what a
price! And it was plain that the crowd considered that
Jack would have a walkover, as the saying went.

Henson and the other umpire entered the ring after
Black Jack and Will, and explained the rules to them
and their seconds. Will and Jack touched hands again.
Henson and his fellow stood back, and the fight was on.

Immediately the noise was ferocious. Women, as well

as men, cheered Black Jack on. Presently, though, when it became obvious that Will was an opponent to be respected, and that the fight might be longer than expected, the noise died down a little.

Beck clenched her own fists. Once, in a silence brought about by the sight of Will hammering Jack rather than the other way round, she found herself shouting, 'Come on, Will, hit him again.' Some of the spectators near her stared at her in astonishment. Beck would have stared at herself if she could. Whatever had possessed her, that she should make such a spectacle of herself? Living wild in the forest was obviously beginning to change her.

After several rounds the fight became more serious in that both men showed signs of the punishing blows which had been exchanged. Will landed a punch on Jack's mouth which set it bleeding. Jack did the same for Will's eyebrow. Jack trampled on Will's feet. Will did awful things to Jack's left arm. The spectators became restless. Things were not going as they should. Henson's fellow umpire tried to cheat Will over the timekeeping between the rounds. Henson would have none of it. He had given Will his word that the fight would be a fair one.

Beck's hands were now in her mouth. As Will staggered away from Jack, narrowly dodging a crucifying haymaker, she leapt to her feet and shrieked at Henson, 'Stop it, I'll agree to anything if you will only stop it. I don't want Will hurt any more.'

Charley Wag rounded on her from inside the ring. 'Shut yer gob, missis. Yer man's winnin'.'

Will winning? It did not look like it from the punishment he had taken. Only the two men in the ring knew how finely the match was balanced. If he had been sparring with Jack in the Gentleman's salon in London, Will knew that he would have beaten him easily. But this was no situation set up for a gentleman's diversion, this was the real, cruel thing, with every dirty trick in the bruisers' book being used.

Nevertheless, he thought that if he could only stay on his feet he would win, for Jack, tiring himself, was growing impatient. A lucky blow from either man could end the contest in a second.

Will decided on trickery. He would pretend that he was weaker than he was, though God knew that he felt weak enough. He began to stagger and to breathe heavily, dropping his poor bleeding fists a little. Black Jack, eager to end a match that was very different from the one which he had expected, saw his man, as he thought, faltering and darted in for the kill. He would deliver the haymaker which was gaining him such a reputation and consign this damned dancing gentleman amateur to oblivion.

In he came in the false belief that his opponent was so weak that he did not need the careful guard he had been keeping. Going in to deliver his haymaker, he left his whole left side open and Will, seeing his opportunity, summoned up the rags of his strength, and did for Jack with his right. The effort had him seeing stars and perilously near to falling over himself.

Jack, though, had already fallen, to lie prone before him. His seconds ran to him to try to revive him. Charley Wag and Bill Pyke caught Will and dragged him to his corner where they supported him on their knees. Charley had a bucket of water and a cloth with which he began to wipe Will's face.

A deathly silence followed Black Jack's fall. It was broken when Henson and his fellow, consulting their watches, announced Will as the winner, seeing that the other man was unable to continue within the stated time.

The fight was over.

Someone shouted 'Huzzah for the *nib sprig*. He's done for Jack right royally,' and the very men and women who had hoped that Jack might do for Will, now cheered Will instead because, improbably, he had done for Jack. And they recognised raw courage when they saw it.

Will, dazed, bruised and bleeding, knew only one thing. That, whatever happened next, he had fought for Beck and won. His seconds helped him out of the ring. Henson said something to him about Black Jack. Will croaked back, 'Tell him not to trouble himself to go to London.'

Charley Wag was shouting to all those in the crowd who had risked their money on Black Jack and now owed him. Even Job looked respectfully at Will—but never mind that. Someone, one of his previous tormentors, took Will's bruised and bleeding paw and shook it vigorously. He hardly felt the pain. That would come later.

And there was Beck, waiting for him.

He tried to smile at her, but his mouth was too swollen and painful. Her eyes were huge and there were tears in them. She put out her hands as though to embrace him, but now that she was near to him she could see the bruises and the burn marks from Black Jack's blows plain upon his face and body. One eye was black and his right hand was swollen. The knuckles of both his hands were raw and bleeding.

She gulped, then said softly, 'Oh, Will...' Leaning forward, she kissed him tenderly on an unmarked patch below his left breast. It was a gesture of affection mixed with pride so unforced that Will closed his eyes before muttering, 'Now, Beck, do not unman me.'

She looked up at him and sparked in her usual brisk fashion, 'Now, Will, how should I do that when Black Jack couldn't?'

Henson, who stood by him, gave a crack of laughter. 'By God, Will Shafto, you've a right game filly there!'

'I know,' croaked Will.

The crowd around them which had roared at Henson's quip now parted to allow Black Jack, who was on his feet again, to approach Will.

'We haven't shaken hands,' he said, his voice as muted as Will's. 'I never thought a Johnny Raw of an amateur would lay me low. I'll lay odds you were taught by a master—but your pluck's all your own.'

'Jackson,' said Will, who was gradually recovering and now stood free of his seconds and Henson. 'The Gentleman himself taught me. I never thought I'd ever need to put his lessons to use.'

He paused. 'You may not wish to hear this, but I'd advise you to ply your trade in the provinces. London's not for you. You'd have your brains beaten out of your head by those who would make mincemeat of me.'

Black Jack lowered his head sadly, to lift it again to say, 'So I suppose—but that doesn't alter what you did. Shake hands then, and all's fair and square between us.'

Will took the proffered hand and shook it. 'I hope they paid you well.'

Jack's grin was rueful. 'Aye, but not so well as they would if I'd beaten you.'

They laughed together, amazing Beck, who wondered how it was that two men who had been grimly intent on stunning the other could so soon afterwards be enjoying a joke together! She would never understand men—but to be fair to them, would men ever understand women?

Will broke into her thoughts. 'Come, Beck,' he said. 'If Mr Henson keeps his word to us, we should be preparing ourselves to leave.'

Henson replied stiffly, 'If I give anyone my word, Mr Shafto, I keep it. But I think that it would be better if you rested here for the next day at least. Otherwise you will scarcely be fit for the long walk you will need to make to find safety and a way home. Charley Wag will drive you in his cart to the road out of the forest. After that you must make your own way. It would not be safe for any of our people to be seen with you.'

'No,' Will said to this suggestion.

But Beck said 'Yes' in her most determined voice. 'You cannot walk far in your present condition, Will, and I trust Mr Henson not to keep us here any longer than is necessary.'

Will was tired to the bone and only wished to lie down, so he gave way, but not before he had assured Henson that in exchange for their lives he would not betray the Luddites' whereabouts. He suspected from something Charley Wag had said that, once he and Beck were gone, they would take no chances but would move to a distant part of the forest where they had another temporary home.

He allowed Beck to lead him to their hut where he lay upon their poor bed and ultimately dreamed strange dreams full of blood and pain, only redeemed by an occasional glimpse of Beck smiling at him and stretching up to kiss him, oh, so gently, on the chest.

Chapter Thirteen

'These shoes don't fit me very well, but I suppose that they are better than nothing if we have to walk a long way tomorrow.'

At Henson's request one of the women had given Beck a pair of her own cast-offs, kept for rough work, so that she might not have to leave the camp barefoot. Will had been allowed to retain those he had been given for the fight. They were sitting in their hut on the following evening. Will's success had brought him a certain popularity. More than one rough fellow had told him earnestly that if that was what he could do whilst he was a gentleman, then if he had trained to be a bruiser, no one could have stopped him.

Will thought that they overestimated Black Jack's prowess, but he did not tell them so. He was greatly recovered, although still sore, and his black eye was inflamed and angry.

But he was affable Will again, friendly and charming to everyone. Beck had washed his face for him, and tried to trim his beard with a pair of scissors. Razors were in short supply in the Luddite camp so he still looked more like a piratical villain than the gentleman he was.

Beck, putting the shoes on one side, came to sit by him on the dirt floor. 'Will,' she said softly, 'I've never really thanked you for what you did for me yesterday. Then you weren't fit to exchange pleasantries with anyone, and today we've been busy preparing to leave.'

Will said, 'Oh, Beck, I only did what a man of honour should. Try to protect my wife, and in doing so, protect myself as well.'

'But at such expense.' She leaned forward to stroke his face on the left side away from his damaged eye. 'You know that I didn't want you to fight that man, and while you did I nearly ran mad, but I only gave way once to my fears and asked Henson to stop it.' She paused. 'And, oh, Will, once I forgot myself.'

Will took her stroking hand in his and kissed its palm. 'Tell me, Beck, how did you do that?'

'Well, all the women were shrieking at Jack to hit you, so when you hit him, I screamed at you, "Come on, Will, hit him again." I scarcely knew myself.' She hid her blushing face in his chest.

Her reward was a laugh. Will dropped her hand so that he might use both of his to cradle her face in his two hands.

'Was I your champion, Beck? Was I?'

'Yes, Will, you were.' She lifted her head to look at him. 'It was scarcely the act of a lady, Will.'

'Ah, but yesterday, Beck, I wasn't a gentleman and you weren't a lady.'

'And today?'

'Today we are what we wish to be,' and slowly, slowly, Will lowered his mouth on to hers.

Here in the forest, anonymous, her unhappy past a distant thing, Beck did not resist him. It was truly as though she were someone else.

Her own hands went up to circle his neck as she vigorously kissed him back. Still holding her head with his left, damaged hand, Will dropped his right one to run it down her body in order to stroke her left breast.

Beck gave a little cry—but did not stop him. She had no wish to stop him. The kiss went on and on and slowly, slowly, Will lowered her on to the bed.

Again he met with no resistance—only cooperation. Was it gratitude for having saved her from Job which moved her, or was it love? No matter. Now was not the time for such needless introspection. Now was the time when the demanding body took over from the questing mind.

He stripped Beck of her scanty clothing; she helped him out of his bloodstained breeches and his grimy shirt so that they lay as close together as a man and woman might before the act of union itself.

And, for whatever reason, she was ready for him at last: her acid tongue and her busy mind both forgotten, as he had forgotten all the reasons why he should not be doing this. He kissed her everywhere, celebrating parts of Beck which she could never have imagined being kissed by any man, until at last she writhed and cried beneath him for consummation.

At first he wanted to be gentle with her, as much for the sake of his own bruised and battered body as for her virginity, but passion drove him on. Once he looked down at her face, also transformed by passion, all her cold command blown away by the wind of their loving, and muttered, beneath his breath so that she could not hear him, 'Oh, how I love and worship thee, my beautiful termagant who cheered me on when I was sore beset.'

For he had heard Beck's frantic shout of encouragement and it had helped to spur him on to his victory over Jack—and over her, as she lay helpless before him, begging for she knew not what.

There, in the rude hut in the depths of the forest, far from the comfort and luxury to which they were both accustomed, Will and Beck consummated the marriage which they had both vowed never to consummate. Even as he breached her virginity she urged him on as she had done in the fight—only the words she used were different—'Oh, yes, Will, yes!'

Afterwards they lay quiet together, Beck cradled against the broad chest which she had kissed in his moment of victory. Presently she slept. If he had hurt her as he made her his, she said nothing of it to him. Before she had fallen asleep she had kissed him on the cheek, saying, 'Oh, thank you, Will, thank you,' as simply as though she were a child who had been given a particularly pleasant sweet.

Quintessential Beck, Will thought to himself before he, too, let sleep claim him, wondering as it did so how she would greet him on the morrow when her head would rule her actions again, and not her heart.

He need not have worried. Beck was up before him, dressing herself for the day in the gown which she had perforce worn ever since their capture. It was stained and torn. Her hair had grown a little so she had tied it back with a short piece of yarn begged from one of the women who had befriended her once it became plain that she was no whining fine lady. Her refusal to be idle had earned her their grudging respect.

She had, indeed, spent much of her time in captivity mending and altering the clothes of the many small children who ran about the camp. Nothing, she found, was ever thrown away: clothes were handed down through the family and then passed on to another until, at length, they fell to pieces.

Carefully though she might dress herself, Beck knew that she looked more like a beggarwoman than the Mrs Will Shafto who, in London, had never been seen other than perfectly turned out.

Her toilet over, she turned to find Will, propped up on one arm, smiling at her. She blushed, and hid her face from him by the simple expedient of bending down as though to inspect her shoes. Her whole body was a testament to last night's loving. Not only did it feel thrillingly alive, but it had aches and pains in peculiar places which she had scarcely known existed before the previous evening.

'Beck,' Will said softly, 'forgive me for last night. I was carried away.'

Forgive him? Why should she forgive him for having been the cause of such pleasure? Dismal reality burst in on Beck. Oh, he must be referring to the bargain which they had broken. Did he regret having broken it?

More to the point, did she?

She stared coldly at him. 'It's a little late for repentance, don't you think?'

Will, who had foolishly assumed that she would understand that he was referring to the haste with which he had deflowered her, not realising that she would interpret what he said as regret for having made love to her, felt as though she had thrown cold water over him.

So they were back to their previous relationship of cool tolerance of one another. He jumped out of bed quite forgetting that he was naked. 'No, Beck. Repentance was not in my mind at all. Celebration, rather.'

Beck stared at the first completely naked man whom she had ever seen. She had thought Will magnificent when he was only naked from the waist up, but now that she was gifted with the sight of a male body as impressive as the nude Greek statues which decorated her various homes she had no words left with which to admire him.

The sight of his long powerful legs and his equally powerful sex were doing strange things to Beck. She gulped, looked away from him, and said, her voice shaking a little, 'You really ought to get dressed, Will. It would be wise to make an early start.'

Belatedly Will became aware of his naked condition. He considered an apology, rejected it. Beck was facing him again, and her expression, whether she knew it or not, could only have been described as excited and anticipatory. He advanced on her, smiling.

Beck stood her ground. She gave an excited little cry when he reached her and took her in his arms. His arousal was plain as he did so.

'Again, Beck, again?' he whispered in her ear.

'Someone might come in,' she gasped.

'Not at this hour of the morning.'

'Won't it tire us—before we set out, I mean?'

'Invigorate us, rather,' Will whispered breathlessly, bearing her down to the bed. 'Don't waste time talking.'

Beck didn't. And somehow, because she was terrified that someone might break in on them, it was even more exciting and her pleasure was far more powerful than it had been on the previous night—and so she told him.

They lay entangled on the makeshift bed. Will said, 'That was what I meant earlier. You were virgin last night, and I was sorry for the haste with which I took you. This morning, now...'

Beck put a finger on his lips. 'No apologies. I could have stopped you both last night and this morning—and I didn't. Now, we really must get dressed.'

She was so matter of fact that she almost set him laughing.

Nevertheless Will did as he was told. The woman who brought their breakfast arrived just as he was pulling his breeches on. She smirked knowingly at him, and at Beck who was busy rearranging herself.

'Summat good for you,' she told them. 'The Mester says as how you'll need it. You've a long walk ahead of you when Charley Wag drops you off.'

And so Charley told them when he drove up in his cart to where they stood with Henson and Job who was still protesting that it was a mistake to let them go.

'I gave my word,' Henson said, 'and they have given theirs. And I don't want murder and rape on my hands. It's not a risk I'm prepared to take. And, Job, you're not to go chasing after them—you hear me?'

Job nodded sullen agreement, and watched Charley Wag drive off with Beck and Will before heaving a great sigh and going off to help the rest strike camp. Even if their recent captives broke their word and informed on them, the authorities would have great difficulty in tracking them down.

Charley Wag took them to the end of the byway— down which Job had driven them into the forest nearly a fortnight ago—before he stopped the cart, saving them at least a mile of their long walk.

'Which is no more than you deserve after the way you fought Black Jack. Follow this byway until you come to the turnpike and walk along that until you reach the first village. Good luck to you both. You're a brave feller,

and your lass is a good plucked 'un, too. I know you'll
not peach on us.'

Will scrambled out of the cart and handed Beck down.
They watched Charley Wag turn his cart round and drive
back in the direction from which they had come. As he
disappeared into the trees Will took Beck's hand in his.

'Come,' he said. 'We have a long way to go.'

He was right. The sun was up, there was no breeze,
and it rapidly grew very hot. Perspiration dewed Beck's
brow and what had seemed a short distance when they
were riding in the coach was a long one when they were
walking. Her shoes hurt her, but she did not complain.

They came to a stream which ran by the side of the
rough track. Will knelt down and drank from it and bade
Beck do the same. Then he tore a strip off the tail of his
shirt, wetted it and made Beck put it round her neck.
Despite her stoicism he could see that she was suffering
from the heat and, by the gingerly way she walking, it
was likely that her feet were blistered.

Neither of them spoke much until, with a sigh of relief, they reached the turnpike where walking was easier.

'Not far now,' Will told her. 'There is a village called
Ashworth nearby, and there we shall find succour. We
must make for the inn, tell our tale, and ask for help.'

Nearby seemed a long way to walk, but shortly after
mid-day they reached the first cottages on the edge of
Ashworth. Salvation was near. Beck straightened up,
held her head high and took her hand out of Will's.
Soon, she thought, soon they would be on their way to
Inglebury again.

There were men and women going about their work
on the road which ran through the village, and they
stared curiously at the two ragged strangers. One man,
well-dressed, gave them a cold glare, and walked into a

large house which stood next to the inn. Will took Beck's hand again.

'Not far, now,' he said.

But he spoke too soon. Behind them the well-dressed man had emerged from the house and was walking rapidly towards them, accompanied by a beadle.

They reached Beck and Will when they were a few short paces from safety.

'Do your duty,' cried the well-dressed man.

The beadle put a hand on Will's shoulder. 'Come with me, young feller, and your doxy, too. We don't allow beggars in our village. Mr Earnshaw here is a friend of the magistrate, and we shall take you to him instanter!'

'No,' said Will, 'we are not beggars. This lady—' and he waved a hand at Beck '—is my wife, and we have been captured...'

He was silenced by a blow across the shoulders from the beadle's staff.

'Don't try to gammon me, young feller. I know your sort...' and he made to strike Will with his staff again.

He was interrupted by Beck who, her face a mask of fury, shouted rather than said, 'Stop that at once. He is telling you the truth. He is my husband, Mr Will Shafto, and I am his wife, who was Miss Rowallan of Inglebury, near Sheffield and we were...'

She said no more, for the beadle seized her and put a hand over her mouth to silence her. Will would have gone to her rescue but a group of villagers, attracted by all this unwonted excitement had come up and, obeying the beadle's shouted instructions, seized hold of him, too.

'Tricksters,' said Mr Earnshaw severely. 'I've met their kind before. Take them to Sir Charles immediately, and he'll see that they're whipped back to the village they have fled from before they become a charge on us.'

It was useless to struggle. 'Do as they say,' Will told Beck wearily. 'We can't stop them and Sir Charles might prove more reasonable than a pack of yokels and a self-important fool.'

He knew that he should not have said anything quite so provoking, but he was nearing the end of his strength. Even so, he was not prepared for the blow across the face which nearly felled him. Beck, sobbing, tried to go to him, but was swept along by the villagers, the beadle and Mr Earnshaw, along the road, up the drive to Sir Charles's fine house where he was about to go into the dining room to eat an early dinner…

Sir Charles Ashworth was large, middle-aged and hungry. He wanted his dinner, having missed his luncheon. The news that Earnshaw, that fussy busybody, had brought him yet another pair of wretches to deal with before he could eat it did not please him.

It pleased him even less when the wretches were pushed into the library where, as JP, he handed out law and judgement. A more ragged pair of rapscallions it had seldom been his misfortune to see.

Will, catching sight of himself and Beck in a long mirror in the hall, would have agreed with him. Ten days in the Luddite encampment had turned him and Beck into persons indistinguishable in appearance from the poor folk among whom they had lived. He was dirty, bearded, and his clothing was both filthy and ragged: Beck, hobbling in her ill-fitting shoes, was little better. He could almost forgive Earnshaw for his misjudgement of them.

But surely all that he and Beck needed to do was to

explain their predicament to this country squire and they would be free again. He misjudged his man. Sir Charles was not stupid but he was set in his ways and, what was worse, had no imagination.

To begin with he would not allow Will to speak. When he tried to explain who they were he bellowed, 'Silence, fellow, and do not speak until you are bid. Earnshaw, pray explain how you came upon this pair of vagrants.'

Nothing loath Earnshaw began his tale of how he had come across them in the village street.

'And what were they doing there, sir? Were they begging?'

'They had not yet begun to do so, but I had no doubt that that was their intent.'

Will, angered, said, 'Nonsense. We were on our way to the inn when we were stopped by…' but Sir Charles did not allow him to finish.

'Be silent, fellow,' he roared, 'or I'll have you gagged.' He turned to Earnshaw. 'Did you have them searched before you brought them here?'

'Aye. The beadle searched them in case they had stolen property on them.'

'And had they?'

'No, Sir Charles, but they had no money either, so they could not have been making for the inn.'

Beck, furious at their mistreatment, called out, 'If you would only allow us to explain…'

Sir Charles cut her off in mid-statement. 'Silence, woman, or I'll have the scold's bridle put upon you. Go on, Earnshaw.'

'That's all. I've no doubt that they would have made for the inn when they had finished begging.'

'Difficult when we hadn't even begun, and didn't intend to,' remarked Beck in her most acid tones.

Something in her manner of speech prevented Sir Charles from threatening her again. He was about to question her when the door opened and a fashionably dressed gentleman came in.

He put up his glass to examine the assembled company before saying in a languid voice, 'What the devil's happened to dinner, Charles? Never say you're having to dispense justice while the mutton grows cold.'

Will stared at the newcomer, that ass, Gilly Thornton, whom he had last seen in Jackson's rooms in Bond Street and had now been sent by heaven to save him—and a more unlikely saviour he could not think of.

'Gilly Thornton,' he said, 'tell these fools who I am.'

Gilly peered at him uncertainly. 'I know the voice, but I'm dem'd sure I've never known anyone who looked like you!'

Will roared at him. 'For God's sake, Gilly, if you don't recognise an old friend when you see him, at least tell me that you recognise my wife!'

'Beck?' drawled Gilly. He raised his quizzing glass again to stare at her. 'Beck, what the devil are you doing in that get-up, and Will, what in the world are you playing at in yours?'

Everyone in the library stared at Gilly.

Sir Charles said in a dazed voice, 'Do you know these people, Thornton?'

'Know them? I should say I do. It's my old friend Will Shafto and his wife. But what they're doin' here in fancy dress is beyond me. Is this some sort of joke, Will?'

'Of course it's not a joke, and if Sir Charles will kindly send the tipstaff and his idiot master away, I shall

be only too happy to explain how we come to be in this
get-up and hauled before Sir Charles as beggars.'

Gilly Thornton turned an unexpectedly shrewd eye on
them both. 'Quite right, old fellow, but before you do
anything in the explainin' line someone should do something for poor Beck. She looks as though she's about to
faint any moment.'

Everyone turned to look at her. He was right. Beck's
eyes were closed and she was swaying gently on her
feet. What no one knew was that she had decided to put
an end to all this nonsense by practising, for once, some
of the female artifices which she had previously despised.

On hearing Gilly's exclamation she let out a small
moan and began to fall sideways towards Will. As she
had expected every man in the room immediately experienced a rush of guilty compunction over their un-
gallant behaviour towards a gentlewoman.

Sir Charles stared at her, shamefaced, and exclaimed,
'Good God.'

Gilly, more acute, cried, 'Catch her, Will.'

Mr Earnshaw, astounded by this turn of events, gog-
gled his bemusement, and the beadle whimpered, beginning to fear for his job now that he had mistakenly insulted and struck two members of the gentry—a class
on whom he normally fawned.

Will, by far the most practical man present, surprised
by Beck's sudden collapse when only a few moments
ago she had been her usual charmingly truculent self,
immediately seized the opportunity which she had offered him to break the tension in the room.

He scooped her up, and turning on Sir Charles, bellowed at him, 'She needs rest and a decent bed. She
hasn't slept or eaten properly for over a week.'

Sir Charles recovered his normal character of a man chivalrous and courteous to all women—provided they were of gentle birth.

'Of course, of course.' He bellowed in his turn, at the gaping footmen who stood at the door, secretly all agog at this untoward commotion in Sir Charles's library. 'Fetch m'lady, the butler and the housekeeper—on the double.'

Beck decided to improve the shining hour. 'A bath,' she quavered, and in case no one took the hint, 'and some clean clothes.'

'Of course, of course, dear madam,' repeated the hapless Sir Charles. 'Pray forgive me my previous discourtesy, forgive all of us...' and he glared at Earnshaw who had landed him in this pickle '...but, of course, we could not have guessed...'

'I did my best to explain,' Will offered from the sofa on which he now sat, cradling Beck, 'but I was forcibly prevented...'

He looked down at her. Her face was turned away from the embarrassed company. She opened her eyes, gave him a wink and then closed them again to the accompaniment of yet another tortured moan. Will was hard put not to laugh. Oh, the naughty, clever doxy! She had succeeded—as usual—in putting everyone in the wrong.

The arrival of Lady Ashworth, the butler and the housekeeper resulted in Beck being carried off to be petted, bathed, found clean garments, fed and generally, as she later told Will, succoured.

As for Will, he was left, still in his dirt, to tell his tale of woe with suitable exclamations of mingled anger and sympathy from everyone except the beadle who had been sent home.

Sir Charles was pacing the library, enraged. When Will had finished, he said with great satisfaction, 'Well, the best thing about this sorry business, Shafto, is that you will be able to lead us to where these wretches are hiding in the forest and put an end to their rebellion.'

Will put on a long face. 'Alas, Sir Charles,' he said earnestly and untruthfully, 'neither my wife nor I have the slightest notion where we were taken. We were captured in the recent storm, after our coach was driven down a byway. In the dark and the confusion which followed we completely lost our bearings. When they released us, we were blindfolded, put in a cart and driven towards the turnpike road in what I am sure was a different direction.

'I also gathered from what was said that the Luddites intended to move camp, as they put it, once we were freed, in case either of us might be able to reveal their whereabouts.'

On hearing this all present, except Gilly Thornton and Will, gave vent to their anger. Sir Charles said abruptly, 'And by the look of your eye, Shafto, you were mistreated. I should think that you'd like to see the whole pack of them hanged or transported.'

Will remembered the starving women and children and the desperation of their fathers, husbands and brothers. He looked around Sir Charles's comfortable library, and thought of the excellent meal which was undoubtedly waiting for them all. He could not condone what had been done to him and Beck, but he could understand why it had been done.

'And their leader,' continued Sir Charles, 'this fellow Ludd, did you come across him?'

Will shook his head. 'No, Sir Charles, nor anyone like him.' Which was true so far as it went, seeing that

Henson was not at all like the roaring captain of men Ned Ludd was supposed to be. But Henson had saved both him and Beck on condition of his silence, and having given his word, and remembering the suffering which he had seen, Will intended to keep it.

Only Gilly Thornton, that frequenter of Jackson's salon, now revealed as Sir Charles's brother-in law, looked sideways at Will once he had been shaved, washed and dressed in decent clothing, and drawled quietly at him, 'What bruiser gave you that black eye and damaged lip, Will, and why?'

So Gilly was shrewder than most gave him credit for. Will laughed and replied, 'A man has to do strange things when he is in the hands of those who hate him, Gilly. I'll only say this, and for your ears alone—thank God I took my practise with the Gentleman seriously.'

'And what does your opponent look like, Will?'

'Worse than I do—and that is the end of the matter. Beck and I are safe and sound again, and wish to forget what has passed since we were dragged from our coach in the pouring rain.'

Will lied. He could not forget, nor did he wish to. Even as he ate Sir Charles's reheated mutton and drank his good port he had at the back of his mind those less fortunate than himself—who had counted himself unfortunate. But he now knew that, in comparison with those among whom he had briefly lived, he was blessed beyond words.

What was worse, his pursuit of heiresses, and his marriage to Beck, seemed the actions of one who was less than a man. That he had come to love Beck was beside the point if all that he had to offer her was the possession of a rogue without honour.

He had been truly a man when he had fought Black

Jack for her, but what would he be if he sank back into the life which he had been living before the Luddites had dragged him from the coach?

The fine food he was eating was as ashes in his mouth because the price he was paying for it was too high.

Chapter Fourteen

'What is it, Will? What's wrong?' For ever since they had returned to London he had been not joyful at their return to normal life, but sombre and withdrawn, quite unlike the man who had made such ardent love to her during the last night of their captivity.

'Nothing,' he said. 'Nothing.' A reply which was not truthful and which did not deceive Beck, but she could get nothing further from him.

They had returned to their London home by a road which did not lead through Sherwood Forest. Beck had sent word to Inglebury for Mrs Grey and her staff to remain there until she came north again in a few weeks' time. London suddenly seemed a haven of peace to her. Will agreed, almost absently, as he had agreed to everything since they had arrived at Ashworth.

Ironically, on the afternoon of the very day on which they had arrived at Ashworth—too late to save them from humiliation—Sir Charles had received a letter from the Lord Lieutenant of Yorkshire asking him to make a search for Mr and Mrs Shafto who had disappeared, with their coach, somewhere between Nottinghamshire and Yorkshire.

The Lord Lieutenant had been alerted by Mrs Grey, who had been in a fever of anxiety once she had discovered that Will and Beck were missing. As Will had supposed, those in the second coach assumed that they had taken a different route in the storm.

It was unfortunate that Beck's courses began at Ashworth so that she and Will were prevented from making love again, just at the very moment when Will might have found in their mutual passion an answer to his problems.

The main one was that he no longer felt that he could continue to be simply Beck's appendage. The more he knew that he loved her, the less he felt inclined to be someone who had no real role to play in her life. Nor did he wish to live off her without giving anything to her in return. In his present position he was nothing more than the stallion whose only purpose was to service the mare.

And all this as a result of fighting Black Jack and listening to Henson's taunts about his never having done a real day's work in his life.

The difficult thing was to tell Beck how he felt, for he was certain that her own feelings of insecurity would result in her seeing his attempts to free himself from bondage, as it were, as an attack on her. Their night of passion in the Luddite camp had made it harder for Will to reach a decision which would hurt her, but what he really feared was that whatever he decided, he would end up by doing so.

Regardless of that, somehow he needed to prove himself. Fighting Black Jack, and winning had been one thing, but it had been done in hot blood. Taking charge of his own destiny would be another and even more terrible thing to be done, and it could not be accomplished in the heat of the moment.

It would mean leaving her.

The more Will thought about it the worse he felt.

He recalled the poem written by the seventeenth-century poet, Richard Lovelace, 'On Going to the Wars', in which he wrote as he left his love, 'I could not love thee, dear, so much, loved I not honour more.'

That exactly described his feelings towards Beck. The more he loved her, the more unworthy he felt. He saw himself as a parasite, nothing more, living on her bounty. Oddly enough, he had not experienced this particular sensation very strongly until after he had made love to her. He had felt then that he was unworthy of her, that she deserved better than having for a husband someone who had married her for her money—even though she had proposed to him, and not the other way round.

In honour he should have refused her. The difficulty was that in the forest by fighting Black Jack he had found his honour again, and having done so he could no longer continue as Rebecca's rogue. Because he had nothing to offer her but his honour, he must free her and himself from their unequal bargain.

It would break his heart to leave her, but he could take nothing further from her, instead, he must give her something: her freedom, and the opportunity to love someone more worthy than himself. He was certain that in the forest she had given herself to him out of gratitude, not love.

He sat down at the escritoire in his room one morning shortly after they reached London and wrote two letters. One was to Coutts Bank, cancelling the quarterly draft which he had caused to be sent north, saying that he would no longer be receiving any allowance from his wife.

The second, and the hardest, was to Beck. She must not know where he was going, only that he had gone.

'My dearest love,' he began, for that was what she had become. 'When you read this I shall be far away. Because I love you, I can no longer continue to live on your bounty. In the Forest I defended you like a man, and now, though it breaks my heart to leave you, I must play a man's part and free you to live and to love someone who deserves you more than I ever can. I must try to support myself by my own efforts and live an honourable life.

'To this end I must break the bargain which we agreed to: a bargain to which I should never have consented. You may believe that it is dishonourable of me, having made it, to break it, but it is less dishonourable than if I continued to hold us to it. I can no longer be Rebecca's rogue because it prevents me from being Beck's honourable husband.

'My heart's darling, believe that this inequality between us would, in the end, come between any chance of our enjoying a happy marriage, and that you should be happy is the one wish of Will Shafto.'

He sealed it, and when he had packed a small bag containing only sufficient clothing for the journey to his new life, he placed it on the writing desk in Beck's room before leaving the house, where he had found love, if not complete happiness with her, by a side entrance so that no one was aware of his departure.

Once in the street he walked briskly toward the inn yard where the coaches left for the north.

Beck had been out visiting her Aunt Petronella. Will had pleaded a headache and the old lady had been disappointed by his absence. She was one of the few people to whom Beck had told the true story of their kidnapping and of Will's fight for her honour with the professional bruiser from Hucknall.

She was a little surprised when she returned in the early evening to find that he was not in. She retired to her room, and called for her maid to dress her in something informal for an evening at home. Her courses had ended and she felt a *frisson* of delight at the notion of celebrating that event by inviting Will into her bed.

Unfortunately the footman who brought the teaboard to her room upon her return thoughtlessly placed it over Will's letter, so that it was not until some little time later that Beck, now growing worried over his continued absence, found it.

She had already asked the butler if he knew where his master had gone, only to receive the reply that he was not aware that Mr Shafto had left the house—something which the footmen on duty confirmed.

This was most unlike Will. He had always been punctilious in informing her of his whereabouts—in complete contrast with her cousin Sarah's husband who came and went without regard for his wife.

It was only when, growing distracted, she sat down at her writing desk that she came across Will's letter, which had been pushed almost out of sight when the footman carelessly retrieved the teaboard.

Where could he be? And why was he writing to her? For she knew Will's hand at once. Agitated, Beck broke the seal and read his letter. For a moment she could scarcely understand it. He could not have left her, he could not, when they had so recently celebrated their

marriage and sealed it in love after he had defended her
so nobly.

And what was this talk of honour? Oh, men's notion
of honour was something which Beck had never understood, and now she understood it less than ever. How
could he say that he loved her, and then leave her, claiming that he did so in the cause of honour?

He had written that his heart was broken, but what
about her poor heart? Was he not breaking hers by writing this…this…sorry rigmarole? The letter lay crumpled
in her disbelieving hand. Shaking, Beck opened it out
and read it again.

This time she read it slowly. Read the words which
told her of his unhappiness about his position in her life
which had come to a head after he had fought Black
Jack. Beck's fight was with the tears which demanded
to overwhelm her; but she would not cry, she would not.

Instead, silently she invoked the heavens. The man
whom she had coldbloodedly chosen to marry for her
own ends had left her for his, and improbably, her heart
was broken, for though he had told her to live and to
love again, her heart was irretrievably given to her
rogue, who had decided to be a rogue no longer.

And she had not the slightest notion where he might
have gone, or what she could do to find him and get him
back again. She might try to tell herself that she did not
care whether she ever saw him again, but it would be a
lie.

In the meantime she would tell no one that he had
deserted her, while she tried to track him down so that
she might throw this letter in his face and call him a
rogue in truth!

Beck could not keep Will's disappearance a secret for
ever. The servants knew that he had walked out of the

house and had not returned, and Beck's absence from
the social scene which she and Will had graced, was
soon commented on. It was Aunt Petronella who first
confronted Beck with her suspicions soon after Beck had
employed an ex-Bow Street Runner to find out everything he could about Will's life before she had married
him, and where he might have fled to when he had left
her.

Aunt Petronella arrived in full fantastic fig, having just
refused to marry the Duke of Durness for the fourth time.
She had been arguing with herself as to whether she
ought to accept him if he ever asked her again, when it
occurred to her that it was time for her to pin Beck down
over what had become of Will.

Beck, when she received her aunt, looked very much
as she always did. Cool and in control of herself. This
had the effect of annoying Aunt Petronella mightily—
she might, at the very least, have had the decency to
betray a little distress at the loss of her husband. She
would, Aunt Petronella thought acidly, have shown more
emotion if she had lost a parlourmaid!

In this she did Beck an injustice. She had no notion
of what it was costing Beck to retain her usual composure. Aunt Petronella grimly decided that she would do
her best to destroy it.

'Well, what have you done with him?' she began, all
aggression.

'Done with what or with whom, Aunt P.?' replied
Beck, full of bland innocence.

'Come, come, my girl, you know perfectly well what
I mean. Where has Will gone? And has he gone for good
after saving you from unimaginable insult in your recent
captivity?'

'I am not your girl, Aunt P. And where Will has gone is as much a mystery to me as to you.'

'Not my girl, eh? Too true—I fear that you are nobody's girl and like to remain so. What did you do to him? Drive him away with your nasty tongue? If so, you are a fool—something which I never previously thought you.'

To her horror Beck's eyes filled with tears. She was near to breaking point: a state which she had resisted for the past week.

'On the contrary, Aunt, we had never been so happy as we were before he left—or so it seemed to me.'

'Oh, I do beg leave to doubt that, Beck. Why did you think so? Was he truly happy? Happy men do not leave their homes and wives without warning.'

'He seemed a trifle distrait, it's true, but nothing more.'

'There must have been something more, and you were too busy, I suppose, playing the iron maiden to notice it.'

The tears were really determined to fall. Beck, in a vain attempt to stave them off, said savagely, 'I'm not an iron maiden, Aunt. Indeed, I'll have you know I'm not a maiden at all…'

There it was, out, and she had not meant to confess it!

Aunt Petronella shook her bedizened head. 'Bedded you at last, did he? Was it too much for you—or him? Found he didn't love you, perhaps, and being your lackey was thus too much. Left without a message, did he—just cut line?'

That did it! Did it royally, in fact. Beck gave a loud cry and flung herself down on the sofa. 'Nothing of the sort,' she sobbed into the cushions. 'He wrote me a letter saying that he loved me and that was why he was leaving me—of all the stupid things! Oh…oh…oh…'

Now the sobs came thick and fast. Aunt Petronella—as she had intended—had finally undone her niece. But having done so, she regretted her handiwork, for she sat down by Beck, took her in her arms and rocked her until the sobs slowly died down.

Beck rested her head against her aunt's breast like a child who had come home to her mother to be comforted.

'There, there,' said her aunt, tenderness succeeding asperity. 'Tell me the truth, Beck, and you will feel better. Do you love him, after all, truly love him, after telling yourself you never would? More to the point, did you ever *tell* the poor fellow that you loved him?'

Beck's answer was a sniffle and a shake of the head. 'Not in so many words. I thought that he must know that I loved him—after…' She could not bring herself to tell her aunt of their one glorious night together in the woods.

Aunt Petronella, ever practical, handed her a handkerchief. 'Blow your nose, child, and tell me what he said in his letter.'

'That he loved me,' confessed Beck over the handkerchief, 'but that his honour would not allow him to continue as we were with him living off me. His honour, Aunt! Are all men mad that they talk of honour so much?'

'I told you that he was a good man, Beck, and so he has proved. He needed to be told of your love. They're different from us, you know, they demand proof. I can only suppose that fighting for you settled something for him in the way of honour. Men do prize honour, Beck, however much we women may think it a bauble. It gives their lives a point which bearing children gives to us. We must not scoff at it, even if we don't understand it.'

'I don't understand anything,' wailed Beck, 'and for this to happen just when I realised that I loved him so much…' The sobs began again, louder and deeper than ever.

'Stop that,' commanded Aunt Petronella sternly. 'At once! Do you want him back again? If so, you must try to find him, not sit here behaving like a ninnyhammer—most unlike you.'

'I *am* trying to find him,' retorted Beck, showing a little of her normal fighting spirit. 'I have hired a man who was a Runner for that very purpose. He is coming to report to me later this afternoon. My lawyer recommended him to me. He says he is a very tiger for tracking people down.'

'Poor Will,' murmured Aunt Petronella, smiling, 'what chance has he of escaping you with both you and the Runner after him?'

'This is not a joke, Aunt,' Beck said, deploying her aunt's handkerchief as a sponge to wipe up her tears. 'On the contrary.'

'Indeed not, but crying won't help, either, even though it comforts me to see that you are human, after all. There have been times when I doubted it.'

Beck sat up straight. 'Mock me, Aunt. I deserve it. For I did not truly know how much Will had come to mean to me until I lost him.'

'Oh, that is frequently the case,' offered Aunt Petronella cheerfully. 'Took him for granted, didn't you? No one likes that. Now, tell me where you think that he might have gone. I could perhaps be of service there.'

Beck dried her eyes and, her manner composed again, she moved away from her aunt and folded her hands in her lap. 'He could be hiding in London, or he may have gone north to his old home. But I doubt that he has done the latter. The lawyer tells me that Shafto Hall is so derelict that no one has lived there for many years. So I have ordered my man to begin by making enquiries around London.'

'And he is due here this afternoon? May I remain until after you have finished your business with him? You will, of course, wish to speak to him alone.'

'Of course, and of course, you may stay. I must tidy myself a little. It would not do for him to find me like this. You will excuse me if I retire to my room and ring for my maid. I shall see him in the study so you may wait here. I shall order the butler to bring you the tea-board.'

Amused, Aunt Petronella watched Beck recover her usual coolly competent self. But now she knew that, beneath it, Beck suffered and bled like the rest of humanity, and that being so, there was hope for her and Will.

'You will be pleased to learn, madam, that I have news for you of Mr Shafto's life in London which I trust might prove helpful, though I have not succeeded in locating the gentleman himself. No one confesses to having seen him since he returned to London with you.'

Jack White, the ex-Runner—for he had retired from his profession to work for Beck's lawyer, Mr Herriott—was a biggish man with a strong face and a body to match. He spoke after a peculiar fashion, mixing slang and good English together, peppered with legal phrases doubtless garnered from his acquaintance with the trials of those whom he had caught.

He fished a notebook out of an inner pocket of his loose grey overcoat which he had insisted on retaining.

'You may be aware of some of what I am about to tell you, so forgive me if I am instructing you in what you already know, but you told me to reveal everything which I discovered whether it be good or ill.

'Mr Shafto was a poor man when he married you. He had a small income, sufficient to keep him in a little comfort, but he seemed, I learned, to be perpetually short of money, although he never gambled. I began by questioning his lawyer friend, Josh Wilmot.' He did not tell Beck that he had actually leaned on Josh heavily in order to get her this information.

'It seems that Mr Shafto did not draw all his income from the bank for his own use, but sent the majority of it away. Mr Wilmot claimed not to know to whom it went. I think that he was speaking the truth. This left your husband on extremely short commons. He supplemented what was left of his income by a variety of means, thus enabling him to appear reasonably well monied in society.

'He took on a series of positions in the evenings, principally with a man named George Masserene who runs a cheap gaming house. He acted there as his chief croupier, occasional bouncer and made up his books. He also kept the books of a number of tradesmen and shopkeepers who could not afford professional help. Mr Masserene told me that Mr Shafto had a gift for numbers and that he was sorry to lose him when he married you.'

Masserene? George Masserene? Beck remembered meeting him in Piccadilly soon after her marriage to Will and the extremely odd conversation which had followed.

'You are sure of this?' Her question was really unnecessary, she knew, but the knowledge that Will had worked hard in the evenings to keep himself afloat was difficult to believe, remembering the usual carefree face he presented to society on those nights on which he was not working.

'Quite sure, madam. I also traced his valet, Gilbert Barry, always known as Gib. He's a right close-mouthed fellow and no mistake. He allowed as how he had not seen his master since he had left his service, and I am inclined to believe him.'

He did not tell Beck that Gib had thrown his head back and laughed after having guessed that Beck wanted Will traced because he had left her.

'You've made my day, that you have. He'd do nowt good for himself until he'd either thrown her shackles off him or had decided to master her, one or the other. Come to his senses at last, has he? I niver believed that she cared tuppence for him.'

Looking at the white-faced woman before him, the Runner thought that Gib might be wrong. She was suffering, no doubt about it, and suffering meant that she cared. But it was no business of his, or Gib's, and so he continued his report.

'Besides Wilmot, I spoke to his other friends, including those who joined him at Jackson's Saloon in Bond Street—and to Jackson himself. None of them admitted to having seen him recently. Jackson said one curious thing: that he had heard that Mr Shafto had taken on a professional bruiser in a match recently, and had beaten him. Did you know that, madam? Any point in following it up?'

Beck shook her head. 'I don't think so. I knew that he had fought a bruiser, and won, but I don't believe that Will would ever wish to be a member of the Fancy. Not his line at all.'

'Well, that's that, Mrs Shafto. Unless you have any other information which you haven't given me yet. I doubt me whether your man is in London—or if he is, no one is telling. You allowed as how he might be in the north. That's a large area of ground—can you narrow it down a little?'

It was Beck's turn to shake her head. 'Leave it with me while I make some enquiries of my own. If I think of anything useful I will tell Mr Herriott to get in touch with you again. In the meantime he will pay you for the work which you have already done for me, and for which I thank you.'

She was a gracious lady whatever the jealous servant, Gib, thought of her. Why would a man wish to leave her? But White knew as well as anyone that the true inward nature of any marriage is a thing known to few beside the principals themselves.

He bowed his way out. Beck sighed and went to tell Aunt Petronella what her man had found out about Will, in particular the information that Will had been earning a hard and painful living before he had married her.

'Which does not surprise me,' said her aunt robustly. 'I always said that he was honourable. What I don't understand, knowing him, is why he never went for a soldier—perhaps he couldn't afford to buy a commission?'

'Now, what do I do next?' asked Beck, a trifle miserably.

'Think of anything odd about Will's behaviour which might prove helpful. You lived with him long enough to know if he said or did anything untoward which might need explaining.'

Beck was morose. 'Everything about Will's conduct needs explaining. For instance, what did he do with his income? The Runner said that he didn't spend it. Why not? Where did it go? There's a mystery if you like, given that disposing of it left him nearly penniless and needing to take on a series of odd jobs such as few gentlemen would expect to engage in.'

Both women sat silent for a time before Beck rang for more tea. It might stimulate thinking.

Aunt Petronella said thoughtfully, 'I never understood why Will didn't buy himself a carriage with the handsome allowance you gave him. For that matter he didn't even spend it on a horse, or refurbish his wardrobe overmuch.'

Beck looked at her, her memory beginning to tell her something she had almost forgotten. 'I asked Will why he didn't buy a carriage—he said that he was thinking about it. So, what did he do with his allowance? Coutts informed me that it was always spent by the end of the quarter.'

She paused, said slowly, 'Do you suppose it was going the same way as the other income of which White spoke?'

Aunt Petronella nodded. 'A reasonable assumption. But does it take us any further on?'

Beck sat silent for a moment. She was having a dreadful thought which she dare not pass on to her aunt. Could it be that Will was already married when he had married her? Did he have a wife and family dependent on him somewhere—and had he disappeared in order to rejoin them?

She shuddered at the mere idea, and to banish it began to speak slowly and deliberately. 'You asked me if there was anything odd about Will's behaviour before he disappeared and I have told you all that I can think of.'

'I suppose that you could ask Coutts if Will was sending the money on to someone by banker's draft—perhaps the same someone as before.'

Beck shook her head. 'Can you believe that, under

these odd circumstances, Will did other than ask Coutts
for confidentiality? And, if so, Mr Coutts would almost
certainly not give me any information.'

'You could always try, Beck. After all, you could tell
him of your sad circumstance and he might then relent.'

'I doubt it, Aunt. But before I visit Coutts Bank I shall
visit Josh Wilmot and George Masserene. Both of them
knew Will before I did and they might be more willing
to talk to me than to Mr White.'

Aunt Petronella rose and kissed Beck. 'Bravo, my
dear. Far better than grieving, you must admit, to go out
and about and try to find your honourable man.'

Beck thought a minute before speaking. 'That depends
on how honourable Will's reason was for passing on the
major part of his income and my allowance.'

'Indeed. But, however painful the reason might prove
to be, you have a duty to continue your search. And the
duty is not only to yourself, but to Will.'

'Agreed.' And Beck threw her arms about Aunt
Petronella and kissed her. For a moment the two women
clung together, wordless. Aunt Petronella could never
remember a time when her niece had offered her spontaneous affection. Adversity is a great teacher, she
thought, and kissed Beck again before leaving her.

Josh Wilmot was so cagey that Beck could get nothing
from him. 'Disappeared, has he,' he said. 'My commis-
erations, Mrs Shafto. Will's a good fellow. I've not the
slightest notion where he has gone. Afraid I can't help
you there.'

He smiled at her. Beck said coolly, 'Mr White informed me that you told him that Will sent the greater
part of his income to a secret address.'

'Indeed. He had a small amount of money left him by

a maiden aunt in the form of an annuity, and he gave away the major part of it. But he did not ask me to perform the business for him. He drew a sum of money each quarter and disposed of it himself. So I cannot help you there, I am afraid.'

Was he speaking the truth? Beck was not sure. But it was plain that he would tell her nothing further.

Josh added, kindly for him, 'You see, Beck, he didn't want anyone to know where the money was going. Not even me. He banked it at Coutts, I do know. But, I'm afraid that if Will asked for confidentiality, Coutts would not pass any information on to you. Against their house rules.'

It was a dead end. Beck thanked him and drove on to the address for George Masserene which White had given to her. He lived in a small villa in one of the modest streets which were being built in north London. Fortune favoured Beck for he was at home: he and his wife and four children ranging in age from five to fourteen.

On arrival a small tweeny showed her into a room furnished in lower-middle-class comfort. It was apparent that George Masserene made a useful income, not a large one.

He came in, smiling. 'Mrs Will Shafto, we have met before, have we not?' He looked around him. 'Will not with you, eh?'

Beck explained. George heaved a great sigh and repeated what Josh Wilmot had told her. 'I've no idea where Will might have gone. I've no idea where he came from either. Only that he was a gent down on his luck—until he married you, of course. Clever and honest, was Will. I could only wish there were more like him!'

'He never spoke to you of his family, and where they might be found, Mr Masserene?'

'He was from the north, he said once, and to be honest Mrs Shafto, in my line of business one doesn't question people about their origins overmuch. Doesn't do, you understand. Will wanted his private life private, and that was that.'

All that Josh Wilmot and George Masserene, and the shopkeepers around the corner whose books Will had kept could offer Beck was a series of testimonials about Will's hard work and his transparent honesty. Gratifying though this was, it offered no clues to Will's current whereabouts.

She told Aunt Petronella and the Duke as much later that evening. All that now remained was for her to visit Coutts Bank, ask for the great man himself and, if he refused to reveal to whom Will was passing on the majority of his money, consider another journey north.

'I'm told that Shafto Hall in Northumberland is a ruin, which leaves me the rest of the district to comb—no small task!'

The Duke said, quietly reasonable for once, 'Unfortunately, I know nothing of his family, other than that his father gambled everything away. They were the last of their line. His mother's family cut her off when she married Shafto, and I'm told that she died some years ago. Report has it that he has nothing left at all in the way of relatives. A dead end, I fear. I asked my old friend Gascoigne if he knew where Will might have gone, but he's as ignorant as the rest of us.'

'How can a man disappear in the England of 1813?' queried Beck. She sank her head in her hands.

Aunt Petronella comforted her. 'Never despair, my

child. Go to Coutts. He can only refuse—but he might not.'

'It is virtually all that is left to me,' sighed Beck sadly. Secretly she was beginning to wonder whether she wanted an answer. Might it not be better, in the long run, to let Will go rather than uncover his secret life?

She could not. For better or for worse, she loved him, and loved him all the more fiercely because she had never expected to love again. At all costs she must know what had happened to him.

And if, once she found him, it was simply to say goodbye to him, because he could never be hers, then that was better than living forever without knowing where he had gone and without allowing her to say farewell to him before he had left her.

She put his letter into her bag and arranged to visit Coutts Bank on the morrow.

Chapter Fifteen

Beck had the status of a great lady in the world of 1813 and Thomas Coutts and his minions treated her as such. She was shown into the bank's parlour where sherry wine and ratafia biscuits awaited Coutts's most honoured clients. Mr Coutts rose and bowed to her.

'What may I do for you, Mrs Shafto?' he asked her after offering her the sherry which Beck refused.

'You may have heard,' Beck said stiffly, for it was painful for her to say it, 'that my husband, Mr Will Shafto, has left me. Unfortunately I do not know where he has gone, and for a variety of reasons, some of them financial, I wish to trace him. I believe that you can help me.'

'No, I was not aware of your husband's departure, and I commiserate with you on it. I will do my best to assist you, if assistance is, indeed, possible.'

Beck leaned forward, her face earnest. 'As you know, Mr Coutts, on marriage I made my husband an allowance, paid quarterly through your bank. I have reason to believe that he spent little of it, but, instead, paid most of it by Banker's draft into the account of another person. If I knew who that person was, and where they lived, I might be able to trace him. I would not ask this information of you were it not that I have exhausted every other avenue which might lead me to him. You are truly my last resort.'

Whilst she was speaking Mr Coutts's face grew more and more melancholy. 'Alas, Mrs Shafto, you ask of me an impossibility. Mr Shafto particularly requested that this transaction remain a secret between himself and the bank, and signed a document to that very purpose. It grieves me to tell you this, but you know as well as I that I cannot breach such a confidence once made.'

'Even,' faltered Beck, 'if to do so might relieve suffering and distress on the part of the person who asks?'

'Mrs Shafto, even if the Regent himself made such a demand of me I could not satisfy him. My word is my bond, and without that my business and that of others, would be at risk. There can be no exceptions. May I add that I deeply regret having to disappoint you.'

Beck would have liked to tell him that his deep regrets cut no ice with her, but for once, held her tongue. It was pointless to make an enemy of a man who was, after all, only carrying out what was asked of him. She allowed him to show her to her carriage and promised to inform him if Mr Shafto should return.

'For,' he said, 'I formed a favourable opinion of him, which, forgive me for saying so, considering his reputation, surprised me a little.'

Another testimonial for Will, thought Beck bitterly. He seems to have behaved well towards everyone but myself!

And what do I do now?

She was still asking herself that question later on that evening. She had sent her supper away uneaten: the sight of it made her feel sick. Although the day was hot she had ordered a fire to be made for she found herself shivering, and even its flames failed to warm her.

She tried to read a novel, but could not, for the future stretched before her dark and friendless. She picked up *The Morning Post* and tried to read that, but could not. She was about to ring for the butler to bring the teaboard in, tea being always recommended for the distressed, when he arrived to tell her that 'There is a person waiting in the entrance hall, madam. He has asked to be allowed to speak to you. He says that he has some information for you which you will be gratified to receive. He says that the matter is urgent.'

'Pray what sort of a person? Does he seem respectable?'

'Most respectable. He has the aspect of a clerk. He says that his name is Smith.'

'Then show him in at once.'

Will! Could he conceivably know something about Will, for that was the only news which could possibly gratify her these days?

The butler ushered Mr Smith in. He was a man of medium height, medium appearance, and medium clothing. Beck could see why the butler thought him a clerk. He was dressed in plain black with a spotless but simple white stock. He bowed in her direction when he entered.

He looked at the butler, who had retreated to the door, and said under his breath, 'Is it possible for me to speak to you alone, Mrs Shafto?'

Beck instructed the butler to leave, which he did after offering her a speaking glance of disapproval.

'What do you have to tell me, sir? The butler said that you were most urgent in your manner.'

'Indeed. I must begin by informing you that I work at Coutts Bank and that I can provide you with information regarding your husband's dealings with the bank. Information which Mr Coutts refused to divulge. For a consideration I would be prepared to offer it to you. You must understand that it is I who deal with your husband's account. This transaction must remain secret between us, for I have no wish to be turned away should it become known that I have breached confidentiality.

'But it seemed wrong to me that a wife should not be aware of her husband's affairs when that knowledge might help her to trace his whereabouts.'

He sniffed and looked pious. 'I could not endure to think of your sufferings, Mrs Shafto, when I had the power to relieve them.'

Beck wished that she could like the man before her. But it did not matter whether she liked him or loathed him if he could lead her to Will.

'How much do you want?' she asked coldly.

Smith—if that were his name—looked surprised. He had met few women who spoke and behaved as bluntly as a man.

'If you could see your way to fifty pounds, perhaps.'

'You are modest, Mr. Smith.' Beck was still blunt. 'Tell me what you know and if it is worth more, then you shall have more. If not, then I will give you less.'

'As you wish. You asked to whom Mr Shafto made regular quarterly payments from his account. A banker's draft was sent to a solicitor by the name of Milburn in the town of Burnside in Northumberland. The draft was made out to a Mrs Will Shafto.'

The room swam before Beck's eyes. All her worst fears had been realised. Will had a wife hidden away, and she, she was the victim of a bigamist who had made her his whore to get at her money and send it to another woman! Why had he left her? Had honour, as he claimed, suddenly overcome him, or had he left because he wished to return to the woman whom he truly loved and for whom he had lied and thieved.

Oh, the monster! If she had begun this search by wishing to find Will so that she could tell him how much she loved him, she would continue it in order to find him and gain her revenge! She would make him wish that he had never been born, the man who had deceived everyone by making them think that he was both brave and honourable!

She suddenly realised that Smith was speaking, his voice anxious.

'Mrs Shafto, Mrs Shafto, are you ill? Shall I ring for your maid?'

Beck sat up straight. 'Of course I am not ill. Far from it. I am well for the first time in months. And for your pains I shall double the money for which you asked. I can give you fifty pounds now and you may have another fifty from the butler if you return in a week's time.'

She went to her escritoire and, unlocking a drawer, took out a purseful of sovereigns and almost flung it at him. 'I do not wish to see you again, understand me?'

'Oh, yes, madam. I shall return in a week. You are most kind.'

'Kind! Kind! I have forgotten the meaning of the word. Take your thirty pieces of silver with you, and enjoy it more than the man you have imitated did.'

She swung round and left the room at once, leaving Smith to gape after her. All that Beck could think of was that, haste, post-haste, she must pack at once, order the carriage to be made ready and set off for Burnside as soon as she and John Coachman had found out where the damned place was.

In the meantime she wrenched from her finger the ring

which her faithless husband had given her and which
she had treasured because he had told her that he had
bought it with his money, not hers.

Had that been a lie, too?

No matter, she would soon confront him with his lies
in the bolthole to which he had scuttled. And when she
got there she would set such a mine under cheating Will
Shafto as would blow him to hell and beyond—wherever
that might be.

Beck's second journey to the north was not so event-
ful as her first, but was more exasperating. She took only
a small staff with her: her lady's maid, Kitty Jackson,
who travelled in the coach with her, two footmen standing at the back, and an outrider who arrived early at the
posthouses where they stayed overnight to make sure
that everything was made ready before she arrived.

She and Will had dispensed with one on their fated
journey to Inglebury, something which they had both
acknowledged later had been a mistake. Neither of them
had wished to travel in overmuch pomp, but Beck, as a
woman on her own in a treacherous world, felt that this
time she could not have too many strong men about her.

The journey was exasperating because it seemed to
take place so slowly. Beck wished that she had not left
Mrs Grey at Inglebury, to look after it until she and Will
returned later in the year. She would have been someone
to talk to. Kitty was so overwhelmed by being alone with
her mistress that she could scarcely do more than blush
and agree with everything Beck said.

Now and again Beck looked down at Will's ring
which, for some reason she did not understand, she had
replaced on her finger in the middle of the night before
she had left London. She had been unable to sleep: the

look on his face when he had given it to her swam into her mind every time she turned her pillow over or tried to compose herself.

At last, to try to exorcise it, she had risen, slipped the ring on again—and sleep had come immediately, as it had done on the night when they had made love. Her own weakness disgusted her when, in the morning, she had not the heart to discard it again.

All the justification that she could offer herself was that it was the one thing of his which was truly hers and no one else's—if she could believe him, that was.

Beck's odyssey took her up the Great North Road, avoiding the Midlands and Sherwood Forest, since this particular route would take them almost to Burnside which Beck had discovered to be a small town not far from Shafto Hall. Which, of course, was not surprising.

Several days' hard driving brought them to Alnwick in the late evening. Beck had reserved a suite of rooms at the White Swan, the principal coaching inn there. Burnside was some five miles distant, on a byway. She felt that she needed a hearty meal and a good night's sleep in a comfortable bed before she confronted her faithless husband.

Only she could not sleep. She rose shortly after midnight to draw the bedroom curtains and gaze up at the moon, the goddess Diana's lamp, the virgin goddess whom she had forsaken when she had allowed Will to make love to her.

Which was, Beck knew, not a completely accurate description of what had happened on that fateful night. She shuddered at the memory, but whether with fear, anger, or frustrated desire at the prospect that he would never make love to her again, she did not know.

Reason told her that it was possible that her long journey might be nothing but a wild goose chase: that Will was not at Burnside, but some place else where she might never find him.

But something, Beck knew not what, was telling her that he was not far away, and that by the time the sun set on the next day she would meet the other, the legal Mrs Shafto.

Her first port of call the following morning was at Mr Milburn's office in Burnside. The town was situated almost at the end of the byway and was typical of those which she had passed through on her journey north. Its small houses were of stone. There was a little market place with a cross in the centre. Behind it loomed grey-blue hills. The people who walked in the narrow streets were dark and suspicious looking.

Mr Milburn's office was soon found. It was the most imposing building in Burnside. Pasted on the wall beside the door was a large notice offering for sale the lands near Shafto Hall, once part of the Shafto estate, but now in the possession of John Whately, Esquire, who wished to sell them.

The clerk who received Beck in his small office conveyed to her his regrets that Mr Milburn was away in Newcastle, representing a client who had been accused of sheep stealing. The fields around Burnside, Beck had already noted, were full of them.

'Then perhaps you may be able to assist me.' Beck had already decided that she would not ask for Will's whereabouts since it was not certain that he had fled to Burnside. Instead she asked, her voice as sweet as she could make it, since she did not wish to earn a refusal by appearing to be an enemy of the woman, 'I am trying to trace a Mrs William Shafto who, I am informed, is a resident of Burnside.'

'Oh,' said the clerk, 'that is easily done. You did not need Mr Milburn's presence in order to learn *that*. Mrs Shafto *was* a resident of Burnside, she rented a small cottage facing the market place, but latterly she has gone to live at the Home Farm.'

'The Home Farm?'

'Ah, you are a stranger in the district. The Home Farm is all that is left of the land around Shafto Hall which used to belong to the Shafto family. The byway ends there, so if you wish to visit Mrs Shafto you will be able to travel down it in your carriage. Is there anything I can do to assist you further?'

Beck had no intention of letting anyone know of the true purpose of her visit.

She rose, picking up her reticule and her bonnet which she had taken off on entering the office. ''No, I thank you, sir. You have already told me all I wish to know.'

Oh, what a lie that was! Her real wish had been that the whole thing had been a fiction promoted by Coutts's clerk to relieve her of her money. Instead she found herself being pointed in the direction of a very real Mrs Shafto.

The clerk followed her to the door, giving her further directions as to where the Home Farm might be found. 'Am I to inform Mr Milburn of your visit?' were his final words.

'Oh, no, indeed not. The matter was concluded when you directed me to the Home Farm.'

The clerk stood in the bow window of his master's office wondering who the fine lady might be who had come with such a simple request. He had been so overwhelmed by her beauty, her toilette—Beck had dressed herself most carefully in her deep blue walking gown with fine lace trimmings—that he had quite forgotten to ask her for her name.

Mr Milburn would not be best pleased with him on hearing that he had committed such a *faux pas*—but then, she had told him not to trouble his master, so he would not.

The longest part of Beck's journey to find Will was the last mile from the little town to the lane which led to the Home Farm.

She stepped out of her carriage, bidding the coachman wait for her. She could see the small farmhouse through a stand of trees which screened it from the lane and the byway which led to it. Beyond the house she could see more fields full of sheep, and some that were given over to wheat and were awaiting the harvest, which was reaped later here than in the warm south. To reach the house she had to cross a farmyard where a collie dog glared at her from his kennel.

The farmhouse had two bow windows at the front and a small porch in which some flowering plants stood in pots on a low ledge. The knocker was of brass and shaped like an imp. She lifted it and rapped sharply on the door. For some moments nothing happened, then the door opened and a large red-faced woman in a black stuff dress and a very white apron stood facing her.

'Yes, Mam?'

Well, by her age and her appearance she was certainly not Will's wife—which was oddly comforting.

'I am informed that a Mrs Will Shafto lives here…'

She got no further, the woman cut her off.

'Aye, that be so. Well?'

'I wonder if I might have a word with her?'

'And who may you be that wants a word with the missis?'

Foolishly, as she now realised, Beck had not considered what she might say in answer to such a question. She did not wish to confess that she was Will's supposed wife if Will were not here.

'I am Miss Rowallan,' she said, for if Will could deceive her, then she was entitled to deceive this other Mrs Shafto. 'I have just visited Mr Milburn who has sent me to you.'

'From Mr Milburn? Come in and wait a moment, hinny, afore I ask the missis if she be willing to see you.'

She opened the door wide and Beck stepped into a small entrance hall with a red-tiled floor of the kind commonly seen in farmhouse kitchens. A warming pan and some dried flowers hung on one whitewashed wall.

The woman disappeared through a rough door made of oak planks and decorated with a wrought iron handle. Beck could hear voices.

Presently the woman reappeared. 'The missis will see you. She's in the kitchen—it's the only downstairs room fit to live in, ye ken, until the house is improved. This way.'

Beck followed her through the door and into a passage from which a staircase rose to the upper storey. Facing them was another oak-planked door which the woman opened, saying, 'Here y'are, missis.'

Beck walked through it, the woman retreating to leave her alone with the kitchen's occupants. The kitchen was large and warm. A fire burned in a huge grate which had a cast-iron spit before it, and a hook from which hung a large cauldron. Brass and copper pans stood on shelves around the room. In the middle of the floor was a well-scrubbed table on which someone—the large woman?—had been making bread.

Seated by the fire was a pretty young woman, a shawl around her shoulders, and a blanket covering her legs. She had some sewing in her hand and a work table by her side. Walking towards her, and waving her hand for Beck to seat herself in a Windsor chair facing the hearth, was a tall, middle-aged woman who bore the traces of great beauty now overworn by age and suffering.

'I am Mrs William Shafto,' she said in a cultured voice. 'I understand from Jinny that you wish to speak to me.'

Chapter Sixteen

Beck stared at her. This was Mrs William Shafto? This woman who, by her age and appearance, could not possibly be Will's wife. It was a wild goose chase that she had embarked on after all.

Mrs Shafto said quietly, 'You seem surprised.'

Beck nodded, swallowed and said in a stifled voice, 'I had understood you to be a much younger woman.'

Mrs Shafto shook her head. 'Alas, no. I am the only Mrs William Shafto in these parts. This,' she added, waving a hand at the young woman by the fire, 'is my daughter, Emily. You will excuse her if she does not rise to greet you. She has been crippled since birth which, as you see, does not prevent her from being useful.'

Emily smiled at her mother and the dazed Beck in response to this tribute, and quietly continued with her work, which was turning an aged sheet.

'Pray will you not sit, Miss Rowallan. I believe that was the name Jinny gave me? Forgive me if I say that you look tired and I would not be inhospitable. I shall ask Jinny to brew us some tea and butter us some bannocks.'

Her legs failing her, Beck sat down. This was all so

different from her expectations that she had no notion of what she might say next, since all that she had intended to say seemed so inapposite. Where was Will? And where was the wife which she had supposed him to be harbouring here?

She looked around the homely room and came out with, 'I had heard that you once lived at Shafto Hall. Mr Milburn's clerk said that you had been residing in Burnside, but had recently moved into the Home Farm.'

'That is true, Miss Rowallan. Forgive me, but may I ask what is the purpose of your visit? It cannot be to learn of my housing arrangements.'

This pleasantly sardonic statement delivered by Mrs Shafto as she sat down in an armchair opposite her daughter reminded Beck so strongly of Will that her brain began to work again, and she knew exactly who the woman before her, and the pretty crippled girl, were.

This, then, was the Mrs Shafto to whom Will had sent most of his income and the allowance which she had made over to him as part of the marriage settlement. He had done so in order to maintain not a mistress, nor a wife, but his penniless mother and his crippled younger sister. He had plainly not told them that he was married, for Mrs Shafto had not recognised her name. Nor had he told them how he had acquired the extra money which he had been sending to them—and had now abandoned.

But where was Will?

Did his mother know of his whereabouts? She certainly appeared to know nothing of his London life.

Even as Beck gathered herself to speak, to ask if they knew where Will might be found, she heard footsteps and voices outside the kitchen door which led to the farmyard.

Her heart sank. This must be the farmer who was responsible for the upkeep of the fields through which she had driven. The door opened and a man in the rough clothing of a working farmer stepped through the door.

The man was Will.

Time, which had, for Beck, been running first fast and then slow, now stopped altogether. No one else seemed to notice. She blinked and time started again.

Mrs Shafto said happily, 'Ah, there you are, Will, most opportune. Perhaps you might be able to help our visitor, Miss Rowallan, who has come to find a Mrs Will Shafto…'

Will's eyebrows rose. 'Has she, indeed? You didn't really need to travel as far as Burnside to find her, did you, Beck?'

Mrs Shafto said, surprised, 'You know Miss Rowallan, then, Will?'

'Indeed I do, mother. In every sense of the word. She is my wife, Mrs Will Shafto.'

Beck licked her lips. She had been far too busy taking in Will's transformation from London dandy to working northern farmer to consider what she might usefully say next. She looked wildly from Will's grave face to his mother's.

Mrs Shafto's showed a mixture of surprise, puzzlement and growing reproach. Her daughter had given a little exclamation and dropped her sewing to the floor from which it was plain that she was unable to retrieve it.

Unable to look Mrs Shafto in the eye after her unmasking, especially when she said unhappily, 'You never told us that you were married, Will,' Beck moved forward, and bent down to pick up the sheet in order to hand it back to Will's sister.

Emily whispered 'Thank you,' and then asked, 'Are you *truly* Will's wife?'

Beck straightened up. 'Yes, truly.'

'Then why did you say that your name was Miss Rowallan?'

'Exactly.' This was Mrs Shafto, her voice now frosty.

Will said nothing, but leaned against the whitewashed wall beside an embroidered sampler declaring hopefully, 'God bless our happy home.'

'Because that was my name, and…' She must say it, she must. 'I was not sure that I was truly Mrs Will Shafto when I found out that a Mrs Will Shafto appeared to live at Burnside.'

'But why did you think that? Will has just told us that he married you.' Mrs Shafto's puzzlement had become extreme.

All of Beck's usual defences against life and its many difficulties were impossible to deploy here. She could not use her sharp tongue, her ability to wound and to control against these two poor women, whose simple goodness was so patent, and who were staring at her rich and sophisticated self in bewilderment.

Spite and wicked vice she could deal with and overcome, but virtue disarmed her. She was suddenly as defenceless as they. And Will was not helping her.

Time ticked by. No one spoke. The fire crackled in the hearth. Emily resumed her sewing. Will's mother sank into an armchair. Will said, sardonically, 'Quiet, Beck? Most unlike you.'

Beck looked around the room. Something inside her snapped. She dropped her head and said in a broken voice, 'Please, Will, help me. Tell me why…' She got no further. She had come here prepared to rail at him, to reproach him for his faithlessness, to mock at the woman for whom he had betrayed her, to have her revenge on him and instead she had found... What?

'Why did you leave me,' burst from her of its own accord, 'when I love you and you said that you loved me. Why? Why? You wrote of honour. Where was the honour in that? To leave me without telling me where you were going.'

On hearing the words 'I love you', Will levered himself off the wall. He began to walk towards her. Beck gave a stifled moan, held out her hands to him, then, her face crumpling, she turned on her heel and ran out of the kitchen.

Mrs Shafto rose to her feet and cried at Will in an accusing voice, 'She was your wife, and you left her, Will, without telling her where you were going. How could you?'

Will, who had almost reached the door, looked at the accusing faces of his mother and sister. How could he explain his apparently callous behaviour to them: the mother and sister who had worshiped him because by some means he had kept them from the almshouse—nay, from the workhouse—to which his father's fecklessness, and then his death, had doomed them.

He was suddenly as frantic as Beck. 'I'll explain everything later, Mother. I must go after her. I can't lose her now.' Without further ado, he, too, ran out of the kitchen. By the time he was in the lane he could see Beck running ahead of him, her skirts lifted to give her greater speed.

He must catch her because she had said, at the last, that she loved him. Why had he been so sure that she cared so little for him that his leaving her would not hurt her so much as it surely had?

More, the one thing which he had not foreseen—

which he should have done—was that somehow she would discover that, through Coutts, he had been sending money to his mother, Mrs Will Shafto, and would instantly assume that this Mrs Shafto must be his wife—which made her—what?

Beck had reached the gate which divided the farm from the lane. Before her was the carriage which would take her away from this place where she had shamed herself. She, who never lied, had lied—and had been royally caught out.

She heard Will pounding along behind her. He must not catch her. He had lied to her when he had written that he loved her. He had lied about his mother and his sister. As a consequence she had assumed all the wrong things about the Mrs Shafto whom he had been supporting.

She was so lost to everything that she was unaware that she was sobbing as she ran, that the tears were running down her face, and were blinding her. She scarcely felt Will catch her up, put a hand on her shoulder to swing her round—to see the ruin which Beck Shafto had become, and all because she had fallen in love with her rogue.

Who was not really a rogue at all, but a man who had been supporting two poor women to the limit of his ability and his endurance. He had lived on the edge of ruin for years in order to keep them from the workhouse, and rather than deck himself out, buy a curricle and gamble with the allowance she had made over to him, he had sent the bulk of it to them to ease their hard lives a little.

She should have had the wit to see that the man she had come to know and love would never have deceived her so cruelly, would never have married her if he had a wife already. The magnitude of her misunderstanding of him overwhelmed her.

'Oh, Beck, what have I done to you?' burst from Will. He tried to comfort her but his very touch seemed to complete her undoing. She had paled, her eyelids had fluttered: she was plainly about to faint. 'Oh, my dearest heart, let me hold you and never let you go. What a pitiful fool I was to desert you.'

Beck heard him as from a great distance. She summoned up the tatters of the strength of mind which had sustained her all her life.

'No, Will,' she managed at last into his rough jacket. 'I was a fool, a wicked fool, to believe that you could have left me because you already had a wife. But I had become so used to betrayal…' She fought back tears.

'Oh, Will.' It seemed to be all that she could say. 'What are we to do?'

'We could go back to the farm and explain ourselves, perhaps.'

'Not yet. I could not face your mother and sister, yet. Oh, why did you not tell me of them? I could have helped them so much.'

Will held her away from him. 'My love, that is part of the problem, my problem, something of which we must speak together before we can resume our marriage. You cannot make matters better simply by doling out your money as the fancy takes you. And, yes, I can see it would be a kindness to all of us if we don't go back immediately. I must be honest with Mother and Emily, after I have talked with you.

'If I had known that you loved me so deeply I would have talked to you before, not left you. But not knowing that, I thought that the kindest thing I could do was to leave you and allow you to start a new life without me.'

Instead of reassuring her, as it was meant to do, Beck's sobs redoubled. 'But I don't want a new life without you. I want my old one—or no life at all. I knew that I loved you when we were prisoners in the forest and I didn't want you to fight that man for me because I couldn't bear to see you hurt. And when you made love to me afterwards, I was in heaven.'

Will was to reflect afterwards on the sad misunderstandings which could part men and women. For the moment he was content to hold Beck to him and stroke her gently until she quietened. He wondered what in the world her watching coachman was making of them!

As Beck hiccuped her way into calmness again he said, 'Let us take a walk together as an old married couple should. Not far from here is Shafto Hall. I could show it to you—ruins are all the fashion nowadays, are they not? Though I cannot promise you a ghost.'

This poor joke brought a watery smile to Beck's face.

'I wouldn't expect a ghost in the summer, Will.'

'I can promise you a dog, though, Beck.' Will put two fingers to his mouth and gave a most ungentlemanlylike whistle, whereupon the collie whom Beck had seen earlier came running out of the farmyard towards them.

On reaching Will it lay on its stomach in submissive fashion, looking up at him with adoring eyes.

'This is Pilot, a working dog. He is not, I fear, a pretty lap dog. I cannot picture you with a lap dog, Beck, I think that Pilot is more your style. He will let you stroke him providing you are gentle. The man who was my tenant here is teaching me not only how to farm, but also how to use Pilot to work with the sheep, before he retires into a contented old age on the only cottage left on the remnant of my father's estates, where he has gone to live since I brought my mother and sister to the Home Farm.'

He could not have thought of a better diversion, one more calculated to dry Beck's tears. She bent down and stroked Pilot, who now transferred his affection to her.

'Pilot may walk with us, Beck, if you wish.'

'I do wish, Will.' She had taken a handkerchief from her reticule and was drying her eyes. 'And you may tell me what made you come here to learn to be a farmer—and why you left me.'

'Yes, I owe you that. Forgive me, Beck, I have been a selfish brute—'

Beck leaned forward and put her fingers on his lips. 'No, Will, if we continue to reproach ourselves for the past we shall never come to terms with the present and, hopefully, the future.'

Will took Beck's arm, and snapped his fingers at Pilot who promptly rose and trotted obediently at his heels. 'This is the way to the Hall. It lies beyond the trees you see before you. There was a drive to it from the byway, but it has become overgrown through neglect. We can walk quite comfortably along its remains, though, and sit on what is left of the terrace.'

Shafto Hall, Beck discovered, was a redbrick building dating back to Tudor times which had been very beautiful before it had decayed into near ruin. Will led Beck to a broken stone bench on a terrace behind the house which overlooked a long slope towards a distant stream. Beyond that were fields dotted with still more sheep, happily grazing.

'I wish I were a sheep,' said Beck as she sat down beside Will, Pilot at their feet. 'Just think how pleasant it would be to have no worries, no notion of the future nor the past, just the delight of grazing in the sun without troubling about where the next meal is coming from.'

'Ah,' said Will naughtily, 'but think what a sheep's destination is, Beck. The slaughterhouse and your plate!'

'But the sheep doesn't know that,' replied Beck incontrovertibly, 'and it is our knowing things which causes us so much unhappiness, is it not?'

'But it causes us so much pleasure, too. Remember our happy night in Sherwood Forest?'

Beck looked earnestly into his face. 'Of course I do. And remembering it makes it even more difficult for me to understand why you left me as you did.'

'I'll try to explain myself. I will say in my defence that I didn't know that you loved me. I thought that night arose out of your gratitude to me for saving you from Job. You never said otherwise, never breathed a word of love to me. Why not, Beck?'

Beck looked away from him and twisted her hands together. 'I can't, Will. I daren't. My life until I met you had taught me a harsh lesson: that I was unloved because I was unworthy. And when, once, long ago, I dared to love, everything went horribly wrong, so I told myself I would never care for anyone again, or, if I did, I would never admit it.'

Her last words were uttered in a voice so low that Will had to strain to hear them. He took her hand in his and saw that she was still wearing the ring which he had given her. The sight of it gave him hope that they might yet have a future together.

'Tell me,' he said at last. 'Tell me what happened to you, Beck, to make you afraid of life and love. The telling might heal you since keeping silent hasn't helped.'

'You will think me foolish...'

'Never that, Beck, never that. Whatever you are, you are not foolish. You may look away from me as you speak if that would make the telling easier.'

So she did—and the words came tumbling out and the hurts of the long-dead years came into the light again, and, as Will had said, the telling brought relief.

'I was not the eldest child. I had a brother, Paul, born some five years before me. I was a disappointment because my father never wanted daughters, only sons to help him to run his business and the lands he was busily buying. He saw himself as the founder of a new noble family. To his great chagrin my mother was sickly and never managed to bear another living child. She was constantly ailing.

'And then Paul was killed when we were out riding together. I will never forget what my father said when I reached home.

'"If one of you had to fall off your horse, why wasn't it you? Why was your brother taken and not you?" He never forgave me for that, nor for the knowledge that whilst I was a good horsewoman, Paul hated horses— he was frightened of them—and the accident happened because of his fear. My father had the horse shot that Paul had been riding, although the grooms with us when the accident happened told him that it was not the horse's fault. Really, it was my father's for he was insistent that Paul learned to ride.

'My mother died soon afterwards as a result of yet another attempt to bear him a son. He said that she and I had been his curse, and he married again as soon as he decently could. But my stepmother was no more fortunate than my mother and, what was worse, she hated me and fed my father's dislike of me.

'You cannot imagine how lonely and unloved I was.

When I was seventeen my father hired a new footman, the son of a yeoman farmer who had had a grammar-school education. He was very handsome. I had seen very few handsome young men, for my father refused to take an interest in me, seeing that he was still trying for a son. Besides, he resented having to supply me with the kind of dowry which would be expected from a man of his wealth. Absolutely everything must go to the son he still hoped to have.

'Robert—for that was the young man's name—and I were thrown together. He talked to me. He said that he felt sorry for me, and I think that I fell in love with him because he was the first person to treat me kindly. What he really felt for me I shall never know. Father said afterwards that Robert hoped that having seduced me and run away with me, he would be bought off. I've no idea whether or not that was the truth. Robert said that he would take me to Gretna, marry me, and then we should go and live on his farm. Now I can see what a foolish plan that was, but then—

'Then I was in heaven because someone really loved me and I loved him. My father always believed that Robert had seduced me, but he had not. He was oddly respectful towards me, as though he could never forget that I was the master's daughter.

'But we never reached Gretna, indeed, we never even left Inglebury House, which was where we were living then. Robert foolishly gossiped about our plans to one of the grooms who went and told my father. We were caught leaving the house.

'You may imagine the scene which followed. Robert was turned away. I never saw him again. My father condemned me to a suite of rooms in the attic where I was allowed to see only female servants. Ironically, my step-

mother, who was increasing at the time, bore my father
a son shortly afterwards but he only lived for a week.

'Like my mother she became an invalid. The doctor
said that she must never bear another child, it would kill
her. She died shortly before he did, so I became my
father's heir; he could never forgive me for that. He
called me his plain stick who had not had the decency
to be born a son. He constantly compared me unkindly
with my beautiful cousin, Sarah Allenby.

'I was certain that he would disinherit me, but he had
quarreled bitterly with his sister Allenby, my aunt, and
wrote in his will that the only reason he was leaving me
everything was because I still bore his name—and was
the last of our line.

'Our line! My grandfather began life as a poor weaver
who took advantage of the changes taking place in the
woollen industry in his youth to make a large fortune,
but my father always spoke as though we had the blood
of Earls in our veins.

'After his death I became Hedley Beaucourt's ward
because my father had said that the Allenbys were not
to have the guardianship of me. Hedley Beaucourt and
the Allenbys badgered me to make the kind of grand
marriage which they later arranged for Sarah. I fought
them off as best I could until I came of age, and I am
so happy that I did because Sarah…poor Sarah…' She
began to cry again, so Will held her close to him and
stroked her chestnut mane until she had recovered herself a little.

'Oh, Will, poor Sarah! Just before I travelled north to
find you—and your supposed wife—Aunt Petronella
told me that Sarah had been found unconscious and injured in the home which her uncle had bought for her
and Wingfield. Wingfield had beaten her senseless and

disappeared. He probably thought that he had killed her. He also hurt Sarah's maid who had tried to protect her...

'And then I remembered that I was told what you had said to the Allenbys when they stopped your marriage to Sarah—that you would have treated her kindly... And I thought of how kind you had been to me—until you disappeared.'

Beck stopped. Everything which she had held inside of her for years had poured out like water from an unstopped bottle. She quivered and trembled in Will's arms, for when she finished speaking he gathered her to him to comfort her—and his merest touch was enough to set her longing for him to do so much more than simply touch her.

She looked up at him for she had something important to tell him. 'You do understand me, don't you? Why I couldn't say ''I love you'' until I saw you in the kitchen just now. I was so overwhelmed that the words flew from me.'

'Understand you? Of course I do and I love you and admire you for your bravery, my dearest.' Will understood at last of what the Duke of Durness had been speaking on their wedding day when he had referred to Beck's sufferings in the past.

'I can say ''I love you, Will'' and because I can do so, you must tell me why you thought that your honour demanded that you leave me. What I find difficult to believe is that honour had anything to do with the matter, but Aunt Peter says that women will never understand what men mean by honour so perhaps you had better not try!'

She paused for a moment before murmuring thoughtfully, 'I love you, Will. Every time I say it, it becomes easier the next time. You will grow quite bored with hearing it.' Mischief in her eyes, she challenged him, 'Now you, Will.'

Will leaned back, still holding her, although like Beck, he was finding that he was longing to do so much more with her than that. But loving must come later when all the misunderstandings which lay between them were cleared out of the way.

He owed it to her to be as frank with her as she had been with him so that they could forget the unhappy past and start life anew, and put the baggage of shame and suffering behind them.

'I can't say that my childhood was unhappy because it wasn't. My father hadn't yet sunk completely into the morass into which drink and gambling had led him. I had—or thought I had—the world before me. And then my father committed suicide when I was eighteen and we, my mother, my sister and I, found that he had left us virtually nothing. Everything had gone to pay his gambling debts except the Home Farm and the few acres around it.

'Oh, we knew that the Hall was falling into ruin, but my father was always telling us that next year he would have it repaired, but next year never came. Before he died I was beginning to understand that something must be wrong, but even then I could not have guessed at the magnitude of our ruin.

'My mother and sister were left with nothing but the small rent from the Home Farm. Shortly before my father shot himself an old aunt left me an annuity and I was able to pass on most of that to her and Emily, just enough to allow them to live in straitened circumstances in upper rooms in a house in Burnside, the village which the Shaftos had owned from time immemorial.

'The worst thing was that I had been trained to be

simply a gentleman living on his acres and his rents, nothing more. I had no profession by which I could earn money to support myself and my two dependents. I was little better than an odd-job man, falling in and out of debt and picking up bits and scraps of employment in order to keep myself, as well as Mother and Emily, out of the gutter. One summer I even joined a band of strolling players—with some success—but the life did not attract me.

'If I had not had Mother and Emily to support I would have signed on as a soldier in the ranks—for I could not afford a commission—but I could not leave them in a situation barely beyond starvation.

'Now you see why I was so desirous to marry a rich wife. Marrying you was their salvation as much as mine. I can only suppose that you found I was here by bullying out of Coutts Bank the fact that I was sending money to a Mrs Shafto in the north—and immediately jumped to the conclusion that I already had a wife, since it was commonly supposed that I was alone in the world.

'What I had not bargained for was not only that the more I knew you, the more I came to love you, but that I soon discovered that I was not cut out to be a kept man: Rebecca's rogue, a man without honour, content to live on a woman without giving her anything in return.

'What finally made me face the truth about myself was fighting Black Jack for you. I had behaved honourably in doing so, but once we were back in society I was again a man without a true occupation, simply someone whom you had married for your convenience.

'If I had known that you loved me I would not have left you as I did, but I would have tried to explain to you then that I must have some reason for living, for accepting your money without giving you anything real in return. So I came back to Burnside to see whether after renouncing everything you had given to me I would be able to keep Mother, Emily and myself in reasonable comfort by learning to run the Home Farm, so that when my tenant retired I could take over from him. I was astonished to discover that hard though it was, I liked the life. I have found a point and purpose in it which I have never known before.

'The work may be hard and menial but it is honourable and I need make no apology for doing it. If we are to save our marriage, Beck, it must be on the understanding that I have some worthwhile occupation. I could not ask you to be a poor farmer's wife, that would not be fair—'

He did not finish for Beck interrupted him eagerly. 'I could restore the Hall, Will, and buy back some of the lands around it. I learned today that they were for sale. And we could improve the farm so that we could live there until the Hall is habitable again. And you can manage Inglebury for me as well. Mr Carter, my agent, is growing old.'

Will shook his head. 'It will not be enough, Beck, for you to shower me with your bounty. We must become partners, only spending our money after joint consultation. If we are to restore the Hall it will have to be done slowly by us, to our taste, and not by an army of workmen from outside whilst we fritter and idle our life away in pointless pleasure.

'I should like to visit London occasionally, but I would not wish to make living there a major part of our lives. I want to be a country squire, living on my acres like Coke of Norfolk does, farming my own land, not simply taking rent from the true workers on it whilst I do nothing.'

Beck sat silent for a moment. She bent down to scratch Pilot gently behind the ears before raising her head and looking earnestly at Will. 'I'm sure you are right to wish that you should be more than an absentee landowner living idle in London.

'I think that I, too, should have an occupation. Mine could be supervising the Hall's restoration and its refurnishing. If Bess of Hardwick nearly three hundred years ago could be a true chatelaine of her husband's lands and possessions, why should I not be? The farmer should have a working wife, after all. I cannot bake or brew, but I can run a great house as I have proved at Inglebury, and the Hall would provide a real challenge for me as learning to be both farmer and agent would for you.'

Will kissed her again, real affection in his voice. 'There speaks my managing Beck! No, I don't object to you managing things—so long as you don't manage me, but leave me something of my own.'

'But you would let me manage our children, Will?' This came out shyly.

'Of course, although when the boys grow up, they would become my responsibility—as the girls would be yours.'

'Boys, Will? Girls? How many children do you plan on having?'

'As many as you wish, Beck. The Hall is big enough for any number, and so is Inglebury, I understand.'

'Any number?' Beck was thoughtful. 'And we haven't even started.'

Will tightened his arms about her. 'What do you mean by that, Beck?'

'Well, we are not getting any younger, Will, are we?

And apart from that night together in the forest we have lived together like a monk and a nun—which is not exactly the way to start a family, now is it?'

'Oh, Beck,' said Will, showering little kisses on her face and neck. 'I might have known that you would be as frank and free a lover as you are in everything else in life. How do you propose that we remedy this sad situation?'

She hid her face in his chest before muttering in a voice so low that he could scarcely hear her, 'Well, we are alone, and not like to be interrupted, and oh, Will, I have missed you so, and I thought that…' Her voice ran out.

'Thought what?'

'That you would never hold me in your arms again. Love me, Will.'

'Now, Beck, now? Whatever will Pilot think?'

'Oh, I had forgotten Pilot.' Her expression was so sorrowful that Will began to laugh. 'No need to worry. I can send Pilot home. Listen,' and he gave a series of whistles which had Pilot on his feet again, his ears pricking.

'Home, boy, home,' said Will, giving a longer whistle after the word home.

Obediently Pilot turned and began to trot briskly in the direction of the farm. 'You see how obedient he is, Beck. Will you be as obedient a wife to me as he is a dog?'

'Only if you agree to be as kind to me as I promise to be to you.'

'Agreed.' Will turned to take her in his arms and lower her on to the grass at their feet, something which he had wished to do from the moment when they had left the farm behind them.

'Oh!' Beck struggled to a sitting position. 'Whatever will your mother and sister think if Pilot returns home without us?'

'That I have sent him ahead.'

'And you will explain to them later something of what went wrong between us?'

'A little, Beck.' He was unfastening his breeches flap, 'but if you don't lie down with me soon I shall think that you have changed your mind about the large family with which you propose to bless me.'

'Oh, I will bless you before that, Will.'

And so she did, there in the open, far from the haunts of men, lying in Will's arms, the sun shining above them, the sheep grazing below, and the birds calling and wheeling in the blue sky.

They were passion's children, and their loving was all the sweeter because it was delayed, and because neither of them had ever dared to hope that they would find the one twin soul with whom they might unite. And afterwards when they were two again, they would carry the memory of being one with them to ease life's burdens.

So Will told Beck when they were lying in each other's arms afterwards. 'I have a confession to make,' he said, 'one which I hope you will not use against me.'

'I would never use anything against you, Will. In future I shall try not to judge anyone, or anything, too hastily. What is it?'

'This. I think that when I left you, always, at the back of my mind, was the thought that, knowing you, if you truly loved me you would be prepared to track me to the polar wastes and beyond to get me back again. Is that what you did, Beck?'

She smiled up at him.

'I didn't track you to the polar wastes, Will, that

wasn't necessary, even if Northumberland is colder than London. But I must confess to employing a Runner, cross-questioning Josh Wilmot and George Masserene and bribing a clerk at Coutts' Bank.'

Will's shout of laughter was a joyful one. 'Oh, that's my wife all over, that's my Beck. Come and have your reward for your perseverance and your determination.'

'Then you're not cross with me, Will, for tracking you down?'

'Cross with you? Of course I'm not cross, and here's your punishment—or your reward—whichever you like to call it.'

With that he bent to kiss her, and one thing led to another so that they celebrated their reunion all over again, only desisting when the sun began to fall down the sky.

Later, much later, the other Mrs Shafto, standing at the window waiting for her son and his wife to return, and guessing what might be delaying them, saw Will walk into the farmyard, his arm around a flushed and smiling Beck.

'Here they come,' she said to Emily, who, her face anxious, was also awaiting her brother's return.

'Oh, Mother, is all well between them, do you think?'

Mrs Shafto watched Will bend his head to kiss Beck when they reached Pilot's kennel.

'Very well, my dear. If his wife drove all the way to Northumberland after him, and he was willing to sink his pride in order to run after her to keep her, then I cannot doubt that, somehow or other, they will find a way to live together happily.'

Beck and Will, now hand in hand, all their misunderstandings behind them, were in full agreement that they would face the pleasures—and the occasional pains—of married life together. Rebecca and her rogue had come home at last.

* * * * *

Historical Romance™

Coming next month

THE VIRTUOUS CYPRIAN
by Nicola Cornick

A Regency delight!
Nicholas, the Earl of Seagrove, was certain that his new
tenant was none other than Susanna Kellaway—the
notorious Cyprian. But if that was so, why was she
shocked at his suggestion that she become his mistress?

DOUBLE DILEMMA
by Polly Forrester

1910 The Edwardian Age
Could this dashing socialite really be the same Geoffrey
Redvers who was Louisa's neighbour and whom she could
barely get a word out of? With her own blend of gentle
persuasion Louisa was determined to solve the mystery!

On sale from 10th August 1998

Available from WH Smith, John Menzies and Volume One

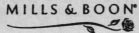

4 FREE

books and a surprise gift!

We would like to take this opportunity to thank you for reading this Mills & Boon® book by offering you the chance to take FOUR more specially selected titles from the Historical Romance™ series absolutely FREE! We're also making this offer to introduce you to the benefits of the Reader Service™—

- ★ FREE home delivery
- ★ FREE gifts and competitions
- ★ FREE monthly newsletter
- ★ Books available before they're in the shops
- ★ Exclusive Reader Service discounts

Accepting these FREE books and gift places you under no obligation to buy, you may cancel at any time, even after receiving your free shipment. Simply complete your details below and return the entire page to the address below. *You don't even need a stamp!*

YES! Please send me 4 free Historical Romance books and a surprise gift. I understand that unless you hear from me, I will receive 4 superb new titles every month for just £2.99 each, postage and packing free. I am under no obligation to purchase any books and may cancel my subscription at any time. The free books and gift will be mine to keep in any case.

H8YE

Ms/Mrs/Miss/Mr....................................Initials ....
BLOCK CAPITALS PLEASE

Surname ....

Address ....

....

....Postcode...

Send this whole page to:
THE READER SERVICE, FREEPOST, CROYDON, CR9 3WZ
(Eire readers please send coupon to: P.O. Box 4546, Dublin 24.)

Offer not valid to current Reader Service subscribers to this series. We reserve the right to refuse an application and applicants must be aged 18 years or over. Only one application per household. Terms and prices subject to change without notice. Offer expires 31st January 1999. You may be mailed with offers from other reputable companies as a result of this application. If you would prefer not to receive such offers, please tick box. ☐

Historical Romance is being used as a trademark.

The Sunday Times **bestselling author**

PENNY JORDAN

TO LOVE, HONOUR &

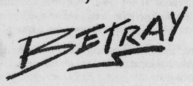

---◆---

Motherhood, marriage, obsession, betrayal and family duty... the latest blockbuster from Penny Jordan has it all. Claudia and Garth's marriage is in real trouble when they adopt a baby and Garth realises that the infant is his!

"Women everywhere will find pieces of themselves in Jordan's characters."

—Publishers Weekly

1-55166-396-1
AVAILABLE FROM JULY 1998